The Captain's Choice

A SAPPHIC SEAS ROMANCE

WREN TAYLOR

EPICEA ⚲ PRESS

TACOMA, WA

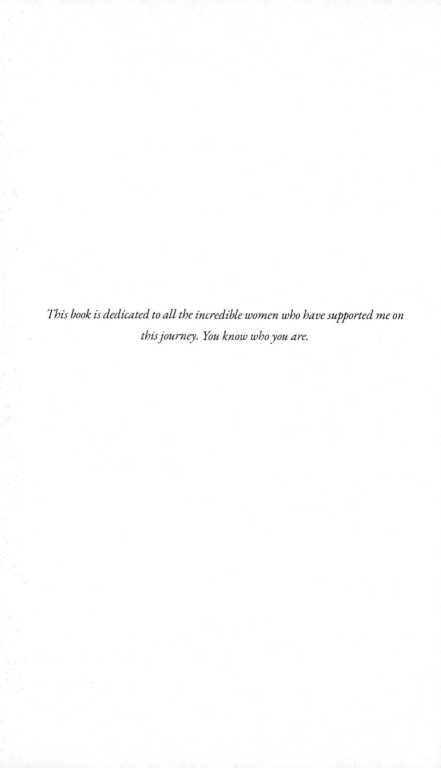

This book is dedicated to all the incredible women who have supported me on this journey. You know who you are.

Chapter 1

JUNE 1707

Mona Lloyd had a problem, and for the first time in her twenty years, she didn't know how to solve it adequately. She had been fretting about what to do for months, and the looming wedding date kept her up late into the night as her mind raced through her options. None seemed sufficient to evade the marriage she had practically been conceived for to cement the alliances of business. It was only a matter of weeks before she would be trapped completely, ensnared in a decades-long plan to enrichen the lives of men at her expense. Most fathers hoped for a son to take over their legacy, but Mona's had wished for a daughter, a suitable match for his business partner and best friend's son.

She couldn't even enjoy the warm June sun that beat down as she helped the maids hang the rest of the laundry on the line strung between two trees on the manor grounds. Damp linens flapped in the breeze rolling up from the sea, and the smells of salt and seaweed permeated the air. It was the first truly hot day of summer. Sweat ran down her spine beneath her stays and pricked at her brow. She dabbed it away with the hem of her apron, feeling the sting as the rough fabric scraped across her sunburned cheeks. Her father would scold her for that, she was sure. Though he allowed her more leniency than most daughters of wealthy merchants were afforded, he still had his limits, and maintaining his image was one. For him, it wouldn't do to have the village think he was working her outside, as though she were part of his staff. Especially not with the wedding so soon.

She should have worn a hat at least, but it was so pleasant to feel the rays of sun warming her hair again. Even with all the windows of the manor opened, the estate still felt stuffy inside– as though the dampness of winter would never fully dissipate, the austerity a permanent feature since her mother's death a decade prior. The joy that used to fill its cavernous rooms had evaporated into the fog of grief and the manor became cold, devoid of the laughter that used to echo through its halls. Mona spent as much time away from it as she could.

"Hurry in, Miss Mona!" Sara, one of the kitchen staff, called to her. "Lunch is to be served soon."

Mona crossed the lawn to the kitchen door, feeling a wave of heat from the hot oven burning as she entered.

"Pardon my saying, Miss, but you look a right mess. Better tidy up afore your father sees." The freckles on Sara's nose twitched as she wrinkled it. Mona rolled her eyes. She was sure she didn't smell that bad, though the morning spent under the sun had taken its toll on the perfect appearance expected of her.

"My father is dining with me today, then?" That was rare, her father normally took his midday meal in his office when he wasn't down at the store in town.

"Indeed, in the formal dining room. I'll send Tilly up to help you get changed."

"No need," Mona said. "He can dine with me as I am, I don't care."

"Mayhap you should. Your future father-in-law is here as well," Sara chastised, and Mona heard the tinge of bitterness underlying the words.

The reminder of Mona's upcoming wedding was a sore spot for both of them, but life seemed filled with sore spots and there was nothing she could do about it. She would be leaving the manor soon, one way or another, and Sara would stay. It would be better that way, a clean break. She would miss their stolen kisses though, their shared understanding of the other's desires. Everything about it was improper, though Mona didn't care much for what society deemed proper. Nonetheless, it was certain to spark a rage yet unseen in her father if he ever found out about the tryst between his highborn daughter and the hired kitchen help, yet neither woman had been able to stop seeking the pleasure only they could give each other.

It was unfair for Sara to be giving Mona that look of betrayal. From the start, Mona had cautioned her that it was a relation born of lust, not love. Sara should have put an end to it the moment she started feeling more. Mona couldn't allow herself to feel bad for her. Truthfully, the maid annoyed her, wagging her tongue too much about inconsequential nothings all the time. The only time Mona could get her to shut up was when that tongue was buried deep between her legs. She shivered, the unbidden thought stirring her desire before she brushed it aside. The time for such follies was over. Mona spun on her heel and stalked off to her room on the second floor to make herself presentable for a meal with the two men who sought to control her fate.

The men were already seated by the time Mona had tucked the escaped strands of copper hair back into its coiffe and sprayed herself with rose scented perfume, changing her pastel outer gown for a more formal deep green that accented her eyes. She'd hoped to avoid notice as she slipped into the dining room, but it was impossible when they were the only two waiting for her.

"You're late, Mona," her father reprimanded as his butler slid a chair out for her to sit across from her future father in law.

"I'm sorry, Father," she said, looking down meekly.

"Apologize to Mr. Howell," he admonished.

"I'm sorry," she whispered again, staring into the bowl of creamy leek and mushroom soup she was served. "Please forgive my rudeness."

"Not to worry, dear, not to worry at all. I'm sure you were quite busy with...er, well, whatever it is you ladies occupy yourself with." Mr. Howell turned back to her father, directing the conversation back to business. "The hay fields are filling in nicely, and I expect a thousand bushels or more come harvest."

"The cost per bushel is up, they had a bad spring season up north this year. We should fetch a pretty sum, even if we only get one harvest off the field."

Mona allowed her mind to drift when it was clear her presence was required as an accessory and a formality, but that she was not expected or invited to participate in the conversation of things that didn't pertain to her. She was there to look pretty and smile graciously, a reminder to Mr. Howell of her father's commitment to their joint business endeavors. They certainly would not be seeking her input on the yield of hay fields and how to extract as much profit from a few acres as they could.

Her half-eaten bowl of soup was replaced with a leg of roasted rabbit accompanied by tender boiled carrots. Mona picked at it, feeling ill despite the tantalizing aroma wafting from the steaming meat. She imagined what they would do if she stood up right there and announced that the wedding was off, if she admitted the truth of her desires to them. Such a proclamation would be unthinkable, and yet, Mona knew she wasn't wrong to yearn for something different. There were other women who lived their lives just fine without men, even if they were denigrated as spinsters by the rest of the town and gossiped about when their backs were turned. Gossip was something she could bear. And there were the widows, two old women who had moved in with each other after their husbands' deaths, seemingly happier than anyone else in town.

"Mona?" Her father asked sharply, pulling her attention back to the table. Mr. Howell stared at her expectantly, and she realized she had no idea what she'd been asked.

"I'm sorry," she said. 'I was just thinking about the wedding and didn't hear what you said."

"Completely understandable, my dear. After all these delays, you must be so excited for it to finally be nigh. I know Rhys is."

"Of course," Mona said, hoping the dread hadn't crept into her voice to betray the lie.

"Anyways, I was only saying how anxious he is to see you again. He has news he wishes to share, swore me to secrecy he did, until he has the chance to tell you himself." Mr. Howell smiled, looking pleased with himself.

"I'll look forward to it then."

The men rose to retreat back to the office and continue their endless discussions of drudgery, but Mona lingered in the dining room after the table had been cleared, staring out the window into the expanse beyond. The manor was up on a bluff that overlooked the sleepy fishing town of Ogmore-by-Sea and the window offered a perfect view of the deep bay. The dining room had always been Mona's favorite room in the manor, a space of light and celebration on which her father had spared no expense to fulfill the wishes of her mother. The piece de resistance was the window that stretched from floor to ceiling. Designed to draw awe and admiration from the important guests her father entertained, it was an architectural marvel with thin panes of glass that were almost perfectly clear, unlike the thick, bubbled glass that was so common in establishments and homes of lesser wealth. Looking from it to the distant horizon always gave Mona a sense of hope and longing. There was more out there, and somehow, someway, she was going to find it.

Mona squinted, focusing on a flash of movement where sky met sea, certain she had imagined it. Though Ogmore boasted a port and a harbor deep enough for the largest of ships, most of their goods flowed into the town over land, the sea-faring merchants and traders preferring to sell their wares in the larger cities where they could fetch a higher price. Her father hadn't mentioned any ships scheduled to arrive, and if anyone in the village would know of the merchants' schedules, it would have been him. Three masts crested the horizon first, white sails standing stark against the cloudless sky. It was unmistakably a ship, and Mona had a good idea which one.

Seven years had passed since *Nimue's Revenge* had sailed across the harbor, but there was no other vessel it could be than the renowned ship that had once called Ogmore home. Though the famed ship was of substantial size, it was dwarfed by the air of mystique and awe that surrounded it and its line of legendary captains. Some said it was the very ship Nimue had sailed upon to deliver Arthur to Avalon, but Mona wasn't sure if she believed that. The townspeople liked to spin stories that were larger than life, maybe to give their little port a greater sense of importance than it had and add a little bit of excitement to their otherwise boring lives.

Boring may have been harsh, but nothing ever happened in Ogmore, not to Mona. Outside visitors came infrequently, and when they did come it was most often agents of the Crown checking in on the village and collecting their dues, or clergy come to peddle their piousness and promises of sins forgiven for the right fee. A ship was different, exciting and rare, bearing spices and spirits from far-off lands that were so hard to come by in the little town. *Nimue's Revenge* grew larger as she passed the outer reach of the bay. Mona had to get down to the dock. She didn't want to miss the arrival that would fuel the town's stories of adventure for years to come, adding to the legend of *Nimue's Revenge*.

The formal dress that had been an annoyance when demanded became a blessing, and Mona needed no time to prepare herself to appear in town. No one would miss her until the evening meal, and by then the news of the *Revenge* would have spread and her absence forgiven. The walk from her father's manor house to the pier that jutted out into the deep bay took the better part of an hour going downhill, and Mona hurried to vie for her spot to witness the arrival. The church bells were tolling jubilantly, and word had traveled quickly that the *Revenge* was on her way. The crowd swelled the closer Mona got to the dock; it seemed everyone had gathered to see the ship and her famous captain disprove the rumors she'd been lost to the waves.

Mona pushed to the front of the dock where the fishmongers were hurriedly packing up their stands to make way for the captain and crew to disembark the massive boat with its three tall masts and dark hull gleaming with droplets of sea mist. It was an imposing beast, casting a shadow across the smaller fishing boats in the harbor as if flaunting its prowess. Mona was surprised to find herself jealous of the scruffy men that scurried around its deck, hauling ropes and shouting to each other. The crew of the ship knew what true freedom meant, sailing on the schedule they set, coming and going as their captain saw fit. She longed to leap aboard and sail far away from Ogmore, the man she was meant to marry, and the life she was never meant to live.

Nothing was wrong with Rhys, but the engagement was arranged by their fathers out of practicality– two rich men desiring to make their estates richer for their progeny– and she had little desire to spend the rest of her days in the company of any man, even one who was charming and gentle and chivalrous and sweet. Most women in town would swoon at the thought of a life with Rhys Howell, but she wasn't most women. Mona had delayed the wedding as long as she could, plying her father with excuses as to why the ceremony should be delayed for better weather, for a finer dress to be made, but the excuses had run out. She knew everyone was becoming impatient.

The dock groaned as the massive ship nudged into it, men aboard throwing ropes down for the townspeople to catch and tie off, mooring it in place. Men hoisted a gangplank onto the deck and the weather-worn crew began offloading cargo, chests and barrels overflowing with the flavors of lands unknown to Mona. The crowd surged around them, helping them carry the crates into the town to be inventoried and sold to the shops and taverns eager to refill their stores. Mona waited patiently, eyes scanning the crowded deck for a glimpse of the famed captain. Only after most of the crowd had dissipated did the cabin door swing open and the leader of the *Revenge* emerged into the late afternoon sun.

Mona's heart skipped a beat, and then another. The Golden Cormorant effortlessly commanded the attention of the few townspeople still lingering on the dock. Her years as captain awarded her a reputation for bravery as well as beauty, her name most often spoken in hushed whispers of reverent admiration for the exceptional woman. And beautiful she was, with hair that shone in a flaxen braid and sea-blue eyes that pierced into whatever captured her gaze from beneath her tanned brow. She dressed in the garb of men, with tanned breeches and a flowing shirt of beige linen that was tied at the waist with a blue sash, but no one would mistake the captain for anything but the woman she was.

It was why the Cormorant had risen to fame in the first place, the popular subject of pub gossip and tall tales told during the dark nights of winter. A woman helming a ship was unthinkable, until Elinor Davies had proven them all wrong. At least, that's what the stories said, and the stories were all Mona had to go on. It was a scandal, but it was one that paid off for the village that was too often ignored by other merchants, so no one dared speak against it.

Mona imagined herself in the captain's shoes, wishing she could effort-lessly exude the confidence and aloofness that allowed the captain to do whatever she pleased. A spark of hope flickered in Mona's soul– maybe the *Revenge's* sudden appearance was a sign, a final escape raft to flee Ogmore and eschew the life that turned her stomach with nausea. No other ships had come through in months, and when one finally appeared it was the only ship helmed by a woman who might understand her desperate need to escape. Mona didn't believe in signs, but if she did, the *Revenge* was as clear of one as any. She tucked a strand of red hair behind her ear and smoothed her skirt, steeling herself to ask if coming aboard was a possibility and wondering if the wrinkles were too noticeable for anyone to take her seriously.

Mona only realized she was staring at the captain when the cold blue eyes locked on hers. She curtsied awkwardly, not knowing what else to do in the presence of such a formidable woman who intimidated and aroused her curiosity. The Cormorant's top lip curled into a sneer, giving her the look of a feral animal that was best not to approach. Apparently curtsying had been the wrong thing to do. Mona blushed, then jumped as she felt a hand at her waist.

"I thought I might find you here, *f'anwylyd,*" Rhys used the Welsh term of endearment, his touch making her skin crawl unpleasantly. "I saw you rush past the shop and was hurt that you didn't stop in to say hello. Come, let's have a drink."

"Don't you need to be at the shop to receive the wares?" She asked, annoyed to have her daydreaming interrupted by the very man she was seeking to escape.

"Your father is handling it. You know he can't trust anyone else to haggle the fairest price, not even his son-in-law." He smiled, and offered his elbow to her. "So what do you say? One drink?"

She sighed, preferring to linger at the dock in hopes of speaking with the captain, but gave no objection as she slipped her arm into his. He led her to the little pub just up the road, a squat building of carefully stacked stones with thick glass windows framed in red. It was the main gathering spot for the townspeople of Ogmore, where local gossip flowed as freely as the pints of ale, and Mona knew it would be teeming with excitement of the ship's arrival. One drink wouldn't hurt, and her father could hardly get mad at her if she was in the company of her future husband.

"Three weeks til I can kiss you," he murmured, pulling her closer. His thumb stroked intimately down the boning at her waist, letting her know he was thinking of much more than just kissing her. "I can hardly wait."

"Right," Mona agreed placidly, careful not to let the disgust show on her face.

Three weeks until the wedding, but not if she could help it. She thought of *Nimue's Revenge* sitting so close in the harbor and felt a pang of guilt at her newfound conviction to find a way onto it. It wasn't Rhys' fault. If she disappeared, the embarrassment would make him the laughingstock of the town, but Mona refused to sacrifice herself for his sake. He wouldn't understand, none of them would.

Rhys held the door for her, then showed her to a quiet table tucked in one of the darker corners of the building, away from the windows that bathed the pub in the mottled light of the setting sun.

"I found us a nice plot of land," Rhys continued, oblivious to her internal turmoil. "On the other side of the back field, you can't even see it from the main house. There's already a well nearby, to water the animals, and nice solid ground to lay a foundation. Father says it's ours as a wedding gift, if it pleases you."

"It sounds lovely," Mona answered, only half listening to his rambling as she scanned the crowd for anyone who had come off the *Revenge*. She just needed a few minutes alone with them, to beg them to plead her case to the captain.

"Would you like to come see it? I'll have a carriage sent round for you tomorrow."

A group of four crewmen were sitting around a table near the door, tucking into plates loaded with laverbread and bowls of *cawl cennin*, a thick vegetable stew garnished with fresh cockles from the bay. The townspeople crowded around, vying to buy them mugs of ale in the hopes that they would be rewarded with harrowing tales of adventures at sea and news from faraway ports. Cheers filled the room as the first barrel of rum was tapped, a taste the sleepy port town hadn't known in the many years since the last casks ran dry.

"To *Nimue's Revenge!*" A man in the crowd raised a cup in toast. "May she ever prosper."

"To *Nimue's Revenge,*" the crowd echoed.

Their roar sent a shiver of excitement down Mona's spine. The crew of the *Revenge* were legends, men who had carved out their own place in the world and earned their fame and fortune along the way. It seemed like such a dream to Mona, to roam the seas and visit all the great ports of the world that she had only read about in books or seen on her ancient tutor's maps.

"Mona? Are you even listening to me?" Rhys covered her hand with his.

"Sorry," she responded, "Just taking it all in."

"I asked if you wanted to try the rum, *f'anwylyd,*" he said, "Since you were probably too young last time there was any in this town."

"I'd like that." Mona twirled a strand of hair nervously between her fingers as she faked a smile.

Rhys went to intercept one of the servers, dutiful and doting as always. For the briefest of moments, Mona wondered if leaving would be a mistake. Rhys would build her a nice home filled with anything she desired, and she could have a nice life, if boring and frustratingly unfulfilling. She could learn to tolerate his touches, give him what he needed in return for his stability and kindness. The longer she pictured an amicable life with him, the faster doubts faded. It would never be enough; she needed more than that. A path out of the town she had never felt a part of, and someone who could love her the way she deserved to be loved.

Rusty hinges creaked as the door to the pub swung open and an awed hush fell over the crowd. Captain Davies stepped in, heels of her boots clicking on the stone floor, her small silhouette framed by the beams of the doorway.

"To the Golden Cormorant!" Another toast was shouted from the back of the room, and the glasses were raised again.

Mona couldn't take her eyes off the captain. The stories had made her out to be larger than life, but she was actually much shorter than Mona, with high, jutting cheekbones and a withering stare for anyone who dared to meet her gaze full on. She had removed the blue sash and her shirt billowed around her, hiding her figure and half-covering the flintlock pistol and cutlass adorning her hips. She swaggered across the room, confidence and graceful strength radiating from her as she passed through the crowd.

"Here," Rhys said, handing her a short glass of amber liquid. "I think you'll like it, it's sweet."

Mona took a sip. It was unlike anything she'd tried, sweet like mead but more heavily spiced. She took another sip, then finished the cup. Rhys was right; it was lovely, and burned quite pleasantly going down, making the whole room warmer as it did. He raised one eyebrow at her but said nothing about her haste in drinking, instead redirecting the conversation back to their pending nuptials. Mona answered his questions as well as she could without lying outright, fearing as she always did that he would be able to read the real truth in her gestures and expressions.

The captain was sitting a few tables over, her presence impossible to ignore as Mona tried to focus on the conversation with her betrothed. When she laughed, it was like bells pealing out the joy of feast days, and her hands painted a picture as she spoke, with fluid motions that illustrated the story she told. A story Mona desperately wished she could hear above the chatter of the crowd. Mona was captivated, her gaze ensnared by the round cheeks that got rosier as the bottle of rum on the table got emptier. Candle flame flickered in eyes that sparkled with the blue of the sea on the clearest summer day. She was everything Mona wished to be, so sure of herself and in control of her world. She was everything Rhys wasn't.

"Your father will hold me to account if I keep you out any later," Rhys said, bringing Mona back to the reality in front of her. "And I've got to finish the ledgers before the morrow."

"In his eyes, you can do no wrong," Mona said. She didn't want to leave the pub, filled with life and intrigue, to return to the grim manor house. "But go if you must, I'll be quite alright here."

Rhys's pleasant expression soured as his handsome features twisted into a scowl. "It wouldn't be proper. We're as good as wed, and you'd dare risk your reputation and mine by staying alone in this pub like a common trollop?"

"You surely know me better than that," she protested.

"Your father has given you too loose a rein for too long. Don't expect me to allow the same." He stood and took her by the elbow, dragging her to her feet. "I'm taking you home now."

Mona looked up at him through watery eyes. "Rhys, you're hurting me." The grip on her forearm loosened as his fingers relaxed, but the reminder that for all his charm and chivalry, she would never be more than one of his belongings smarted more.

"Is there a problem here?" The captain stepped in front of them, blocking their path through the crowded tables to the exit. An enormous man loomed behind her.

"Not at all," Rhys said smoothly.

"I was asking her," the captain said, looking at Mona.

Mona thought her heart would leap from her chest as all her breath left it. "No," she finally stammered as Rhys's fingers clamped down once again. "No problem."

The captain held her gaze a moment longer, then shrugged and stepped aside. Mona had to nearly jog to match Rhys's pace as he pulled her outside. He only slowed when the merry sounds of the pub were lost to the winds that whipped up from the bay.

"What's gotten into you lately?" He stopped abruptly in the road and spun her to face him.

"What do you mean?"

"Every time we've spoken in the past month, you've seemed entirely disinterested. You barely respond, and now you defy me? In public, for anyone to see my humiliation?"

"Rhys, I'm sorry. It won't happen again." Mona would make sure of that, no matter what.

"No. It won't." He sighed. "Show me your arm."

He grabbed her hand before she could offer it and lifted it to inspect her forearm. The red prints of his fingers were visible in the bright moonlight. He trailed his hand across it, his touch gentle, then lifted her hand to his lips and kissed her knuckles. Mona shivered.

"Are you cold, my love?" He asked tenderly, misinterpreting her shudder. He removed his coat and draped the gray, woolen garment around her shoulders.

"Thank you," she said, confused by his sudden reversal to kindness once more.

"I know it must be daunting for you, to leave the only home you've known and start a life with me. But I promise to care for you well, and keep you away from harm, even when you can't see it."

Chapter 2

E LINOR CRUMPLED THE SHEET of parchment in a tight fist. This was not why she and the crew of her ship had finally returned to Ogmore-by-Sea, and if this was how they intended to treat the bravery and sacrifices of *Nimue's Revenge*, it would be the last time the town would be graced with her presence. Surely long enough had passed that the debt was repaid, and she no longer needed to concern herself with a forgotten village and a promise made long ago.

She had no loyalty to Ogmore beyond that of her former captain and mentor, the feared Captain Greybrow. She wasn't even from the town that he had sworn an oath– to himself, no less– to supply years before she ever stepped foot on the *Revenge*. But she had given him her word as he lay dying seven years before, that she would helm his beloved ship and continue to supply his beloved town. No, she owed Ogmore nothing, but to Greybrow she owed everything– for granting an opportunity to a scared street urchin whose sneaky hands were slated for a chopping block after picking one too many pockets.

Greybrow hadn't asked any questions when she darted onto the *Revenge* mere moments before it pushed off to sea; he'd just sighed paternally and handed her a bucket and a mop and told her to get to work. In time, he taught her to navigate and how to adjust the sails, load a cannon and shoot a pistol, and she had risen in the ranks to eventually become master gunner of his ship, much to the unspoken chagrin of the many men who now called her Captain. For seven years, she had answered to no man, nor would she that day, even if his title was duke and his letter demanding. She uncrumpled the parchment to read it again.

To the Esteemed Captain Elinor Davies, otherwise known as the Golden Cormorant;

Due to recent reports of piracy from the Crown's ships in the Atlantic and Caribbean, deemed to have been carried out by your vessel Nimue's Revenge, the Earl of Caernarfon requires that Nimue's Revenge remain docked at Ogmore-by-Sea until such a point in time that he is able to travel to Ogmore-by-Sea to investigate these claims. Your cooperation is most appreciated in this matter.

Piracy. She scoffed. Based on what she had seen at sea, the Crown's navy was no impartial judge as to who was a pirate or not. Her crew wouldn't take kindly to the insinuation either, charges of piracy could cost them their livelihoods, or their lives. She tried to avoid seizing merchant ships flying the Crown's flag, but she had a crew to answer to and the opportunity had presented itself at just the right time to secure them enough gold to stave off mutiny. None of the sailors had been killed, nor their ship taken, so accusations of piracy seemed like quite the overreaction.

Not that the letter mattered, she would simply ignore it and set sail before the Earl even knew she had been there. No one could stop the *Revenge* from leaving. The townspeople could try, though she doubted they felt any great loyalty to the distant peer who ruled according to whispered information and blackmailed threats. And the townspeople adored her, though she had no earthly idea why. She supposed tales at sea became more monumental as the long days passed, and normal encounters turned into far-fetched shanties when the alcohol flowed at the pubs near ports. None of them would risk their lives or livelihoods against her cannons or her men's cutlasses.

"Has word already been sent to the Earl that we're docked here?" She asked the townsman whose name she had already forgotten. Lloyd or something, it didn't matter. Just another wealthy man looking to curry favor with those he saw as powerful. She wondered if she counted in that number.

"Don't think so, Captain Davies, but I'm sure they will soon enough. Going to make a run for it, are you?"

She glared at him. She'd thought the wax seal looked odd, as though it had been carefully scraped free and then remelted into place. His question all but confirmed her suspicion that the letter had been read before being passed along to her. There was no such thing as privacy in a small village like Ogmore. All the more reason to leave, and quickly.

"The *Revenge* does not run away, this accusation simply has no merit. We have a Letter of Marque as a protector of the Crown's interests at sea. All the business we conduct is perfectly legal, and this accusation is an offense."

"Then surely it would be a simple matter to await the Earl's arrival and show him this letter yourself," the man implored, raising an eyebrow at her. "I'm most certain my shop would hate to be accused of selling stolen goods, and doubly so if they were stolen from the Crown."

She laughed, more from disbelief than any humor in the situation. What did the man think his shop had been selling for decades prior, if not stolen goods plucked from unsuspecting ships in the waters of the Caribbean? Elinor rolled her eyes. Men. Always seeing only what they wished to see. Everything they dealt in was stolen goods, ripped from people whose lands they plundered, then changing hands again as the ships from different nations battled to bring the prize home to their own lands.

"We're on a tight schedule to keep," she said curtly. "Just here until she's loaded up and off we sail. My crew wasn't made for life on the land."

"If you disobey the Earl, and therefore the Crown, the waters you sail will become that much more dangerous," the man warned. "Your Letter of Marque will be revoked."

Elinor shrugged to hide how much his words bothered her. "Danger at sea is nothing new to the *Revenge*. We cherish anything to break up the monotony of the endless blue expanse."

Her fingertips drifted to the cutlass at her hip. She was getting out of practice with the delicate blade, she wouldn't mind an easy fight or two to refresh the skill. He was finely dressed, and she wondered how much gold he carried. It would be an easy matter to relieve him of it. The man noticed where her hand lay and took a step back, as if she was considering using it on him. Coward. He would never survive life on her ship, and he ought to show a little more respect for those who did. She spun and left the room without so much as a goodbye, out of patience for the politicking of men.

She found Tristan– her most loyal friend and the quartermaster of her ship– leaning against the wall of the shop as he waited for her to return. He was flirting with a young woman who batted long eyelashes at him from beneath her bonnet as she traced the scar on his forearm with slender fingers.

He'd gotten the wound in their most recent skirmish, a gash from a cutlass deep enough that she'd been afraid he'd lose the arm. He'd laughed it off in his usual fashion, joking that it would make him even more intriguing to the ladies. It seemed he'd been right. Elinor cleared her throat, not wanting to interrupt but needing to reclaim her quartermaster from the pretty woman distracting him from business.

"Captain," he said, nodding his head respectfully as fell in step beside her. "What news of the Earl?"

"None to be concerned with," she replied, waving his concerns away with feigned confidence. "I see you've made a new acquaintance."

He grinned and ran a hand through his short, dark hair. "Can't help that the ladies fall over themselves for me. Jealous?" He teased.

"Not at all. None of the women in this town are my type, they're too stuck up and concerned with looks and status to hold any appeal."

"Right," he said, as he always did when he disagreed with her. "Or maybe the great Captain Davies finds herself, dare I say, *intimidated* by them?"

"Certainly not, I just don't have time for such follies here. We sail in three days." Elinor crossed her arms, frustrated by how easily he saw through her.

"So soon?" Tristan asked, surprised. "I was just arranging to dry dock the *Revenge,* figured we'd stay a few weeks at least, clean her well and rest long before we sail again."

"The crew will have sated their lust on the little entertainment this town has to offer and the *Revenge* will be heavy in the water with provisions to recross. We can't stay here forever."

"There's a wide gap between three days and forever, and the men are in no rush to cross again. Why are you?" Tristan peered down at her, and Elinor was certain he was reading her soul.

"Wales bores me. Aren't you ready to go home?" She hated hiding things from him, but it was necessary for the time being. She would tell him the real truth of the letter soon enough.

"For some of us, Wales is still home. I was hoping to go visit my Nan," he said. "It's been years and I fear her time is short for this world."

"How far is she?" Elinor asked, taking pity on her devoted right hand man– Greybrow's nephew and her only crewman who still had family in the tiny fishing village. He was the one who had pushed for a return to Ogmore, and she realized his reasons were more personal than she'd thought.

"Half a day's ride inland if I can find a fast horse."

"Find that horse and go to her," Elinor instructed. "I'll handle everything here. We sail Wednesday morning with the tide."

He thanked her, and they walked to the dock in easy silence, gathering stares of admiration from the townspeople as they went. No other port gave them such a welcome, and the attention made her uncomfortable. All the more reason to leave as soon as possible and return to a place where expectations didn't weigh as heavily upon her.

Unlike her crew, the town of Ogmore held no entertainment or allure for Elinor, so she reboarded the ship, crossed the timber plank deck, and entered her cabin. The wooden bar thudded as she dropped it into place, locking herself into the one place she could be alone to untangle her thoughts. She lit a candle, then slumped in a chair at her table in the center of the living quarters, exhausted from maintaining a constant pretense of control.

Piracy. Beneath her facade of annoyance and nonchalance, the charge was frightening. Captains who were investigated for piracy were never found to be innocent, and her fate was as good as sealed if she chose to stick around in Ogmore for the Earl to come investigate her. It was absurd. She only ran her ship the way Greybrow had run his, in a way that allowed her crew to live contently and die honorably as privateers. Not pirates.

That their work involved relieving certain merchant ships of their wares was of little import. It was for a noble cause, to weaken the French and Spanish that threatened the Crown and supply her subjects with the goods they needed. But how was she to convince an Earl of that, when she could scarcely convince herself?

Elinor unrolled a creased canvas map, the names of far-off locales scrawled in French script amongst the fanciful illustrations of beasts that lurked in the depths below. She needed to decide where the *Revenge* would set her sails for next. The Caribbean lay before her, each island on the map offering a different temptation. Nassau maybe, or Tortuga. Even the coast of Hispaniola was alluring, if dangerous, offering greater treasure as the Spanish increased their presence there.

She sighed, imagining the lush Bahama Islands, with their warm seas and white sands. A visit to Nassau would boost her men's spirits, and she could recruit new ones to replace those lost in the last fray. It was a convenient location to intercept ships, especially the Spanish ones that carried gold from the New World and other valuable goods like rum, and sugar. Yes, Nassau would be a welcome balm to her soul after months on harsh seas and the dreary dampness of Wales that persisted even when the sun shone.

The chair groaned as she pushed it back and walked over to her windows that overlooked the quiet town with its boring people, a sharp contrast to the debauchery and revelry found an ocean away. Her men filed up the gangplank like ants, loading crates onto the ship, ammunition for her guns and food for the journey ahead. Half her crew was still below decks in their hammocks, sleeping off the raucous night before at the town's pub. She would let it slide, just once. They had earned a rest.

Chapter 3

*D*EAR *RHYS,* MONA WROTE, then scratched out. Too casual for the
message she needed to convey. She grabbed a fresh sheet of the
expensive paper, knowing her father would cringe at the waste, and dipped
her quill into the pot of ink again. It didn't matter, she wouldn't be there
to receive his scolding. *Rhys,* she started over. That was better. Straight to
the point and without room for him to interpret doubt from her words.

I'm truly sorry to do this to you, and I don't expect you to understand. I
can't marry you, nor can I continue a life here. I am eternally grateful to
you for these months of kindness, but my future lies elsewhere. I wouldn't
have been a good wife to you. Please extend my apologies to your father on my
behalf. Mona.

She squinted at the letter in the dim candlelight, examining the cursive
for signs that would give away her hand had been shaking as she wrote it.
Finding none, she folded it, wrote his name on the front, and left it on
her father's desk. One of the floorboards let out a horrendous creak as she
tread upon it, and she froze. No one in the house stirred, and she continued

on tip toe, pausing every few steps to listen for signs that someone was approaching to stop her. She'd taken care to give no sign she was leaving, no reason for her father or his staff to suspect anything was amiss.

Leo, her ornery black cat with a chunk missing from one ear, meowed as she crept through the kitchen. She shushed him, bending to stroke him one last time as a tear slipped from the corner of her eye. Out of everything at the manor, he was what she would miss the most. He purred and stretched his neck at her touch on the top of his head and she almost changed her mind. As soon as she stepped through the door, everything would change, and she wasn't ready. She needed more time, but she didn't have it.

"Be a good kitty," she choked out. "Eat all the mice in the larder and watch over the manor."

She pushed through the door before she broke down sobbing. It was a silly thing to be so emotional over, after all, Leo was just a cat, but she would miss the way he ran to her for scraps she snuck from the table for him, or the way he pawed at her feet for affection when she was near. Outside, a salty breeze whipped strands of hair loose from the bun pinned at the nape of her neck. Mona hitched up her skirts and darted down the street, sticking to the shadows even though no one was out to question why she was about at such a late hour. She didn't look back until she reached the docks, but when she finally did it was with tear-filled eyes. Ogmore was the only home she knew, and it had given her a comfortable life. She gazed over every building fanning out around the small bay, committing them to memory in case she never returned. The pub, the shop her father owned, the dressmaker where Mona had spent hours selecting fabrics and being fitted for the latest styles, all shuttered against the dark of the night.

Her eyes drifted up the hill to the manor, bathed in the light of the moon overhead. No candles flickered in the windows, her escape was still unnoticed. She knew the decision to leave was rash, but it had to be. She'd only learned that the *Revenge* would be leaving when her father mentioned it over supper the evening before, and Mona was forced to commit to the plan sooner than she anticipated. She hadn't even had time to pack a valise, not wanting to rouse suspicion in the staff or her father, so she would be stepping onto the ship empty-handed and without invitation. It wasn't ideal, but it was her last opportunity, and she was determined to make it work.

Mona crept up the gangplank and onto the vast ship, at least ten times larger than any other vessel moored in the bay. Small waves lapped at the hull, breaking against it in tiny splashes. A man slept on the deck, slouched against a crate. Mona didn't dare descend the hatch into the underbelly of the ship, where the rest of the crew was sure to be if the snores emanating from below were anything to judge by. She couldn't be discovered until after the ship had left, so they would have no opportunity to drag her back to her father. And Rhys. She was glad she would be far from their fury when her notes were read.

The ship rocked like a cradle being swung by the hand of an invisible mother, invoking a distant memory of her own. The motion was comforting. She looked around her new home. The deck was lined with cannons, and Mona gave those a wide berth. She knew nothing about the intimidating weapons, and she didn't want to risk brushing against one and setting it aroar. A pile of crates was lashed to the wide deck at the rear of the ship, and she slipped behind it, squeezing between the wooden boxes and the polished rail. Her underskirt caught on a nail and she yanked it free, holding her breath as the fabric ripped. The night remained silent.

Her pounding heart slowed as the minutes passed and no one approached. She leaned against the crates and dozed until the sound of yelling on the deck woke her up. Streaks of dawn's first light glowed red on the horizon and reflected in the inky water beyond the rail. The manor staff were surely awake by now, and she wondered how long it would be before they noticed her missing. How long would it be before her father noticed the letters on his desk? A few hours at least, he never entered his study until after the breakfast meal. She craned her neck for a glimpse of the manor, but it was hidden from her vantage point.

Come on ship, move, she thought, as if she could make it happen by power of will alone.

"Hoist the sails! Now!" The captain bellowed further up the deck, as if in response to Mona's silent plea. "We need to catch the tide."

"Captain," she heard another voice protest, "You sure it's a wise idea? I ne'er seen clouds red like them at dawn before. Storms a brewin' just past the bay."

Mona heard the men muttering at this and she glanced up at the clouds above. They were an alarming shade of crimson, a sure sign of rain coming inland.

"You may ne'er have, Reddy, but the *Revenge* has, and always lives to tell the tale!" The captain responded, asserting her authority but laughing as she did.

The men whooped and cheered, their exuberance sending a ripple of excitement down Mona's spine. This was what she had been waiting for, yearning to be a part of, and her dream was so close to becoming a reality.

"We sail on!" The captain's voice rose above the din again, the proclamation bordering on arrogance, and the men seemed to eat it up.

Mona shivered with delight, and a little bit of fear. She hadn't known what to expect on the ship, but so far it seemed just like the stories had told. The Golden Cormorant was just as formidable as the songs written about her, and the men listened to her. Respected her. It was remarkable. The great sails flapped loudly in the breeze as they were hoisted overhead on masts that towered as tall as any tree in the woods surrounding Ogmore. Heavy ropes thudded against timbers as they were untied from the dock and reeled onto the deck of the ship. The wind caught the sails and, with a great jolt that would have caused Mona to lose her balance if she wasn't bracing against the crates, *Nimue's Revenge* began to move across the water.

"Turn her," the captain yelled.

The ship tacked right, turning away from the shore to follow the coastline around the bay. Mona watched until the dock was no longer visible and the town of Ogmore was just a speck in the distance. The gentle rocking that had lulled her to sleep in the bay was more pronounced in deeper water, and her stomach churned with the unfamiliar movement until she clambered to her feet to retch yellow bile over the railing.

"Hey," a man yelled behind her, closer than any of the other voices had been.

Mona looked up, startled, and realized he was talking to her.

"Get out from back there," he ordered. "It's not safe."

She knew she would be discovered eventually, she just hadn't expected it so soon. She inched past the boxes until she was face to face with a tall man. His hair was black as a raven's feathers, and his eyes burned with anger. She recognized him as the intimidating man who stood behind the captain in the pub a few nights prior.

"What are you doing here?" He growled.

"I need passage." Mona raised her chin as she'd seen the captain do when staring down men, hoping he didn't notice her hands tremble.

"This ship's no place for a woman like you." He sneered at her. "Best I take you to the captain, afore one of the other mates finds you out here or the storm tosses you over."

He grabbed Mona's arm and began dragging her across the deck. She pulled away, shocked at his audacity in touching her, a betrothed woman. No, not betrothed any longer. Not that that fact gave him any right to touch her.

"I can walk quite well on my own, thank you," she said primly, though the pitching of the ship was making it difficult to keep her balance.

The chatter on the deck subsided as the men working noticed the commotion and stopped what they were doing to stare. The gruff man ignored them and led Mona past the tall masts and rigging, under the flag of the British Crown, and to a door set beneath a balcony flanked by two flights of stairs.

"Got a problem, Cap," Tristan called, pounding on the door.

It swung open with a creak and there she stood, the Golden Cormorant in all her close-up glory. She frowned at Mona, who squirmed under the gaze. The captain was sizing her up, assessing her from top to bottom as though Mona were some curious specimen whose value needed to be determined. The captain must have decided she posed no threat, because she jerked her thumb towards the cabin.

"Take her in there. I'll be in in a moment."

The man pulled Mona inside the dim cabin and shut the door behind him. The cabin was presumably large for a ship, though it was much smaller than any of the bedrooms at the manor and much more sparsely furnished, with a simple bed under a thin mattress and cabinets lining the walls. A pair of silver candlesticks that alluded to wealth unseen were in danger of sliding off the table in the center of the room as the ship rocked, and the man jumped to catch them before they hit the floor. He tucked them into a drawer near a row of windows overlooking the back of the ship, offering a glimpse of the storm clouds that rolled in above as portended by the fiery sunrise. Mona heard the captain outside as she raised her voice to address the crew. Her words were muffled by the thick wood door, but Mona could still make them out.

"Listen, you lot, and listen well. I don't know who this woman is or how she came to be on our ship. But I am going to find out. And if I hear any of you's laid a finger on her or had anything to do with this, the fish'll have that finger for their evening meal. Do I make myself clear?"

"Aye, Captain," they responded with one voice.

"Good. Finish your chores and get below, the storm'll be blowing soon."

"Aye, Captain!"

The door swung open again, this time caught by a gust of wind that made Mona jump as it slammed against a cabinet bolted to the wall.

"Where did you find her, Tristan?" The captain crossed her arms and glared at Mona.

"Top deck, behind the crates at the stern." He pointed towards the rear of the ship, and Mona noticed a wicked scar snaking up his forearm, gleaming pale against his tan skin. The injury looked recent, but fully healed.

Some of the tension melted from the captain's face, softening the creases between her brows. She turned to Mona. "Don't you know it's bad luck to have a woman on a ship?"

Mona was taken aback by the question and frowned in confusion.

"It was a joke," the Captain said without smiling. "Which of my men brought you on board this ship?"

"None of them," Mona replied.

The captain raised an eyebrow at her but didn't say anything.

"I just need passage." Mona looked down, embarassed by how deftly the captain made her feel inferior.

"This isn't a passenger ship."

"I know," Mona whispered, "But I couldn't wait for one and had no means of transport to a larger port. I was running out of time."

"For what?"

"A wedding to a man I knew I couldn't marry." Mona saw no reason to lie, and hoped the independent captain would take pity on her. She glanced out the porthole window, even though the town was far out of sight. They would surely know she was gone by now, and another pang of guilt knotted her stomach. No, that was seasickness, she realized too late as she retched again. A flicker of a smile cracked across the Captain's stony face as she handed Mona a handkerchief.

"You'll get used to it. Where are you seeking passage to?"

"Boston," Mona said as she wiped her mouth. It was the only city she knew by name in the colonies.

"Boston? Too far off course. We're going to Nassau."

Mona smiled wanly. She had never heard of the place. "Nassau will do."

Chapter 4

E LINOR SIGHED AND RUBBED her temples, trying to decide what to do. She didn't have rations for a stowaway, and she had no desire to have a pretty, young woman on board the ship to distract her men from the hard labor of sailing. Her threats could only do so much to guarantee the woman's safety, and she didn't want any additional responsibilities. She crossed the room and pretended to examine the books on a shelf as she considered her options. This new development would pose difficulties, but she couldn't help but feel sorry for the young woman who was so desperate to escape marriage that she snuck aboard a ship to cross an ocean.

"We could turn back," Tristan appeared by her side, whispering the suggestion. "We're less than a day out. Return to port, kick her off, wait out the storm, and sail tomorrow instead."

Elinor shook her head. She still hadn't told Tristan about the letter from the Earl, and she wouldn't until they were far out to sea. He was nobler than she, and would want to face the accusations head on to prove their legitimacy as privateers. He was naive. Elinor knew the bloodlust was growing among the ruling class as their coffers shrank due to stolen profit at sea. Tristan wouldn't understand how quick men were to blame women for their woes, or how standing for themselves was a risk she couldn't take. There would be no proving their legitimacy, as long as she was at the helm.

"We're not turning back," she insisted. "Don't you recognize her?"

He shook his head.

"The girl from the pub the other night. With the man that looked a hair away from roughing her up. I'm certain it's her."

"All the more reason to take her back. He didn't seem like someone to trifle with."

"I can't do that. Not if she's unsafe."

"We can't put her down with the crew. I don't trust them out of our sight. It took them long enough to come around to you."

"I know," Elinor hissed. "We'll put her in Scab's quarters, and move him below deck."

"He won't like that."

"He doesn't have to like it, he just has to do it. Tell him we'll give him a greater share of the next treasure we come across, taken from my own cut." She nodded to the door, indicating she wanted him to see to it immediately.

The corner of his mouth twitched, and Elinor knew he had more to say but would keep it to himself until he had a chance to do so privately. His discretion was one of the things that made him such a good friend. He bowed his head to her slightly, then sauntered out of the cabin to attend to the unsavory task of evicting the master gunner from the sleeping quarters he had earned with his rank on the ship.

Elinor turned back to face the woman across the room. Her skin was sallow with seasickness, but her expression was resolute. The unwillingness to show fear was admirable, even if she looked to be no more than one of the simpering women in town who threw themselves at her men for a temporary thrill. The dress she wore was an entirely impractical frock that put her femininity on full, distracting display, and Elinor had to tear her eyes away from the exposed cleavage that invited her gaze to wander lower and lower.

"What's your name?" Elinor asked.

"Mona Lloyd," she said, lifting her chin. The quiver in her voice was barely perceptible, but Elinor saw straight through the feigned bravado.

"Mona Lloyd," Elinor repeated. The surname Lloyd was familiar to her, but she couldn't quite place it. "If you want to stay on my ship, you have to abide by my rules."

Mona nodded. "Of course."

Elinor tsked. "Rule number one: Don't agree to things if you don't know the terms." The woman had a lot to learn if she was going to survive on the *Revenge*, and the eagerness to please was something that would have to be done away with if she wished to survive among the cutthroat crew.

"Ok then, what are the rules, so that I know what I'm agreeing to?" Mona asked, green eyes clouded with suspicion.

Elinor smiled tersely. She was a quick learner at least, and suspicion was a healthy response. "We abide by a code on this ship. No lying to the captain and no thievin' from your shipmates. Keep your weapons fit for service, not that that one applies to you," she added, since Mona was clearly unarmed. "No gambling, no fighting, no fucking, not on the ship. Leave all that for the shore. Don't talk about the business of *Nimue's Revenge* with anyone outside this ship, nor betray her to any enemy lest you wish your own death at our hands. Understand?"

Mona paled at the mention of death, but she nodded. "I understand."

"Good. And if the conditions aboard my ship are not to your liking, you are welcome to see yourself off it at any time. But if you do find yourself in the ocean, you're on your own. No way to save you then without risking one of our own." Elinor gestured out the window where the ocean stretched as far as the eye could see. "Tristan is the Quartermaster of this ship, he's having a room prepared for you. His command on board this ship is to be followed as closely as mine. Any questions?"

"When do we arrive in Nassau?"

Elinor laughed. "Months."

"Months?" Mona echoed, eyes widening. "Surely the Atlantic isn't so broad."

"Months," Elinor confirmed, wondering if the woman had any idea what she'd gotten herself into. "Three, maybe four, depending where the wind blows us."

A life at sea was a last resort for many, and a life that few could survive, and certainly not one suited for a well-born lady. Even if one could withstand the long hours of grueling labor required for safe crossings, there was always a risk of disease from living in such close quarters without proper washing. Elinor had lost three men to bleeding bowels on the journey back to Wales, all gunners sent to their final resting place somewhere in the murky depths below. Those left unscathed by disease found danger elsewhere, be it in the skirmishes the ship routinely engaged in to replenish their stores of food, drink, and gold or in the seedy port cities where they moored to get their fill of women, gambling, and wine. And now even the Crown was turning on those they once employed, with accusations of piracy being lobbed at any privateer who they no longer favored. The great Captain Kidd had been hanged in London only a few years prior, his body left the sway above the Thames as a warning to all those who would consider following his wake. Elinor was certain it was nothing the young woman from Ogmore should be caught up in.

It was a lonely life, as well. She encouraged camaraderie among her men, but relationships were forbidden during their long months on the ship in pursuit of prey. Attachments were dangerous and could be severed with one swift slice of a cutlass, one echoing shot from a pistol, even one errant wave from the sea. It was truly no place for a woman as soft and naive as Mona seemed to be, yet Elinor couldn't stop her resolve weakening as she studied the woman in her cabin. Her wealth was obvious from the cut and rich color of her dress, though Elinor didn't think she was titled. At least she hoped not, or kidnapping would be added to the case against her for piracy. Mona noticed Elinor staring and blushed, the pink spreading across her cheeks to lend her a healthier hue.

"You can't wear that on my ship," Elinor said with more harshness than she intended. Not because the foamy green dress clung to Mona's waist, drawing attention to her feminine curves. Not because the stays forced Mona into an upright posture that thrust her bosom forward and offered a titillating display framed by delicate white ruffles. Not because it was so distracting that every time Elinor laid eyes on it she could think of nothing other than stripping it away to see what treasures were hidden below.

Mona looked startled, and stared down at her dress. "I've got nothing else."

"Nothing?" Perhaps the woman was as foolish as Elinor had initially thought, if she had really embarked on a voyage of months with nothing but the impractical clothes she wore.

"I'll find you something of mine for now. Skirts and ships don't mix. Too much to get snagged up on." Elinor moved to her wardrobe, digging through to find something that would fit the taller, broader woman. "Plus, the more you look the part, the less my men will stare."

Mona took the clothes she was handed, a worn pair of trousers with a patched hole in the knee and a loose linen shirt that could pass for white in dim lighting. Elinor turned, giving the woman her privacy. She heard Mona fumbling with the unfamiliar garments, and then heard her exasperated sigh.

"Can you... I can't..." Mona stumbled over the words. "Could you help me loosen the stays?"

Elinor felt her temper flare as she turned back around. Was the woman so incompetent she couldn't even dress herself? That would never do. Mona had removed her overdress and petticoats to pull on the breeches, the bottom hem landing mid shin and revealing shapely calves. The fabric was too tight on her thighs and hugged her hips, drawing attention to the tantalizing curve of her bottom. Elinor was immediately inclined to order her back into her skirts, practicality be damned. If she wanted to protect the woman from the leers of men on the ship, the new garb wouldn't do the trick. If anything, the breeches made her more alluring, and left less to the imagination.

The stays were made of thick fabric with heavy boning running the length of the garment, encumbering the movement of the wearer. No wonder Mona seemed so stiff, so formal. Elinor couldn't remember the last time she had worn such a thing, even if it was considered a requirement for women of society. She was not a woman of society and refused to deign to their conventions. Mona turned, revealing the intricate criss-crossing laces that pulled her waist to unnatural definition, and Elinor wondered how she even managed to breathe.

Elinor was hesitant to touch her, even under innocent pretenses, and her fingers shook as she reached for the tight laces. It had been so long since she touched another woman. There was no place for such moments of intimacy on the ship, especially not for her, and she fumbled with the knot, the skill of unlacing lost to years without practice. The willing women she most frequently encountered were already unclothed, and the act of loosening the stays caused a flash of desire to burn within her. The men of her crew had been able to slake their thirst at the sleepy port, but she had not, for her desires were unheard of and unsatisfied by proper society. She wondered if Mona could feel her hesitation.

"How did you even get into this thing?" Elinor asked to break the tension rising in the room.

"I had help from my maid," Mona confirmed.

Elinor's suspicion was correct, she was from money, likely the daughter or niece of the shopkeeper in Ogmore-by-Sea. That could be a problem, depending on how jilted her betrothed was by her disappearance, and how important he was to the Earl. Elinor's fingers brushed against the bare skin between Mona's shoulders, smooth as a windless sea and unmarred by the scars of a difficult life. She felt Mona stiffen at the touch and quickly moved her hands away, the warmth of Mona's skin lingering on her fingertips as she focused on unstringing the laces while touching Mona as little as possible. Finally the garment was undone, and Mona inhaled deeply as the stays fell away, not bothering to cover herself and preserve her modesty. Elinor forced herself not to look, suppressing the curiosity that asked if Mona's breasts were as perfect as they'd teased from beneath the stays, if the skin on her stomach was as soft as that of her back.

"Thank you," she whispered, pulling the linen shirt over her head. It was a better fit than the trousers, but still clung too tightly to Mona's ample chest and left too little to the imagination. It would have to do. Elinor would just have to stay away from her until they reached the Bahamas, just as she had ordered the men to. She couldn't afford any more distractions.

"Can you work?" Elinor changed the subject without acknowledging the thanks.

"Of course I can," Mona replied sharply. She sounded offended by the question, but Elinor didn't think it had been unreasonable to ask.

"Good, because you'll have to earn your keep here. The men won't like giving handouts of their hard-earned spoils to stowaways, no matter how pretty they might be."

"I want to help." Mona raised her chin defiantly, and Elinor was relieved to see most of the color had returned to her face. "I'm not seeking free passage."

A knock sounded at the door, a pause, and then another rap. Tristan.

"Enter," she called.

"Her quarters are ready. Scab's none too pleased about it, though."

Elinor hadn't imagined he would be. Scab, short for Scabbard, was a cantankerous old sailor who had earned his nickname by surviving a well-placed thrust to the gut from a sword. He'd earned his rank as master gunner many times over, his background in the Crown's navy an indispensable asset for the ship, and he would see the eviction from his private quarters as a personal slight. But there was naught to be done about it. She couldn't put Mona down with the crew.

The boat swayed hard to the right as it was tossed by a rising swell, sending Mona scrambling for a handhold to keep her balance, and Elinor was struck again by her incompetence at sea. Inconsiderate was another negative trait she could add to the growing list, as the woman clearly hadn't thought through the imposition her presence would cause for the *Revenge* and her crew.

"Tristan will show you to your cabin," Elinor addressed Mona. "When your work is done for the day, you may walk about the upper decks while the sun is above the horizon. When night falls, you're not to leave your cabin unless the ship is sinking. Never go below decks to the crew's quarters unless accompanied by me or Tristan. If you do, I will not be responsible for what happens to you."

"I understand," Mona whispered, and Elinor could see she truly did by the fear that flashed in her eyes. Even the most naive woman could understand the dangers of men.

Elinor's crew knew she had no tolerance for men who laid hands on unwilling women, a crime punishable by death on *Nimue's Revenge,* but it was better to take no chances. Their lust had been satisfied temporarily at port, but long weeks with no one to warm their beds could drive the sanest of men mad. There had been moments in the past where the crew thought to test her authority and failed, but steering them away from this kind of temptation on board the ship would be a trial she had never faced before.

Elinor mouthed a silent thank you to Tristan, who led the girl from the room. She followed closely behind, stepping out onto the deck of the massive ship. The storm was rolling towards the land as the *Revenge* fled from it. They would have to cross directly through the squall, facing it head on and hoping they wouldn't be blown too far off course. Lightning streaked across the sky, a jagged flash of white followed shortly by a clap of thunder so loud she felt it in her chest. She could doubt her decision to sail in it later, as it was far too late for that decision to be undone.

"Tie everything down, including yourselves," she yelled. Her voice was nearly drowned out by the gusting winds, and only the men nearest to her could hear the command. She walked the length of the ship repeating the orders. "Hang on to your hats boys, she's going to be big."

Chapter 5

*Y*OU'RE NOT TO LEAVE *your cabin unless the ship is sinking.* The Captain's orders echoed in Mona's mind with each swell of waves that sent the ship tilting violently from side to side. How was she to know if the ship was sinking, enclosed in the musty cabin that smelled of salt and sweat and– after her arrival in the room– bile? She had never even been on a ship before, except the one time Rhys had taken her rowing on a day when the waters in the bay were calm. The sea hadn't seemed a violent place then.

If her choice to leave was wrong, it was too late and there was no use wallowing in guilt about it any longer. She was trapped on the *Revenge*, for better or for worse, until they reached the mysterious, far-off port of Nassau. Even the word was exhilarating on her tongue, foreign and sweet like the rum she had tasted a few days before. Nassau. She should have paid more attention when her tutor dragged the large maps before her, teaching her the geography of places she thought she'd never visit.

Another wave crashed against the ship's hull, pushing it so far to the left that Mona was sure that it was the one that would send her running from the cabin into the dark night. Not that she could make her way to the door if she wanted to, the ship was leaning at such a severe angle that she could do nothing but cling to the frame of the bed and pray it would right itself again. Sure enough, it did, overcorrecting and listing back to the right.

Months, the captain had said, casually. Mona couldn't imagine spending even one night in such a state of terror and misery, let alone months. If it continued like this she would surely go mad and launch herself from the ship and into the ocean just to put an end to the torment of her turning stomach. She wondered how the captain did it as she doubled over again, wracked with dry heaves since her stomach had nothing left in it to empty.

At some point in the night, the terrible rocking ceased and Mona drifted off to sleep. She awoke to bright light streaming through the cracks between the planks of wood that made up her door. Though her brow was still damp with sweat, her stomach had settled, and growled in complaint of its treatment and lack of food the day before. She stretched and was reminded of the strange clothing she had fallen asleep in, garments that still smelled like the captain who had worn it before her. Longing clenched between her thighs, a reminder of why she had left Ogmore to begin with. The captain had been clear with her expectations for conduct on the ship, yet Mona was unable to stop herself from remembering the way her fingers had brushed across the skin of her back and left her aching for more.

She cracked the door open and peeked outside, the blue sky and shining sun a welcome sight. Men were scurrying about the deck, adjusting the sails and polishing the heavy cannons that lined each side. The ship crested gentle waves and was propelled forward by the wind. She opened the door a little wider and slipped out. No one seemed to take notice of her except for Tristan, who stepped away from the small group of men he was instructing to come speak with her.

"Good morning, Lady Lloyd," he greeted her with a smile.

"Just Mona," she corrected. "I'm not a Lady."

"Sleep well?" He had to be teasing her. There was no way anyone on the ship could have had a pleasant night's rest.

She shook her head, remembering how terrified she had been in the violent storm, tossed around her cabin like a child's rag doll. "Terribly."

"That was nothing," he said. "Strong, aye, but short. The *Revenge* has seen squalls that last for days, that make even the toughest man call out for their mothers."

Mona shrugged, trying to seem nonchalant. If the captain could manage, so could she. "I won't be calling for mine; she's dead," she finally said, struggling to keep her tone casual.

"As is mine," Tristan said with a knowing glance that said he saw right through her tough facade. "I was raised by the *Revenge*. You'll still call for her in your darkest hours."

"I'm not afraid," Mona insisted, even though she was.

"Then you're dim-witted. On a ship like ours, the fearless become the dead. Though maybe that's your wish. You did step willingly aboard a pirate ship and you're damn lucky it was this one."

"Pirate ship?" Mona's jaw dropped in shock. *Nimue's Revenge* was a merchant ship, the finest in Wales. Or so the stories told. She fended pirates off to deliver goods, but none of the tales had ever implied she engaged in piracy herself.

"Aye, she is, for all the Captain pretends she's not. How else do you think we come by all the goods to supply Ogmore-by-Sea and the villages? Charity by my uncle, it was, during the famine, but not paid for by his purse."

"I see," Mona said carefully, although she didn't. It was unthinkable, for pirates were evil, and for all their gruffness, she had seen nothing that implied the crew of the ship was the scourge of the seas.

"You don't believe me?" Tristan asked.

"No, I do," Mona stumbled over the words in the wake of the shocking admission. "I just thought... I mean, you seem so well educated. I didn't know pirates..."

"Knew how to speak properly? How to read and write? Of course we do, most of us anyway."

"I didn't mean any offense," Mona insisted.

"None taken," Tristan said. "Come with me."

She followed him across the deck, no longer escaping the notice of the crew going about their morning tasks. A low whistle behind her was cut off by a sharp glare from the quartermaster, but everyone else pretended to ignore her as she was led into the narrow galley at the rear of the ship. The floors were covered with sheets of tin that gleamed in the sunlight and caused spots to dance in front of her eyes if she looked at them too long. A single plate of food sat on a table at one end of the room, sliding back and forth slightly as the ship rocked.

"Miss the breakfast call again and you won't have none," Tristan warned. "The boys voted to make an exception for your first day. You might do well to thank them for it."

Mona was indeed grateful to have some food, though the meal had long gone cold. She ate the two boiled eggs and chunk of bread hurriedly, as if at any moment Tristan might change his mind about allowing her it. There was even half an apple, and even though it was mealy, she savored the sweetness as the juices ran down her chin.

"Don't get used to that, either. The food is only going to get worse til we reach the Caribbean."

"I'll survive," she finally snapped, sick of his patronizing tone. He took her to be some naive child, who stumbled upon the ship by accident, and she resolved to prove she was no burden upon them.

"We'll see," he said. "Clean up the mess here, then report to me on the deck when you've finished."

He strode out of the galley, letting the door slam behind him. Mona didn't know what to make of the man, who flipped between kindness and gruffness, and she found that odd. Normally she had a good read on men and their intentions, was able to charm them with a well-timed smile or turn them away with a cold shoulder, but Tristan had given none of the reactions she was accustomed to.

She looked around the small kitchen and groaned as she finally noticed stacks of dirty wooden plates and tankards for the first time. When the Captain had asked if she could work, she imagined mending, maybe some dusting in the private cabins, or even helping with laundry, but nothing like this. She'd never had to lift a finger in the kitchen before; her father employed people for that. She had no idea where to even begin.

Mona took her time cleaning the plates, carefully scrubbing any trace of food from them so as to avoid any further criticism from the quartermaster, or worse, the captain. She rinsed them with salty water that she assumed someone had drawn up from the sea, and tossed the wastewater from the window, where it fell three stories or more and splashed into the waves below. She rested a moment, wiping her brow as she gazed at the horizon and enjoyed the quiet moment of solitude on the bustling ship. All she could see was the blue of the ocean stretching in every direction, and she was struck with a feeling of isolation, as though the ship was alone and the rest of the world had ceased to exist. Perhaps it had, and she didn't even know it.

The sun was high in the sky when she finally finished, satisfied that the work had been completed to perfection. She strolled across the deck to find Tristan giving orders to another man, and stood patiently to the side while he finished.

"Tomorrow, it should take you half as long," he chided her. "What were you doing in there, daydreaming?"

"No, I was working," she corrected, indignant.

"Work faster. You're already behind. Griff, Reddy!" He waved over two men who could almost pass for twins that were working nearby.

Mona smiled at them and dropped into a small curtsy out of habit as they approached. One repeated the gesture back, mocking her.

"You're with them til supper, Cap wants the decks clean enough to eat from," Tristan ordered.

Mona sighed at the idea of more work. She had been hoping to return to her chambers, her hands were tender from scrubbing so many plates and she was still tired from the fitful night of sleep before. This was worse treatment than any of her father's staff received, she was sure of it. It was remarkable there were any men willing to work on the ship under such abject conditions. Surely they wouldn't expect this of her every day or she really would walk off the ship to take her chances with the beasts below.

"Come on then, miss." One of them– Griff or Reddy, she wasn't sure yet– spoke to her with a smile.

Mona took the bucket she was handed and followed the two men over to an area around the cannons. They were her age, more or less, but moved with the confident ease of men who were skilled masters of their domain. She wondered how long they had been on the ship, and what circumstances had led them there. They seemed pleasant enough, but it was clear that they were not in a talkative mood, so her questions remained unasked.

A stiff brush bobbed in the bucket, and she retrieved it. More salt water stung the fresh blisters on her palms. She ignored the pain. She knew she couldn't give them any excuse to see her as weak, and she would be damned if they caught her complaining. The wooden planks that made up the deck were smooth, probably from being cleaned so often and so vigorously, but they still hurt her knees as she crawled across it scrubbing. The trousers felt tight across her seat as she bent forward with the brush, and she could feel Griff and Reddy staring at her from behind as she worked.

"Do you do this every day?" She asked, hoping the question would break their gaze.

It seemed to work, and one of the men reddened at having been caught before quickly looking away.

"Sometimes twice," the taller one replied. He was a gangly thing, all limbs with a face pocked by long-healed disease. She thought he was probably Reddy, a name that seemed to fit his ruddy complexion.

"But why?" The decks looked clean enough to Mona.

"Mostly to prevent a fire." He nodded towards the row of cannons. "Every one o' them's filled with powder, and powder don't mix too good with wooden ships. One spark on a dirty deck, and we'll be meetin' the monsters below eye to eye."

"That makes sense." Mona scrubbed harder, spurred on by the frightful picture the man painted. She was ashamed by her lack of knowledge about the sophisticated weapons the ship carried, and all the precautions necessary to make their passage safe. Perhaps Tristan was overbearing for a reason, and they were right to question her ability.

The quartermaster was nowhere in sight, but she dared not ease her pace of scrubbing once she knew her own life might depend on it. She let her eyes drift around the deck as she worked, looking for the aloof captain of the *Revenge*, but the Golden Cormorant was also absent from the deck. Mona wondered if they were with each other, and felt a stab of jealousy imagining the handsome quartermaster receiving the undivided attention of his captain. They were too at ease with each other, their shared glances too intimate to be anything but the type of relationship the captain had warned Mona against forming on the ship. Perhaps the code didn't apply to them as leaders on the ship, but it hardly seemed fair.

An hour or more passed, and any thoughts of fairness faded from Mona's mind as she struggled to keep pace with the two other men in the little deck crew she'd been assigned. They seemed to never tire, covering each quadrant of the deck with brusque efficiency. Mona's back cramped from being bent over too long without reprieve, and she stretched quickly to soothe it before carrying on with the work. She could rest when she was alone in her cabin again, she just needed to make it through the afternoon.

"Tell me about the captain," she said, trying to hide how winded she was from the exertion she was unacclimated to.

"What's to tell?" The ruddy man shrugged and looked to his friend.

"What's she like?" Mona asked.

"She's as lucky as they come. Gets out of every scrape richer. Knows this ship better than everyone, and lets no one forget it."

"She's cold, but not cruel. Unless you cross her."

"I don't plan to," Mona said, wondering what they meant when they spoke of cruelty, then deciding not to ask what she didn't want to know.

Chapter 6

ELINOR AND TRISTAN STOOD side by side with their arms crossed, mirror images of each other as they observed the newcomer from the balcony above the captain's quarters that overlooked the top deck. He was the only one on the ship with whom she could let her guard down, his steadfastness putting her at ease. Her crew was loyal to her, of course, but only because she paid well and gave them ample opportunity to indulge in their pleasures between voyages. Their loyalty could turn as quickly as the tide. Tristan was more like a brother, someone she would trust with her life even if she ran out of pieces of eight to distribute for the favor of preserving it.

"How is she?" Elinor asked her right hand man.

"Weak, lazy, and next to useless," he laughed.

"Next to?" Elinor raised an eyebrow, allowing him a rare smile.

"Well, she's good to look at, at least."

"She is, but the code applies to you, too, Tristan. Keep it to looking," Elinor reminded him, not surprised he was attracted to the redhead with the entrancing green eyes. She was exactly his type, lithe and limber with plump, pouty lips and a beguiling smile that would make even the chastest monk forget his vows were she to turn it on him. Elinor wasn't at all surprised that her quartermaster had fallen under the woman's enchantment.

"And what about you?" Tristan teased. So he had noticed her staring, too. He knew she shared his proclivity for women.

"Especially me," she said, not in the mood for his jokes. Her love life, or lack thereof, was a sore spot between them.

Tristan knew Elinor better than anyone alive, knew her reasons to avoid attachment, yet for years he had still pushed her to look for companionship. She refused to entertain the idea that it might be with Mona, and she doubted Mona would reciprocate the interest anyways. Life was cruel in that way, and frustrating. They just needed to make it to Nassau, and she would be back in Lisbet's embrace again, warm enough for the coin she paid for it. She would give the crew a long repose there, a month or more if their money lasted. They had earned it. But first they had to make it.

"Summon her to my cabin for supper this evening. I still have questions about her," Elinor instructed.

"I'm sure you would," he prodded, but she shut him down with a look that said the time for joking was over. Serious once more, he asked, "What are you planning to do with her?"

Elinor frowned. "I haven't decided yet. That's why I need to speak with her."

"Having her on board is another risk we may not be able to afford."

"I know that," she said.

"If we run afoul of the Crown's navy–"

"I know that," Elinor cut Tristan off before he could finish the thought. A well-off woman on their ship would only arouse suspicions of kidnapping when they carried no other passengers. At best there would be a bloody battle, at worst, a hanging for her and all her crew.

"Could toss her overboard," Tristan suggested with a playful glint in his eye. "Might solve a lot of problems."

"Oh, stop it." Elinor shoved him and he exaggerated stumbling and catching himself on the rail of the balcony. "She stays on board the ship til we drop anchor at Nassau."

"If we do see the Navy we could give her over, though," Tristan suggested, serious again. "They can't accuse us of trying to ransom her if we're shoving her on them without asking for coin. Tell 'em the truth, she stowed away."

"No," insisted Elinor, sighing. It was time she finally told him the truth about the letter in Ogmore. "We can't engage the Navy. They're likely to be seeking us, if not now, then soon."

"Seeking us for what?"

"Piracy, Tristan. The Earl sent a letter demanding the *Revenge* remain docked until I could be questioned about accusations of piracy. That we left will be good as an admission of guilt to them, and it will be our necks on the rope."

He crossed his arms and glared at her, as upset as she knew he would be. "So that's why you were in such a hurry to leave. When were you going to tell me?"

"Now," she replied.

"Bit late, don't you think?" His jaw clenched, and though he remained outwardly calm, she could see the vein that always twitched in anger rising across his forehead. "Seems something you might have seen fit to tell me, oh, I don't know, *before* we fled an official summons. We could have talked sense into the Earl, but now you put us all at risk."

"We always knew this was coming."

Elinor and Tristan had been raised on Greybrow's stories of the glory days of the Caribbean, when privateers lorded over the seas and made their merriment wherever they saw fit, backed by letters of marque from the Crown or local island governors that gave them free reign to attack any ship they saw as a threat. But Port Royal was no longer a haven for the privateers turned pirates, whose letters of marque were being rescinded as the nearby town of Kingston grew. The Crown's net was tightening, and the ports that offered a safe haven for those whose gains were ill gotten were dwindling.

"You can get off my ship in Nassau if it no longer pleases you," she added ruefully, knowing he wouldn't take her suggestion seriously.

"Never," he said softly. "I belong to the *Revenge* and am at her captain's service as long as she sees me fit for the responsibility. But, Ellie—"

"Don't tell the men about the letter," Elinor instructed, cutting him off before he could say something that force her to acknowledge the bubbling guilt over keeping the secret from him. "No need to cause them worry."

"They know well enough what we do here, Ellie," he said. "You're the only one who pretends to be something that we aren't anymore."

"We're still good people."

"We aren't," he said curtly. "But it doesn't matter. It's too late to go back."

A few hours later, Elinor sat in her cabin and scribbled in the ship's log about the conversation she'd had with the quartermaster. His concerns still bothered her, and she shared them. Hopefully the woman would provide satisfactory answers. As if he'd heard her thoughts, Tristan rapped on the door three times, then entered with the young woman in tow. Mona curtsied, a ridiculous gesture that put her genteel upbringing on full display. That was a habit she would have to break if she ever wanted to be taken seriously on the ship.

Elinor nodded in greeting to the duo. Was it her imagination, or did Mona's gaze linger on Tristan's a bit longer than necessary as he held the door and she mouthed her thanks? Not that Elinor was jealous, of course. That would be ridiculous. She didn't even know the woman and there was nothing to be jealous of. Mona did look lovely though, if a bit less clean than the day before. Elinor thought it suited her, the salt-stiffened hair curling seductively at her temples and around the nape of her neck, where it had escaped from the pins holding her bun tightly to her scalp.

"Sit," Elinor invited as she gestured to two empty chairs at the table. Tristan looked at her, and she read the question in his eyes. She nodded. She needed him to stay, to be a buffer between her and her desire. Or to help her pry answers from Mona, should she be too unwilling.

Elinor poured a tankard of grog for each of them, mixed with the rum from one of her personal bottles, then joined them at the table.

"How do you find our ship, Miss...? What was it again?" Elinor asked her guest, feigning indifference.

"Just Mona," the woman replied, looking down. "*Nimue's Revenge* is lovely. Truly."

Elinor thought that was probably the first time the word lovely had been used in conjunction with her ship, and fought the smile that teased at the corners of her mouth. Tristan was less successful in disguising his own snicker, and Elinor kicked him under the table.

"Tristan tells me you find the work too difficult," Elinor tested her.

Mona's eyes widened and she looked at Tristan as though he had betrayed her. "Not at all. I'm sorry if I'm too slow, I'm just not used to it. I will get used to it, though, I swear."

"For the record, I never said anything of the sort," Tristan protested, turning the betrayed look to Elinor before reassuring Mona with a smile. "You did well today, seeing as it was your first day and all."

"To our newest crewmate, then," Elinor said, raising her cup and an eyebrow at how quickly Tristan's attitude towards the newcomer had changed when the pretty girl was sitting right beside him.

Three mugs touched in the center of the table, and each drank deeply. Elinor waited until the silence became uncomfortable and Mona shifted in her seat. She found it was better to take her time when seeking information about people; it gave her an opportunity to study their movement and judge if they were telling a truth or lie. Of course, this was no true interrogation, as the woman had no treasure for Elinor to take and seemed unlikely to be a threat to the *Revenge*.

"Who are you, really?" Elinor finally asked.

"No one important," Mona said, looking quickly to the right and back again. Possibly a lie, one to follow up on.

"You're related to the shopkeeper, are you not?"

"He's my father," Mona admitted. So, it was as Elinor expected.

"And the Earl of Caernarfon entrusts him with official correspondence. Why?"

Mona looked taken aback by the question, then shrugged. "He never spoke to me about his business. It wasn't my place to know." A believable lie, but a lie nonetheless, Elinor was certain.

"Why did you stow away on my ship?" Elinor asked through gritted teeth. Mona was avoiding answering her questions, and it frustrated her. Tristan's glance confirmed Elinor's suspicions, the woman seemed to be more important than she was letting on.

"I told you, I needed to leave before a wedding I didn't want." This time, Mona's green eyes stayed even on Elinor's, and there was earnestness in her tone. That seemed to be the truth, at least.

"To the man in the pub?"

Mona nodded.

"What's in Boston?" Elinor changed the subject quickly, hoping to catch her off guard.

Confusion.

"Why were you seeking passage there?" Elinor pressed.

Recognition lit in Mona's eyes as she seemed to finally recall the answer she had given the night before. So Boston had been a lie, as well.

"No reason. It was just the first place I could think of," Mona admitted.

"Will your fiancé be looking for you?"

Mona shrugged again.

"Answer a question when your captain asks you," Tristan admonished, any trace of the earlier flirtation gone from his voice. He knew when she required him to be serious.

"Let me rephrase," Elinor said. "Does your fiancé have the money to be looking for you?"

"I guess so," Mona said, almost too softly for her to hear. "I'm not sure. I don't know who he would send to look, though. None of the boats in Ogmore would survive the Atlantic. And he won't know we're going to Nassau, unless someone in town knows."

Elinor glanced at Tristan, seeing that he shared her concerns in his deep brown eyes and wary frown. The sooner they got the woman off the *Revenge*, the better. Wealthy men were powerful men, and it would do them no good to have another one searching for them.

"Why couldn't you marry him?" Tristan asked.

"I just couldn't." Mona looked away. She was hiding something, Elinor was sure of it.

"Was he cruel?" Elinor pressed. She hadn't liked the way the man had handled Mona in the pub, having seen it too many times before.

"No, no more than any other man," Mona said.

"Or maybe you're pregnant by another man and afraid of his reaction?"

"I'm quite sure I'm not," Mona said, "but I didn't love him. The marriage was arranged by our fathers, to strengthen their business. I never had a say. And, I, uh, didn't care to share his bed."

Elinor pretended not to notice Tristan staring at her. It didn't mean anything. Not wanting to share one man's bed said nothing about the dozens of other men Mona Lloyd could surely have her choice of. Rich and beautiful? Elinor was sure her father had suitors knocking down his door for a chance at her hand. Tristan kicked her under the table, trying to get Elinor to meet his gaze, but she continued ignoring him.

"How does your father know the Earl?" Elinor asked again, hoping the sudden shift in subject would be enough to jar the truth from Mona.

"His business partner is the Countess's nephew, I think, or some relation."

A knock at the door cut her questioning short, and one of the powder boys entered bearing a tray with three steaming bowls of stew. They ate in silence as the sun sank below the horizon, Mona yawning audibly between bites, exhausted from the long day of labor her body was clearly unaccustomed to.

"Leave us and return to your quarters," Elinor dismissed her when the table was cleared. She had more questions, but they could wait until the girl was better rested.

Elinor rose to see Mona to the door, barring it behind her. She took a swig of rum straight from the bottle, then passed it to Tristan. Out on the deck, the men were reveling in the rising moonlight, a sharp contrast to the intensity with which they had battled the storm the night before. Bottles were passed about and shanties would be sung into the wee hours of dawn until the men passed out in their hammocks if they still had enough of their wits to stagger below deck, or on the main deck if they didn't. Their celebration was a relief to see. A happy crew made a happy captain, for as long as the rum flowed they would follow her wherever she led them.

"What did you make of her answers?" Elinor asked.

"Earnest," said Tristan. "I think she was telling the truth. Mostly."

"She wasn't very forthcoming with the information."

"Would you be? She doesn't know us at all. Probably just doesn't want us to send word to her father or fiancé when we get to port. Worried we'll send her back."

"It's a fair concern," Elinor laughed, "As that's exactly what I intend to do with her. Do you realize who her fiancé must be?"

"No?" Tristan shrugged.

"Someone close to the Earl, if all she was saying was true. Her marriage was a business arrangement and her father does business with a relative of the Countess. This could end badly for us, Tristan."

"If it does, it's too late to do anything about it now. Her father could have multiple partners and she may have nothing to do with the Earl. Maybe you should give her a chance," Tristan countered. "Like my uncle gave you."

"That's different."

"Is it, though?" Tristan raised a dark eyebrow, challenging her.

"I was a child, it was easy to adapt. And no one was looking for me. Besides, the last woman I gave a chance..." Elinor trailed off, unable to speak the words.

"It's not fair to let Abigail cloud your judgment of Mona."

Elinor knew he was right, but she wasn't ready to admit it.

"She likes you," Tristan said.

"Doubtful," Elinor laughed at the absurdity of the idea.

"She couldn't take her eyes off you. Looked like she was ready to devour you instead of the stew."

"Don't be ridiculous." Elinor had seen no indication that her desire was reciprocated, and she didn't want it to be. Captaining the ship was hard enough without the distractions of a woman who wanted her back.

"Yet she said she had no desire to share a bed with her fiancé, even though he isn't unkind to her. I doubt she would mind warming your cabin, if you gave her a chance."

"Go to bed, Tristan, and stop concerning yourself with mine. Have you forgotten the code?"

"You're no fun anymore," he sulked. "Come join the crew on the deck for one drink, at least? For old times' sake? It would mean a lot to them, I'm sure."

"Not tonight," she turned down the invitation. She wanted to be alone. She couldn't stoop to fraternizing with the men, even if all her success was on their labor. It was too big of a risk. One wrong word would undo the years of work she'd done to earn their respect, one slip could ruin everything.

Tristan left, and she lay back on her wide bed. The plush feather mattress was a luxury compared to the wooden planks with straw mats in the other quarters, or the lines of hammocks hung deep in the bowels of the ship for the lowest ranking mates to sleep on. Elinor loosened her belt, thinking about what Tristan had said. It was true, a Captain's life was a lonely one, and her cabin did get cold on the nights when it seemed their voyage was neverending, but that was the way it had to be. Had to. She would never show that weakness again.

She let her fingers trail down her stomach, trying to remember what it felt like when the hand belonged to someone else. Seven months and seventeen days. Not that she was counting. Elinor didn't need anyone else to give her the satisfaction her body craved. Her fingers had learned to do the task well enough themselves, drawing on old memories of unbridled ecstasy to coax forth the waves of her release. But when she closed her eyes, it wasn't Lisbet's face that filled her mind, nor Abi's. Her fingers burned as she imagined they way they brushed Mona's pale back, aching with regret that she hadn't been able to reach back out for more. Her core ignited with the thought of releasing Mona's hair from the pins to ripple across her shoulders in a resplendent wave of copper, and dampness seeped from her as she imagined brushing that hair aside to kiss the soft skin of Mona's neck.

Elinor slid her hand under her waistband and cupped herself with her palm. She could summon Mona back to her cabin, order her to the bed, and lay claim to every inch of her. A tempting idea, but impossible. She parted her slit with one finger instead, her muscles clenching in anticipation. It brushed against her most sensitive parts, causing a tingle to shoot down her legs. She slid the finger back down, joined by a second on the search for her slick opening. She arched her back as she entered herself, straining for the angle that would give her the quickest release. She massaged herself slowly, feeling the wetness increase and begin to spill from her. When she was gasping for air and her walls began to clench around her hand, she withdrew them and stroked the tiny hood covering her most sensitive spot. Her legs trembled and she bit back a cry of pleasure as she rode the wave of ecstasy, then lay still. She didn't need anyone to warm her cabin, she thought as she basked in the calm spreading through her limbs after the orgasm. She was just fine alone.

Chapter 7

A S THE WEEKS PASSED, Mona found herself becoming more comfortable with, and even enjoying, the routine of life at sea. The blisters on her hands had hardened over into tough calluses, and the hours of scrubbing no longer hurt. She had begun to loosen up around the men on the ship, cracking jokes with them and telling stories of her childhood to pass the time. In turn, they taught her the songs of the ship that heralded the bravery of captain and crew, and explained the real stories behind them, which were often much less heroic than they were portrayed. She knew which one was Griff and which was Reddy, along with dozens of the other men with wondrous names like Scabbard, Loosey, and Patch-Eyed Jack. Even Tristan's gruffness had faded as he realized she was capable of more than he thought, including following the rules.

The more distance she gained, the less she thought about her old life in Ogmore and those she had abandoned there. Any regrets of leaving had quickly been washed away by the acceptance Mona found on the ship. The men treated her almost as an equal, respecting her in a way Rhys never had.

As time stretched, it began to seem as though she had spent her entire life on *Nimue's Revenge*. Her footing had become surer, and she no longer had to clutch at the rails when a particularly large swell passed. Even her stomach had ceased with its protestations and become used to the constant motion, just as the captain had promised.

The captain was the one aspect of the ship Mona still couldn't figure out. She had been summoned to supper three more times, and had no better idea of who the captain really was than she did on the day the *Revenge* docked in Ogmore. The crew spoke carefully of her, their respect plain as they danced around Mona's questions with half-answers and platitudes. Yet, when the captain stepped out onto the deck, Mona could scarcely tear her eyes away from her, so entranced was she by her very presence. When the captain spoke, it took all of Mona's willpower to focus on the commands she was giving instead of how it might feel to kiss her soft, pink lips. Mona caught herself longing to don her heavy dress again, folded so carefully into a chest that hadn't been reopened, if only to have the Captain's fingers at her back unlacing the stays one more time.

Mona sat back on her heels, trying to rein in the thoughts that stirred her loins. She had chores to finish, it wasn't the time to be imagining such fantasies, especially not as the captain was walking across the deck right towards her.

"The swabbing can wait this time," she said brusquely. "Go to my cabin and bar the door, don't come out until Tristan or I come for you."

Mona scrambled to her feet. "Why? What's happening?"

"Hopefully nothing." The captain frowned. "But a ship's been spotted, and I need you off the deck and out of sight. That's an order," she added when Mona hesitated.

"Aye, Captain," Mona responded, and hurried to obey. She was annoyed that no one else had been given the order to hide, but it was clear the captain expected no argument from her.

"Ahoy, men!" The captain yelled behind her. "All hands to the deck and ready your guns but hold your fire! A ship's sailin' our way."

Mona slipped into the cabin but left the door ajar so she could see what was happening on the deck. Her heart raced from excitement, there was finally something to break the monotony of endless days of labor. All the stories she had heard had only made her want an adventure of her own more desperately, and it seemed she was about to be a part of one. She wondered if she might make it into a song one day. Certainly not if the captain ordered her to hide every time a ship was spotted. It wasn't fair.

The deck teemed with dozens of men called up from the lower levels of the ship, carrying heavy cannonballs to each station. Mona could have helped with that, if they'd allowed her. The powder boys, the youngest of the crew, ran gunpowder to the men waiting beside the heavy guns. She knew she was capable of that, too. At least she would be more careful than the boys, who were spilling across the deck she had just swabbed. Whether there was to be a battle or not, she would certainly be scrubbing it again. The captain marched around the deck shouting orders, her golden braid gleaming under the afternoon sun.

"What flag?" A gunner called out.

"The Crown!" Tristan shouted.

"Hold your fire," yelled the captain. "Let's see if she approaches."

"Coming right for us," Tristan responded. "You'd better get belowdecks, Cap."

"What, and miss the fight?" She yelled, raising her pistol in the air.

The men on the deck cheered, raising bottles to their Captain as they readied themselves for battle. Goosebumps raised on Mona's arms. It was a sight to behold. The men transformed from disciplined workers to fierce warriors right before her eyes, affixing fierce scowls to their faces and snarling their intent to kill. Up until that moment, Mona had still harbored a bit of doubt that the men were actually pirates. The men were too civilized and Tristan was known for his playfulness, and she had almost convinced herself that the whole thing was an elaborate ruse at her expense. Nothing she had seen aboard the *Revenge* had indicated the crew were anything but dedicated sailors with a knack for finding trouble. Nothing until the other ship came into sight.

Mona saw it then, a great English warship even larger than the *Revenge* with the colors of Britain flying high upon her mast. She counted two decks, each with a long row of cannons pointing directly at them. Even knowing nothing about ships, she could tell this was not one to be trifled with. She held her breath in anticipation, wondering what she was meant to do if the captain or Tristan never came for her, if the huge English vessel would sink them to the bottom of the ocean. Surely there was no way the *Revenge* could win in a fight against such a beast built from the endless coffers of the Crown.

"Hold," the captain yelled, tucking her long braid under her shirt and pulling her three-cornered hat lower onto her head. "Hold!"

The other ship was approaching so quickly Mona thought they were going to be rammed, and she braced herself in the doorframe for impact. None came except for a slight bump as the ship came to rest beside the *Revenge.* A man appeared on the opposing deck, wearing a British naval uniform.

"Where is your captain?" He bellowed.

The crew looked to the Golden Cormorant, who in turn looked to Tristan. She nodded slightly, and he stepped forward.

"I am the captain of this ship," Tristan replied.

"Command your men to lower their weapons and step away from the guns. We are boarding your ship."

Mona shut the door all the way and fumbled to get the heavy bar in place, then pressed her ear to it so she could still hear.

"By what authority?" Tristan's voice was muffled by the thick wood.

"By the authority of the navy of the Kingdom of Great Britain." The response was faint.

Mona decided it was more frightening than exciting when she couldn't see what was going on, but she didn't dare unbar the door. The captain had given her an order that she didn't dare defy.

"We're simple merchants, returning with an empty ship but for our rations to see us through," Tristan protested. "There is no need to board us, no need to search, you'll find nothing untoward here."

"Seems a lot of guns and a crew too eager to fight for a merchant ship."

"We run routes to the Caribbean, lots of pirates these days. Though we're grateful for the Crown's protection, you don't always get there in time. So we had to take our protection into our own hands. You understand, I'm sure, that one can never be too careful."

"Indeed. Yet we'll still need to search the ship. Lots of pirates these days. You understand, I'm sure, one can never be too careful," the captain of the other ship parroted Tristan's words back to him.

There was a long pause, so long that Mona thought the men had moved out of earshot, but then she heard Tristan's response.

"Board us if you must, but make it quick. We're on a tight schedule."

Mona heard footsteps on the deck, and then someone pushed against the door. She stifled her yelp and leaped back as she heard the knocks, furtive but soft.

"Unbar the door, Mona," she heard the captain hiss. "Then hide."

"Aye, Captain," she whispered back, and heard the footsteps dart away.

She removed the bar and peered around the room. Though it was the largest cabin on the ship, the quarters were still small, and the hiding spaces were few. There was a large chest at the foot of the bed, but surely it would be one of the first places someone would look if they were searching for indications of piracy. Chests were where treasure was kept, even the simplest child knew that. The wardrobe was another option large enough to hold her, but with the same problem. She heard more footsteps outside the door and dove under the bed, crawling to the furthest corner and curling into herself. It wasn't ideal, but it seemed the best the cabin had to offer, and maybe she could pass unnoticed in the shadows and dim light. The door to the cabin creaked open, and the boots of two men entered.

"I've no doubt you'll find all of this highly unnecessary, Captain," Tristan said. "May I offer you a drink?"

"Wouldn't say no, Captain... what was it again?"

"Buell. Tristan Buell," he replied.

"Captain Buell, the name seems familiar," said the Englishman, "But I just can't place it."

"You're no doubt thinking of my uncle, the Greybrow. Saved one of you lot's ships when Kidd set upon it off the coast of Wales."

"Ah, yes, that does ring a bell. And, forgive me if I misunderstand, but your uncle was also involved in, how should I put it, some of the more nefarious aspects of seafaring?"

"The accusation offends me, sir. I assure you, *the Revenge* is involved in no such dealings. Never has been, and never will be."

"No offense meant Captain, none at all. I must admit it is quite a relief to run across another vessel flying the Crown's flag. Too many Spanish in these waters, you know. Surely you won't mind if I just poke around a bit, due diligence and all?"

"Be my guest," Tristan invited, though all trace of pleasantry was gone from his voice.

Mona held her breath as the English captain went to the wardrobe first. Her heart thudded in her chest, and she wished she could hold it as well, certain the two men could hear it racing from across the room and her discovery was imminent. She heard cabinets being opened and slammed shut, then the screech of wood as drawers were pulled out and rifled through.

"Everything does seem to be in order here," the Englishman finally said.

"Excellent," Tristan said, tone relaxed again. "I'll see you back to your ship then?"

"Very well," the voices faded as the booted feet shuffled back out of the cabin. "It was a pleasure making your acquaintance, Captain Buell, and Godspeed on your journey."

Mona didn't dare move from her hiding spot until the real captain of the ship appeared in her cabin, accompanied by Tristan.

"You did well," she praised him.

"Got damn lucky," he replied. "They weren't looking for a fight today. Didn't even ask to see our letter."

"You always do." A chair scraped across the floor as the captain took her seat. "You can come out now Mona, the danger has passed."

There was no graceful way to extricate herself from her position under the bed, so she used her elbows to crawl as she wiggled her hips to thrust herself forward and emerged, blinking, to see the captain and Tristan both staring at her. Her cheeks burned hot, and she knew she was blushing, feeling as though she had just been birthed into some intimate moment she wasn't meant to be privy to. She scrambled to her feet, brushing dust from her clothing.

The captain waved her over. "So, you witnessed your first big battle at sea and lived to tell the tale."

Mona laughed nervously, not knowing how else to respond. It had seemed a lot of build up for nothing. Preparation, overreaction, and then... nothing.

"It's true, though," the captain insisted. "That's how they go more often than not. Ships are boarded with no shots fired. Of course, we were lucky we had nothing on board of interest to the British Navy. Were we headed the other direction, fortune may not have been on our side."

"Today was a battle of wits," Tristan added. "Next time it may be a battle of force. We prepare for both."

"I understand," said Mora. "But why did I have to hide?"

"The same reason I did and let Tristan speak for me. Women have no place on ships, not in the eyes of the Navy." The captain sighed, pulling her braid back out from under her shirt, then elaborated. "Women on vessels that aren't carrying passengers are cause for suspicion. There's only one type of woman that helms a ship, and it's the kind the Crown wishes to eliminate. Even in our garb, it's well clear you're not meant for this life. Your speech is too educated, your accent too Welsh, and you can't even wield a weapon. They would assume you to be our prisoner, and if they knew you were someone of import it would be mine or Tristan's body swaying in the breeze o'er the Thames."

"You have me mistaken," Mona corrected. "I'm not important at all, certainly not enough for the king's navy to give a whit about me."

"Perhaps, perhaps not. It's not a risk I can take, for myself or my men."

The ship lurched as her sails caught the breeze and propelled them forward once more, and Mona contemplated the unfairness of it all. The captain had shown herself to be a more than capable leader of the crew of dozens of men, and they seemed eager to let her lead.

"If that's true– that women have no place on ships– then how did you become captain of the *Revenge*?"

The captain and Tristan shared one of their long looks, where it seemed they were having an entire conversation through barely perceptible eye movements, each reading the other's mind. Mona scowled. She knew she had no right to envy the ease of their relationship, but she couldn't help it. Especially because she couldn't figure it out.

"That's a long story that spans many years, and one we don't have time to tell now. Get back to the deck and finish swabbing," Tristan ordered. "Your mates are waiting."

Chapter 8

S ALTED BEEF, PICKLED CABBAGE, and the small, round discs called
sea biscuits that were meant to pass for bread lay on the table in the
captain's quarters. Elinor was reminded why she so rarely crossed the Atlantic. Four weeks into the journey, and all the fresh food on board was long
gone. Traversing the open ocean was one of the more unpleasant aspects of
sailing, and the clear waters of the Caribbean with its isles of abundance
filled her with a longing so intense she could almost smell the fruit stands
at the market in Nassau, still months away. Her navigator assured her they
were on course and heading into warmer winds soon, but it still wasn't
soon enough for Elinor as she faced the miserable rations once again. To
make matters worse, Tristan had taken it upon himself to invite Mona for
supper.

Mona ate her ration with seeming vigor, and Elinor was begrudgingly
impressed again by the woman's tenacity. If she had complaints, she didn't
voice them, and Tristan said she was keeping up with her tasks as any
crewman would. No one looking at her now would suspect her genteel

birth, so tanned was her skin from hours under the sun, her hair loosened from its prim coiffe to fly free in the salty breeze. Yes, Mona was earning her keep, and for that Elinor was relieved, as her men didn't take kindly to any who didn't pull their weight.

Tristan cleared his throat. "So, Elinor, Mona asked how you became captain. Where does the story begin?"

She glared at him. She hated when he called her by her name in front of the crew, and that extended to Mona. It was too familiar and undermined her authority and station on the ship. He looked appropriately chastised at the slip.

"What do you know of the *Revenge*, Mona?" Elinor asked.

"Not much, I suppose. *Nimue's Revenge* is renowned in Ogmore, of course, because of Greybrow, but all that happened before I was born."

Elinor nodded for her to continue, curious to know what tales the villagers had woven over the years.

"It's said he was a farmer during the great famine, and whilst he was out digging in his field, he disinterred the bones of the very ship that ported Arthur to Avalon. He knew it was a sign that he could save the town, but not by farming, so he took up the life of a sailor and ventured far, returning with goods to last the town a whole year."

Tristan laughed. "There's some grain of truth in that to be sure. Greybrow was my uncle, and he did supply the town during the famine, but he was also known as the best captain to sail the Caribbean, taking on crew without regard to their circumstances and offering them a better life than they could have dreamed of." He smirked at Elinor, though he needed not have; the underlying message of his words was clear.

"We were raised on this ship," Elinor chimed in. "He was like a father to me. He established the code on this ship, one we mostly still live by today. Do you know how a sailor gets their name?"

Mona shook her head.

"It's given to them by their crew, as a sign of respect. Graybrow earned his because he helmed the ship so long his hair turned gray. It's rare for a privateer to last two years on a ship, but he made it more than twenty."

"How did you get yours?" Mona asked.

Elinor flushed, embarrassed because she felt her moniker was still unearned. She could still remember that day as though it was yesterday, even though more than fifteen years had passed. "He gave it to me, shortly after I came aboard. I hate it."

"Tell her the story," Tristan urged. "It will help her understand."

Elinor knew he was right. "I came to *Revenge* when I was seven. Greybrow took me under his wing immediately, but his crew was none too happy about it. Women are bad luck on ships, you see, and they blamed me for a spate of it. None of it was my fault, but sailors have their superstitions."

"We were sitting lame in a dead wind," Tristan took over the telling, reprieving Elinor of the emotions that were rushing to the surface as she remembered the old crew's vitriol against her, just a child at the time. "Another ship set upon us, wishing to lighten our load. We were low on powder and had no good means for a fight. The crew wanted to toss her overboard, hoping the tides of luck would turn with her off the ship, but the moment she was dragged on deck, the winds filled our sails. We were able to outrun them with ne'er a shot fired."

Mona was hanging on to the tale with rapt attention, and Elinor was perfectly fine to let Tristan continue it. That way neither of them would hear the crack in her voice when she spoke about the man she considered a father, who had saved her life in so many ways. She hoped Greybrow would be proud of her and the way she had run his ship.

"When we had reached a safe distance, my uncle, Greybrow, paraded her around the deck, proclaiming her a symbol of good fortune for the *Revenge*. He declared her the Golden Cormorant, gold because her hair shines like the riches we seek and the cormorant because they're the luckiest bird a sailor could spot."

"So that's how you became the captain? Because they think you bring them good fortune?" Mona looked at Elinor, green eyes wide with awe.

"I do bring them good fortune. But yes, that's the beginning of how I became the captain of this ship. How I became bound to her, at least," she replied, sighing. "We did tell you it's a long story."

"I want to hear everything." Mona leaned forward.

Tristan poured her another drink, and Elinor drank the dram in one swallow. It steeled her nerves as it slid down to her stomach. She needed to pull herself together, to be the calm, collected captain that Mona expected her to be. It wouldn't do at all to be seen as some emotional wreck.

"Even if the crew saw me as lucky, I still had to work twice as hard to earn their respect and show them I really belong here. But it wasn't until Greybrow's final battle that they believed I could lead. And even that's still thanks to Greybrow intervening. And Tristan. I wouldn't be here without him." Elinor was getting flustered, telling the story all out of order. Tristan had always supported her, but she still wondered if there was a part of that resented her for stepping into the role that seemed to be his destiny.

"I think he always meant this ship to be yours. Your mind is sharper for battle, and mine better attuned to the needs of the crew. We balance each other well." Tristan read her mind again.

"We fired on a ship we couldn't take," Tristan filled in the gaps for Mona. "My uncle took a round from a pistol early in the battle, and while I tended to him in the cabin, Elinor– Captain Davies– though she was the master gunner at the time, led the *Revenge* to an impossible victory. My uncle didn't survive to see it, and the crew voted for Ellie to take the role."

"They wanted Tristan as their captain. He was already quartermaster of the ship then, and they thought it was right for the second in command to step to the helm. Maybe it was, but Tristan refused their nomination. Said it should be me." Seven years later, Elinor still didn't understand why he had given it up. It was something they had both dreamed about as children, when they'd run around below deck after their chores were done. Each pretended to be captain of their own ship, and engaged in mock battles, occasionally recruiting older crewman to join in their games.

He smiled at her. "It was a good compromise, and what my uncle wanted."

"And easier for the crew to live with. Tristan handles the day to day and most of the interaction with them, and they respect his authority there. And I lead them to victory in battle and fill their pockets with pieces of eight." Elinor leaned back in her chair and crossed her arms. She still didn't understand why Tristan had insisted they tell Mona everything. Well, not quite everything. Even he knew some things were unspeakable. The whole supper was probably just a ploy for him to spend more time with Mona under the watchful eye of the captain, so none of the crew could accuse them of any impropriety.

"I think it's incredible," Mona said breathily, leaning in even further. Her red hair gleamed tantalizingly in the candle's flickering light and Elinor had to fight the urge to reach out to brush away a loose strand that had fallen across Mona's eye and tuck it behind her ear.

"Do you?" Elinor arched an eyebrow, forcing herself to remain unmoved as she wondered if Mona even realized that her shirt's wide neck gaped open when she leaned forward, offering a glimpse of the full bosom beneath. She pried her eyes away. Surely Mona was putting on the show for Tristan's benefit, but her eyes were still locked on Elinor's.

"I do," Mona practically purred, "Tell me more."

"What else would you like to know?" Elinor asked stiffly, pretending she didn't notice the delightful, rosy flush that was creeping across Mona's chest.

"Everything," Mona repeated, enunciating every syllable. Elinor barely heard the word. Mona's lips were too distracting as she formed it. Her face seemed to glow in the candlelight, and the sun had brought a smattering of tan freckles forth to dance entrancingly across her cheeks.

Tristan cleared his throat. Elinor had almost forgotten he was still there.

"The hour's getting late, I think I'll be retiring to my cabin now," he said, halfway between a statement and a question.

Elinor knew if she shook her head he would stay. It would be the wiser thing to do, to avoid the temptation of being alone with Mona, a temptation she had managed to avoid for nearly a month. It wasn't just a physical longing, though that was strong. It was a need for closeness, a deeper urge to connect with someone like her, someone who would understand all the things Tristan simply could not. She realized he was still looking to her for a response, and she nodded to the door. He rose, tipping his hat to both of them, and they were alone at last.

More rum. Elinor needed more rum. She poured herself a glass, and offered the bottle to Mona. Mona filled hers, and the women drank, each searching the other's face for the answer to a question left unspoken.

Mona spoke first, her face flushed. "Where is Nassau, anyways?"

"I can show you," Elinor said quickly, grateful for something to do with her hands that might keep them from reaching out to Mona. She retrieved a map and unrolled it on the table. "Come look."

Mona walked around the table, hips swaying in her distinctively feminine way. She must have been doing it on purpose. She didn't sashay like that in front of the crew. Or maybe she did and Elinor just hadn't noticed. It was probably all wishful thinking on her part. Mona's sleeve brushed Elinor's as she stood so close Elinor could feel the heat of her body.

"I always dreamed of seeing more of the world," Mona said. "I just never thought it would happen. My life was determined for me before I ever got a chance to live it."

"And now you are. I just hope you don't come to regret it."

"Never. And I wanted to thank you for not throwing me off your ship."

Elinor nodded, accepting the thanks. "It was the right thing to do. It's what the Greybrow would have done. Once I recognized you from the pub, I couldn't send you back. You looked so miserable with him."

"I thought I hid it well," Mona said. "No one else ever noticed."

"It was your eyes," Elinor said, remembering the look of dread that had clouded Mona's otherwise beautiful face that night. "It was like they were pleading for help."

"I don't want to talk about Rhys anymore. You're much more interesting to me."

Elinor laughed. "I don't see why. I'm not that interesting. My life is this ship, and always has been."

"So where is it we're headed?" Mona leaned in even closer, peering at the map.

Elinor pointed to a small chain of small islands on the outer reaches of the Caribbean below the Spanish colony of Florida.

"Those are the Bahama Islands," she explained, and pointed again. "And that is New Providence, home to the port of Nassau. Or what's left of it, anyways."

"What do you mean, what's left of it?"

Elinor quickly explained the raids on Nassau, ordered by the French and Spanish authorities on the neighboring islands to staunch the bleed of piracy into their waters. When the first raid had been unable to suppress them in 1703, they mounted another attack just three years later, reducing Nassau to nearly nothing. Nearly. Elinor had heard tell that the privateers were coming together there again, forming a new haven to replace Port Royal as a home for their debauchery replete with taverns and inns, shops and whores all willing to relieve the privateers of their coin.

"And where are we now?" Mona asked.

Elinor slid her hand north, drawing a rough circle in the middle of the Atlantic ocean. It was labeled *Mer du Nord* on the old French map that had been plundered from a ship she had sent to the depths some five odd years before, the lettering slightly faded from years of use. "Somewhere around there."

"So far yet," sighed Mona.

"Getting bored with life on our ship?" Elinor teased.

"Not at all." Mona bit her lip. "I find it fascinating."

"What will you do when we get to Nassau, anyways?"

"I don't know, I hadn't thought that far. I suppose I'll seek passage to the Colonies, to start."

Elinor laughed. She hadn't quite figured out if the woman was too brave for her own good, or just too naive, but something about it was charming nonetheless.

"That will be hard to come by now, I think."

"Well, maybe I could stay with the *Revenge* for a while then? I'll work hard, I swear it."

"No." Elinor couldn't bear the thought of having her on board any longer than necessary, just out of reach. While it may have been adventure Mona craved, the ship was no life for a woman like that. "I'll secure your passage to the Colonies. There are a few captains that owe me the favor. You may have to wait awhile for the right ship."

"How long is a while in Nassau?"

Elinor shrugged. "Could be days, could be years. No right way of knowing who is coming and when, assuming any of them are still alive. But don't worry, I'll find you your passage. You have my word."

"Do you want so badly to be rid of me, then?"

Yes. The temptation was driving Elinor wild. "Just a desire to see you safely on your way to whatever you're searching for."

Mona pointed to something else on the map, a detailed illustration not far from where Elinor indicated the *Revenge* was sailing. It was a great, scaled beast, drawn to appear the size of a frigate with menacing tusks and large, webbed feet like those of a gull.

"Have you ever fought a monster before?" Mona asked.

"Many times," Elinor said, "Though not as they're pictured here." She wasn't sure the sea beasts of legend even existed. She had never seen one, and she had been on the seas as long as anyone.

"What do you mean?" Mona asked.

"Some of the most fearsome monsters are the men out on these seas. But I have fought them and I have won." And lost, but Mona didn't need to hear about that. Elinor took another drink to wash the bitter reminder of failure away. She was beginning to feel the warmth of the alcohol rising on the back of her neck, making her bolder and the question burn stronger.

Knowing wouldn't hurt. She covered Mona's hand, still resting on the map, with her own.

"Tell me the truth, Mona," she whispered, feeling her palm tingle where it rested upon Mona's. "What is the real reason you didn't want to marry him?"

Green eyes met hers, searching for the answer Elinor wanted to hear. Elinor kept her face still, careful not to show any emotion. She didn't want Mona to say what would appease her as captain, she wanted to truth of Mona's inner feelings. Her heart pounded as though it was begging for escape from her chest.

"I..." Mona hesitated, then leaned down and pressed her lips against Elinor's. She pulled away before Elinor could kiss her back. "I'm sorry."

"Shhh," Elinor hushed her, pulling Mona to her again.

Her lips were just as sweet as Elinor had imagined and tasted lightly of the vanilla that was used to spice the rum. They were soft, too, even as they pressed hard against her. Elinor brought free hand to Mona's neck, brushing back the briny waves of red, and pulled her even closer. She felt Mona's sharp inhale as their chests brushed against each other, and Mona responded hungrily. The ship rocked in the swells of night, and the women rocked with it, swaying as they clung to each other desperately.

Elinor pushed Mona backwards to sit on the table, and Mona answered wrapping her legs around Elinor's waist as they kissed. The bed beckoned just across the room. It would be so easy to carry her there, lay her down and explore her body by the full moonlight streaming through the window. Elinor moved away from Mona's lips, kissing down the side of her neck to taste the salty skin near the collar of her shirt, each little gasp begging Elinor to continue. Mona's hands ran down Elinor's back to tug at the hem of her shirt.

Elinor pulled back, disentangling her hands from Mona's hair. "We can't do this."

"Why not?" Mona tried to pull her back, but Elinor resisted.

"We can't." It was against the code for one, and besides, Elinor didn't need any distractions in her life. Couldn't afford any new attachments.

"Because of Tristan?" Mona said sadly, looking away.

"Tristan? What does he have to do with anything?" Tristan was the furthest thing from Elinor's thoughts.

"Aren't you and he...? You seem so close."

Elinor laughed bitterly. "It's not that. Tristan is like a brother to me, nothing more."

"Then what?" Mona pouted with lips slightly swollen from their embrace, and Elinor had to look away before she kissed them again.

"We just can't. Not on the ship. It's against the code. Go to your quarters, Mona," Elinor demanded, slipping back into her role as captain as she pretended pulling away didn't hurt..

Mona obeyed without further protest, stopping only at the door to look back wistfully, before slamming it shut behind her. She was mad, but Elinor expected her to be. More than that, she was likely hurt and confused, both things Elinor had wished to avoid. She cursed Tristan for leaving them alone. He must have known where it would lead, and now it was too late to take back. Knowing Mona wanted her too was far worse than wondering. She should have never fallen into the trap. The map lay askew on the table, and she straightened it. Six weeks to Nassau, if the winds held. She just had to have enough willpower to last until then, and Mona could become another painful memory, nothing more.

Chapter 9

"OPEN THE DOOR, MONA!" Tristan called, his bellow followed by three loud raps on her door. "You're late."

"Go away," she yelled back. "I'm feeling unwell."

It was true, her head ached from drinking too much rum then crying long into the night and her eyes were so swollen she could barely see through them. She couldn't be seen on deck in such disarray. The men would talk. Of course, they would talk if she didn't appear for her chores either, but at least she wouldn't have to face them. She didn't care anymore what they thought of her.

"Let me in," Tristan insisted, pounding on the door again. "Mona, that's an order."

When it was clear he wasn't going to leave her alone, she rose to unbar the door, groaning as she went. He pushed past her and shut the door behind him again.

"You were fine last night. What's all this now?"

Mona felt the tears welling up in her eyes and blinked them away, hoping he didn't notice. She didn't want him to think her weak, and how was she supposed to explain that her heart was breaking to someone who surely wouldn't understand. She opened her mouth to tell him she was fine, but different words spilled out.

"She rejected me," Mona sobbed, covering her face with her hands as she broke down again. "She doesn't want anything to do with me."

"The captain?" Tristan clarified, though there was no one else on the *Revenge* that Mona could have been referring to.

She nodded, wiping away tears that were quickly replaced with new ones of embarrassment. "I just don't know what I did wrong. Everything seemed fine, and then it was like a wall went up and she pushed me away."

"Give her time," Tristan said, patting her awkwardly on the arm. "You didn't do anything wrong. She may come around yet."

"How can you say that? You don't even know what happened."

"I know the captain. I'm sure she didn't intend to hurt you like this. She's just slow to come around."

"I don't understand."

"She has her reasons, and they aren't mine to tell. Give her time," he repeated. "Now come, the dishes are waiting."

Mona allowed Tristan to take her by the arm and lead her across the deck to the tiny galley.

"Take all the time you need," he said, "But not too much. Griff and Reddy will be wondering about you."

She worked absentmindedly, allowing her hands to do the task they had memorized while she stared out the window at the blue expanse looking for signs of the monsters that had dotted the map. Time seemed endless out on the open ocean, yet the map had betrayed the truth, that they were ever churning towards their destination and that her days on *Nimue's Revenge* would eventually come to an end.

She should have never kissed the captain, but she hadn't been able to hold back. Words had seemed too inadequate to explain why she'd need to leave Ogmore, and the kiss seemed the only way to convey what she needed the captain to understand. How else was she to explain that it hadn't been one man, but all men she rejected in her flight from Ogmore? And the kiss had been perfect, passionate, right up until the moment it wasn't, when the captain pulled away with pain in her eyes. Mona just wished she knew where she had gone wrong. She had been so sure the captain was eyeing her with the same desire she felt, and when the captain laid her hand on Mona's... Mona couldn't think about it any longer. She splashed cool sea water on her face to wash away the tears, but just burned her sun-chapped cheeks. She couldn't dawdle any longer, she was needed on the deck.

That night, another storm blew up, tossing the ship around in the waves. Mona couldn't help but remember her first night on board the ship, full of trepidation and horribly sick. This time the storm excited her more than it frightened her, even as she had to cling to the bed to not be tossed out of it. If the ship went down in the night, she thought, at least she would go down knowing what it was like to feel the captain's mouth on hers, even if the moment had been too brief. She couldn't regret that.

When the storm died down, the strong winds remained, pushing along *Nimue's Revenge* on her southern trajectory. The sun stayed in the sky longer and the nights got warmer as the weeks went by, but Mona never received another invitation to dine in the captain's cabin. In fact, the captain seemed to be avoiding her altogether, refusing to meet her eyes when their paths crossed on the deck and spending most of her hours enclosed in the cabin or alone at the helm of the ship. Even Tristan seemed to be giving

Mona a wide berth, barking orders but exchanging none of the pleasantries and gentle teasing she had grown accustomed to from the quartermaster.

Mona had nearly worn holes in the knees of the breeches given to her by the captain due to all the time she spent on her knees scrubbing in them, but no one could say her section of deck wasn't the cleanest on the ship. She sat back to look at her progress when the ship veered hard towards the starboard side, jolting with the change of direction, and Mona slid across the deck until she caught herself on one of the eight pounder cannons, so named for the weight of the balls they fired. The deck was a flurry of activity as the crew abandoned their posts to rush to the railing.

"What is it? A ship?" She asked Reddy, who was closest to her, as she scrambled to her feet.

"No," he said, "I can't see one."

"Hope nothing's wrong with the boat," Griff chimed in. "That was a hard turn."

Mona peered out at the horizon, seeing nothing but blue water and blue sky dotted with clouds. The crew were yelling in confusion, trying to figure out why the ship had made the sudden shift. The captain stood at the helm and was glaring at Mona, Tristan at her side. Mona felt her cheeks get hot under the withering stare. She still didn't understand what she had done wrong to cause the captain's ire.

"We're changing course!" The captain shouted. "Heading for Carolina."

Another place that Mona had never really heard of, one that sounded only vaguely familiar from her tutor's ramblings. The crew seemed to know it well, though, and erupted in protest at the news.

"Thought we were going to Nassau," Scab shouted back.

"The plan has changed."

"We didn't vote to change it," Griff yelled. "What happened to our choice? You promised Nassau. We demand a vote."

A cheer of assent rose from the crew. Mona knew many of the men, including Griff, had wives or favored prostitutes in the abandoned port city that they were so eager to get back to. Truth told, she was disappointed with the news, too. The closer they got to the isle, the more the men talked about how lush and beautiful it was, painting scenes of opulence Mona couldn't even imagine. She had been looking forward to seeing it, if only to know if it lived up to the wondrous reputation the men bestowed upon it.

"Lots of traders run through the Carolina settlements," the captain explained. "The pickings will be easy, and your pockets will be heavy with coins when we reach our beloved isle of New Providence."

The men grumbled a bit amongst themselves, then grizzled old Scab spoke up, his voice somber.

"If it's the Carolina your sights are set on, it'll not be with our help. Change the course and we'll surrender to the first ship we come upon, be she Crown or pirate."

Mona could tell the captain was frustrated, and she scowled at the dissidents in the crew before finally conceding to a vote.

"Step forward then, one at a time, and let your voice be heard, then. Nassau or Carolina?" The captain looked to Tristan first.

He looked from her to the crew and back. "Carolina."

Scab stepped up. "Nassau."

Griff was next. "Nassau."

One by one, the rest of the ship's crew cast their votes to determine their destination. She had hung back at the rear of the crew, assuming she had no voice as a passenger on their ship, so she was surprised when the captain called her name after everyone else had gone. She hesitated, torn between wanting to please the captain by saying Carolina and wanting to see the Caribbean island everyone spoke so highly of. Not that it mattered. The votes were clear, and the crew would overrule their captain.

"Nassau," she replied.

"Correct the course then," the captain ordered Tristan. She whirled, but not before Mona caught a glimpse of angry tears in her eyes, and stomped back to her cabin.

Chapter 10

"WHAT WAS THAT ABOUT?" Tristan asked as he stepped into the cabin without knocking, his anger palpable in the stuffy room. "Since when do you have any interest in seeing the Carolina? And why didn't you talk to me first?"

"It's the closest port," Elinor said through gritted teeth, keeping her back turned to him.

"Is something wrong with the ship?" Concern crept into Tristan's voice.

"No, she needs to be careened but nothing that can't wait." Elinor sighed impatiently, frustrated that he was questioning her judgment. She didn't need to explain her reasoning to him, she just needed his support.

"Then what?" Tristan took her by the shoulders, gently, and spun her around to face him.

"I need her off my ship," Ellinor spat out, tears running silently down her face. "As soon as possible."

"Mona? What did she do?" He guided her to sit on the bed then handed her the bottle of rum.

"She's weak, lazy, and next to useless," Elinor parroted his words from the woman's first full day on her ship.

"You know she isn't. I had my doubts, but she works as hard as any man on this ship, maybe harder. Elinor, what is this really about?"

Elinor swallowed desperately, trying to rid her throat of the lump that had formed there. She blinked against the tears that welled in her eyes, but she couldn't stop the drops that escaped to run down her cheeks. It was humiliating, and she felt her cheeks flush hot with anger. She had lost control of her ship and lost control of herself. It was unfitting of a captain.

"Because I started to care for her, dammit! I didn't want to like her, and then she kissed me, and now I can't stop thinking about her, and she's becoming too much of a distraction. Which makes this too dangerous for her to continue. You know that."

"Oh, Elinor," he said, pulling her into an embrace, and she knew he was thinking of Abigail, too. "She wouldn't have wanted this for you."

"Don't tell me what she would have wanted," she snapped and pulled away. The wound was too raw, and she didn't want his pity for something that was her own fault.

"I know you miss her," Tristan said softly. "But don't you think five years is long enough? You can't punish yourself forever."

Elinor drank angrily from the bottle, crossing the room to slam it down on the table as rum overflowed her mouth and spilled down her chin. How dare he talk about Abigail to her? He knew it was forbidden, they all did.

"Leave," she demanded.

He ignored her command. "You can't run from it forever, Elinor. You have to forgive yourself."

I can't let it happen again, she rebutted silently. She pointed at the door. "That was an order from your captain. Get out."

"Give Mona a chance. Or at least an explanation, you owe her that much."

"Tristan..." Elinor warned. He was pushing her limits with his defiance, and she didn't want to discipline him. She would if she had to, though.

"You don't see how many mornings she's arrived at breakfast with eyes red from crying. You know you're hurting her. Tell her why. Tell her about Abigail before we get to Nassau or I will."

"Get out!" Elinor screamed, reaching her breaking point and not caring if the whole ship heard her. She drew her cutlass and advanced towards him. "You overstep too far. Never speak her name on this ship again, or I'll have your tongue out. Am I clear, Quartermaster?"

"Aye, Captain." He frowned, clearly taken aback by the full force of ire she had never turned against him before, placed his hat back on his head, and left.

She drank the last swig of rum, and hurled the bottle against the door as it closed behind him. The bottle shattered, shards of expensive glass exploding across the room. Abigail. She sobbed the name into her mattress, hoping it muffled her cries. Her first love, so long gone that her face was but a memory so blurred by time that Elinor could scarcely conjure it from the recesses of her mind anymore. Tristan was right, she admitted to herself begrudgingly, Abi wouldn't have wanted her to live like this. Abi, so full of love and ready to share it with everyone, would have wanted Elinor to seek it again. But what Abi would have wanted didn't matter. She wasn't the one left behind.

The five years since her death had somehow passed in the blink of an eye, yet every day spent without her was agonizing torture. And that had been the point, to torture her until her last day. Abigail, her first love, with the eyes that glittered blue like the stillest waters around the cayes of the Caribbean, who had stepped onto her ship and into her heart. For seven months they had sailed the waters together, going from island to island, taking spoils where they found them, and delighting in each other's company. With Abi by her side, their victories were guaranteed.

Until night they lost. They hadn't even known the ship was upon them until the first cannons were fired. Her crew fought valiantly, but they hadn't been able to stop the other ship from boarding the *Revenge*. They had just left port with lightened pockets and a lighter ship, and the other captain was angry not to find the spoils he was searching for. But they had found Abigail cowering in Elinor's cabin, and dragged her out to the deck. Neither pirate nor prisoner, they knew she was someone's wife, an easy target to manipulate the crew into submission. When Elinor tried to stop it she was tied to the mast, incapacitated as Abigail was tortured in front of her. The screams still haunted her dreams. They had first extracted the information they wanted, and then the pleasure before tossing Abi's barely-conscious body over the side of the ship. Elinor sobbed as the memory replayed before her eyes.

Elinor had gotten her revenge, chasing the ship down and cutting the man's fingers from his body one by one as he begged forgiveness for his sins. Forgiveness was not hers to offer. He had taken the life of the only one who could absolve him. When he had no fingers or toes remaining, she ordered him to be tied to the end of a cannon and had an eight pound ball shot through him as his blood drained into the ocean. Indeed, she had fought monsters, and it had turned her into one as well. When it was done, she wrote the new law into her code, that no man or woman should lie with another on her ship. Spouses and lovers were to be left ashore, if the men choose to have them, so they couldn't be used against them. And Abigail, her dear Abigail, was never to be spoken of again.

She knelt to pick up the shards of glass as her anger abated into grief. She'd never believed in the pirates' talk of curses put upon them by the supposedly wicked women they had scorned, but she supposed this was hers; destined to roam the seas with the one thing she wanted most always beyond her grasp.

Then Mona had come. It was easy to long for her company when she thought her advances would be rebuked, just another woman to admire from afar. Knowing that the longing was reciprocated made it impossible to be around her. The anger Elinor had felt in the weeks since the kiss was misplaced and she knew it, but that made it no less real. It wasn't Mona's fault that she wasn't Abi. It wasn't Mona's fault that any of it had happened, yet she couldn't help but resent the woman who fit in with the crew and pulled her weight more than Abi ever had. Who was tough in ways Abi never was. And in the darkest corners of her soul, the part she dared never access for fear of what such thoughts would bring, she was angry with Abi. For never having learned to fight, or even to wield a flintlock in defense. For laughing off Elinor's fears. For distracting her the night of the attack, convincing her the ship she swore she saw across the inky water was a figment of imagination, to be ignored until it was too late. For begging for Elinor's life and exposing herself as a target to manipulate Elinor's resolve. For dying and leaving Elinor to pick up the pieces alone.

But most of all, Elinor was angry with herself, for after all the resentment and excuses were stripped away there was no one else to blame for that night. She was the captain of the ship, and she had made a mistake. A mistake too many others had paid for with their lives. She would not resign Mona to the same fate, and as soon as they reached Nassau and secured her passage onwards, any obligation she had to the woman was done.

Nassau. Elinor's cheeks flushed anew. It was the first time her crew had voted against her wishes. Even though Tristan had supported her outwardly, the men still thought they knew better how to run her ship than her, and the public rebuke stung. A new thought clenched her stomach with fear; maybe her days as captain were coming to an end. They could remove her any time they wanted, and if they thought she was no longer fit for the job, she could think of a few who might try for it. Over her dead body. The *Revenge* was all Elinor had left, and she would be damned if she lost her ship, too.

Chapter 11

SIX DAYS PASSED BEFORE Mona saw the captain again after her decision to change course was overruled. Tristan seemed to be brooding as well, and the overall mood on the ship had taken a turn. She supposed it was to be expected, they had been confined to the floating mass of carefully hewn and tarred timber for too many weeks, and though no one on the crew would deny their love for the sea, she could tell they all yearned to be on dry land again and ached for the company of others.

The water in the barrels had gone musty with age, and Mona found herself turning more and more to the spirits the ship still had good stock of, if only to avoid the rancid taste. When it was discovered that half of their remaining meat was crawling with maggots, most of the men still opted to eat it anyway. It was that or a slow starvation. She thought of the stories that had circulated Ogmore, the days of endless adventure in exotic locales, and scoffed. If she ever went back she would tell them how the stories were false, life at sea was filled with drudgery and hard work, boredom that never ceased, and food that would make one long for just a spoonful of the most basic leek soup. She swore to never scorn the simplicity of a bowl of *cawl cennin* again.

And if she'd never left? Mona allowed herself to consider what her life might have been. Married to Rhys, maybe already pregnant with his heir. Her hand went to her stomach at the thought, and her mood lifted. No matter how dull things seemed on board the ship, the days were surely easier than the life she had been doomed to. Even if she had made a mess of things with the captain.

Mona stood at the rail of the ship watching the red sun sinking slowly below the horizon. The hour was getting late, but she had a few more precious moments to be outside before she was exiled to her cabin for the night. A breeze rustled her shirt and she wrapped her arms around herself, more out of habit than actual chill. A flash of movement in the corner of her eye made her jump, and she realized the captain had crept up and was standing right beside her.

"Good evening, Captain," she said formally, dread creeping in as she wondered what she had done to earn the individual attention of the woman who never spoke to her.

"Mona, I..." she trailed off and took a deep breath. "If I've done anything to cause you distress, please know that was not my intention."

"I'm fine," Mona said, taken aback by the near apology.

"It's nothing you did," the captain continued. "My duty to the ship must come first."

"I understand."

Mona thought the captain would leave as quickly as she had come, but she leaned forward to rest her forearms on the rail. She looked older somehow, as though the journey from Wales had been particularly taxing. Her hair still shone like gold in the setting sun, lending her an air of regality.

Mona was reminded of a queen looking out over her realm, fitting for the captain who was said to dominate the seas. Her eyes were closed as the spray of waves misted across her face, and Mona sensed a deep anguish coming her. Mona wished she had some words of comfort, but knew the captain wouldn't take them kindly, so instead she stood with her until the silence became uncomfortable.

"This isn't the first time I've run away from home," she said to break it, talking more to herself than the captain. "Though this is the farthest I've ever gotten."

"Oh?" The captain opened her eyes and looked at Mona.

"When I was seven or eight, my father was set to punish me, I don't even remember for what anymore. I just remember thinking I wouldn't allow it to happen, so instead of going to his study I went into the kitchen, stole some bread and cheese, and ran off into the woods. Took the staff all of twenty minutes to catch up to me, and cost me double the lashings than if I had just accepted the punishment up front."

"Why are you telling me this?" The captain asked warily.

Mona shrugged. "I suppose so you know I don't regret my decision at all. I feel more at home here than I ever have before." Mona stopped short of asking to stay again, knowing the request was futile.

"You've done well to adapt. Good thing, too, because you'll have another long journey from Nassau to the colonies." The captain seemed to hear Mona's unspoken question, and shut it down quickly.

Mona pretended like the rebuke didn't sting, and fiddled with the hem of her shirt so as to have a reason not to meet the captain's eyes. Everyone knew the ship was hurting for crewmen, and hoped to pick up more willing hands in the Islands. She didn't understand why she couldn't join them, and why the captain was the one who seemed most against it. She, of all people, should know that Mona was as capable as any. It had to be the kiss. Mona had misread the situation, and it had ruined everything for her.

The sun was just a crescent sliver hanging over the ocean, the sky darkening rapidly in its wake as the first stars appeared in the night. Laughter filled the deck and the crew passed bottles around, the warm evening a welcome backdrop for their carousing. Mona often wished she could join them in the evenings, but the captain had ordered her to be in her cabin after dark. The unfairness of a rule that seemed to only apply to her grated. Sensing she couldn't make things worse with the captain, Mona figured it didn't hurt to ask for a little more freedom to ease her loneliness.

"Why can't I stay out later with the crew on the deck?"

"Because I don't trust them with you and I'd rather not have to kill any of them."

"None of them have done anything even remotely untoward," Mona protested. "I can look after myself, you know."

The captain looked her up and down slowly, assessing. "I very much doubt that. Any of my men would subdue you quickly in a fight."

"It's not fair! You won't even give me a chance." Mona felt like screaming in frustration, but it was clear the captain already thought her a child, so she settled for crossing her arms across her chest. "What have I done wrong?"

"I gave you a chance by not tossing you into the bay at Ogmore. Don't make me regret it."

"It's clear you already do," Mona said, tears pricking in her eyes.

"Mona," the captain whispered, her voice catching on the name. "Don't cry. I only care for your safety. Can't you see that?"

"What about my happiness? What good is safety if I'm doomed to long for something I can't have? Ogmore was safety, and it wasn't enough."

"And you think this is?" The captain scoffed.

"I think it could be. All my life, no one has ever seen me. They see my father's money. Friendships were permitted only when they were advantageous for business or status and I could never trust anyone. It's different here. The crew doesn't care about that, just that I can pull my weight." Mona said carefully. "Of course there are still things I'd need to learn."

"Like what?"

"How to shoot or wield a cutlass, so I'm not entirely defenseless if we come across another ship. I could run powder for the cannons. I want to be able to help, not hide." Mona couldn't tell if it was her imagination playing tricks in the fading light, or if the captain really paled at the suggestion.

Finally, she shook her head. "What you need to learn is women like you don't belong on ships like mine. I'll not let you carve out a place for yourself here."

"What do you mean, women like me?"

"Rich, spoiled, naive. Raised to look pretty and not much else."

"Is that what you really think of me?" Mona was hurt. Hadn't she shown she was more than that?

The captain shrugged and looked away. It was the first time Mona could remember the captain being afraid to meet her eyes.

"Well, you're wrong. I'm not rich, even if my father is. I have nothing, no coin to my name and only the clothes I arrived in. I work as hard as anyone else on the *Revenge*, and I'm not as naive as you think." Mona swallowed her pride. "Please. Just give me a chance. I have nothing else."

It was impossible to read the thoughts behind the captain's stony face as she glared at Mona. Mona wondered if she was really thinking it through or just keeping her on edge, toying with her emotions and giving her false hope before delivering a crushing verdict.

"I'll consider it," the captain said, relenting a little.

"Thank you," Mona replied, stopping herself just before she curtsied. Old habits were hard to rid herself of. "I guess I'll be off to bed, then?"

The captain nodded, and Mona felt a flash of disappointment as she turned to cross the deck back to her lonely chambers. It was hard to even think of bed without imagining the captain with her in it, and something in the captain's cold rejections only stirred her desire to be wanted more. She paused at her door, looking back to see the captain still staring at her.

***

Three days later, Tristan approached Mona on the deck as she was finishing swabbing around the cannons.

"Come with me," he ordered, striding off towards the stern of the ship before Mona could even ask what was happening.

She trotted behind him, catching up as they arrived at the back of the *Revenge*, the same place where he had found her stowing away those many months before. The crates that had been stacked there were dismantled as they were emptied, and most of the rear deck was empty.

"The captain has decided you're to learn how to shoot," Tristan said.

"Really?" Mona said, grinning.

Tristan shrugged. "She said you talked her into it. Have you even held a pistol before?"

"Of course I have," Mona replied, indignant at his teasing. "Once. But it was a long time ago." Tristan didn't have to know that it was her father's and he had only let her hold it briefly to stop her whining. His idea of a compromise, since he wouldn't allow her to participate in the hunt.

Tristan handed her the weapon, and she lifted it gingerly, testing its weight in her hands as she worried it might go off unbidden. Tristan noticed her hesitation.

"You can't be afraid of it."

"I'm not," Mona said, even though she was, a little. "Is it safe?"

Tristan laughed. "Safe? She's meant to kill people. Of course she isn't safe. But treat her right, and she probably won't kill you."

Mona thought he could just as easily have been describing the captain as the weapon in her hands.

"First, powder," Tristan said, tilting the barrel of the pistol up and pouring the black grains down it. "Then the ball."

He showed her how to wrap it in a scrap of cloth and use the ramrod to push it down into place. Then he showed her how to pull back the frizzen that covered the flashpan, and drop more fine black powder there.

"So the flint has something to ignite," he grunted by way of explanation. "In a battle, you should be able to do that all in thirty seconds, any more and you won't be alive long enough to fire again."

"So it's ready now?" Mona asked, cradling the pistol cautiously so as not to disturb it's combustible contents.

"Just cock, aim, and shoot," Tristan said, pointing to the blue water trailing behind them. "Off the ship."

Mona pulled back the cock and raised the flintlock, arm trembling under the weight. Tristan covered his ears and nodded to her. Her finger brushed the trigger and she flinched, waiting for a sound that never came. She pulled it a little harder, and felt the weapon explode in her hand, sending her reeling backwards as she almost dropped it to the deck. Her ears were ringing and she felt Tristan behind her, steadying her.

"Load it again," he instructed, handing her the powder. "This time plant your feet wider, so you won't be thrown back with the shot."

She repeated the process, exactly as he had shown her, and when he nodded his approval, she fired again. It was easier when she knew what to expect, was able to brace herself against the rocking of the ship and the recoil of the gun.

"Again," he said.

When he was satisfied she had learned as much as she was going to for the day, he took the weapon back. Her hand felt light without the weight of the pistol and was covered in dark residue from the shots she had fired. The sharp smell of gunpowder lingered in the air.

"Clean up here," he ordered, nodding to the bucket and mop that were never far. "Then you may join us on deck, if you so desire."

"Really?" Mona asked, glancing towards the sun. By the time she reswabbed the deck it would be past dark, and she didn't dare defy the captain's orders.

"Only until I retire to my quarters," he clarified.

Mona's arms and shoulders ached from the hard work of firing the gun after an already long day of physical labor, but she pushed through it and made quick work of cleaning the small deck. The sounds of the crew's evening revelry were rising on the main deck and she was eager to join them for the first time.

"Mona!" Reddy called as soon as she stepped around the corner. "Sit," he offered, abandoning the crate he was perched on. "Tristan was just going to dance for us."

The crew bellowed with laughter as Tristan turned redder than the just set sun and shook his head. "I was not."

Mona sat on the edge of the crate, smoothing imaginary skirts as she did. She didn't want the men to see how nervous she was. Even though she had spent months in their company, this was different. Somewhere to her left, a bottle was being pressed into her hand. She took it and drank deeply, feeling the familiar burn followed by warm spices and sugar as the rum slipped down her throat.

"Dance, dance!" The men were still encouraging Tristan, pounding their fists on crates to make a rhythm. One of the crewmen pulled out a tin flute and began playing an upbeat tune.

Finally Tristan shrugged, then got to his feet as the men scooted their crates back to form a circle around him. The pounding became louder as Tristan stepped to the center of it, nodding his head in time to the rhythm before his feet began to move. Mona watched with rapt attention as he performed a series of quick steps, jumping high into the air to end with a flourish as he locked eyes with the man next to Reddy.

The man rose to the challenge, joining Tristan in the center of the circle as the rest the crew cheered and the bottles circulated once more. Mona drank again, grinning as the second man responded in a flurry of steps of his own, spinning and stomping before throwing the challenge back to Tristan.

"He's really good," Mona said to Reddy as the quartermaster quickened his pace.

"Aye, the best on the ship, but it's rare he'll join us anymore," Reddy replied.

"Why's that?"

"I don't rightly know. Spose he's busy running the ship," Reddy said, then shrugged. "Or the captain keeps him on a short chain, like you."

"She just wants to keep me from harm," Mona said, jumping to the captain's defense, though she didn't know why. The crew seemed harmless enough; no one had even given her a second glance after she had taken her seat among them.

"She's not wrong in her concern, but none of us would ever hurt you, Miss Mona. You're one of us now."

Mona felt her heart swell as the second man in the circle threw up his hands in defeat, laughing as he gasped for air. Reddy's acceptance meant more to her than she could put into words, so she just grinned happily and handed over the bottle of rum. Tristan returned to his seat as two more men took places in the circle and the flute player struck up another tune. Mona laughed and clapped along with the music as they danced, each trying to outdo the other with increasingly elaborate leaps and spins as the hour grew later. She yawned, and Tristan was beside her instantly, as though he had been watching for the moment she displayed any signs of tiredness.

"Time to get you to bed, Mona," he said. "The hour's late enough."

He escorted her to her cabin door and tipped his hat.

"Thank you," she slurred. "And tell the captain thank you, as well. I had fun tonight, for the first time in a long time."

Chapter 12

Everyone on board *Nimue's Revenge* was on edge, Elinor could feel it every time she stepped out onto the decks. They were hungry, not just for food, but for the excitement of a battle at sea and spoils to spend when they reached the Bahamas. Elinor was ready to give it to them, if the opportunity presented itself. She opened the cabinet and removed a flag, black as the sea under a moonless night, with a white skull in the top left corner, and the mighty *Y Ddraig Goch*, the red dragon of Wales that had been the battle standard of Arthur himself, adorning the bottom right.

The ship was entering the trade routes, and soon they would lower the flag of the Crown that offered them safety and camouflage in unfriendly waters to raise the flag Greybrow had designed so many years before. The original had long since been lost, rent beyond repair in some skirmish years ago. Elinor trailed her fingers over the fabric, feeling the raised scars of thread that rippled across its surface. The careful mending she had done was nearly invisible, the flag's implied threat as intimidating as ever. Elinor was anxious to see her flapping in the wind again.

Yells rose from the deck, mingling with the soft sea breeze that floated through her open windows. She supposed she should go see what the commotion was about, but Tristan was already knocking at her door with his familiar staccatoed raps. He barged in before she could even reach the door to open it.

"We've sighted land!" He rushed to Elinor and gathered her in a hug, spinning her around before setting her back down. "Finally."

"Finally," Elinor echoed, going to the window to look out. Sure enough, there was a tiny spit of sand emerging from the ocean, many boat lengths away still.

"You've got the flag out," Tristan said from her table in the center of the room. "Planning something?"

"Just making sure she's in good repair before we need her next," Elinor said, eyes still locked on the land in the distance.

"But is the *Revenge* ready?"

"The men are. The ship, well, you can tell how slow she is. We won't be doing any outrunning, but I think we can still manage some outgunning."

"We're so close to land now, why not just scrape the hulls first and take our spoils after?" Tristan asked.

It would be the sensible thing to do, but it was a risk Elinor could no longer afford to take. She voiced her concerns to Tristan. "They already overruled me once on the Carolinas, I can't upset them further. They're hungry for blood and for gold, not more work."

He tsked. "This is different, Elinor. Careening would be for the good of everyone. The *Revenge* is still your ship, treat her well. What would Greybrow do?"

"I don't know." She shrugged. "His crew never defied him."

"The men are still with you."

"Until the kegs run dry. We can't go ashore until we replenish that at least, or there really will be mutiny."

"You worry too much," he said, slinging an arm around her shoulders. "Make your decision, but make it with confidence. You know you'll always have my backing."

"Worry keeps us alive," she countered. "I'll think on it. For now we continue the course to Nassau."

"Worry may keep us alive, but it also keeps us from living." Tristan squeezed her shoulder, and Elinor knew he wasn't just talking about the crew.

She also knew he was right. In her concern for those around, she was losing sight of the real goal. All the crew needed from her was prosperity, full pockets that would buy them the happiness they needed in a world that had too often been cruel to them. She never used to doubt her decisions, but everything had changed since Mona boarded the ship and she had lost sight of herself.

"We fight first," she stated before she could change her mind again. "The flag wishes to fly. It's been too long."

Tristan smiled, and Elinor wondered if that had been his intent all along. He'd always had a way of presenting options to her that made the right choice clear.

"We won't be able to run, so we'll have to trap them," she mused. "We'll signal distress to lure them in, turn our guns on them before they have time to flee."

Tristan pulled out the map and laid it atop the flag on the table, studying the chain of isles that marked the eastern entrance to the Caribbean.

"There should be a fair few ships well loaded and leaving on their fall crossings," he said. "If we're here, we can anchor between these islands and try to intercept a Spanish ship leaving Hispaniola." He pointed out the locations on the map.

"Here," Elinor said, placing her finger on a narrow bay just beyond the main shipping corridor between two smaller islands with no marked settlements on them. "It's close, and well hidden."

"I'll let the navigator know," Tristan said, rolling up the map and setting it aside. "And you'll tell the men?"

"Yes," Elinor agreed. "After supper. What rations do we have left in the hold?"

"Not much, but enough for a few weeks more," he replied, frowning.

"No matter. We'll be full up on supplies in a few days time. I want the men to feast tonight. They've earned it."

Tristan was still frowning, the lines etched between his dark eyebrows reminding her of the scowl Greybrow so often wore. His displeasure was apparent, but Elinor wasn't able to make out the root of it.

"What troubles you?" She finally asked when the moment of silence between them had gone on too long.

"Mona," he replied, barely louder than a whisper, as though he feared speaking her name. "This course will put her closer to harm's way."

"I suppose we'll see how well you've taught her then." Elinor laughed off the concern, faking bravado for his sake. "You said she's a good shot."

"It's not her I worry about as much as you. Will you be able to bear it if harm befell her?"

"As well as I would bear harm coming to anyone on this ship," she lied. "I can't put her before them. Maybe we could use her after all."

"Do I dare ask?" Tristan said cautiously.

"Bait, Tristan. A merchant might pass by a ship, especially if they spy our cannons, but their honor won't allow them to ignore a woman in distress. We'll use her to lure them in."

"I see," he said. "'Tis a clever plan, but–"

Elinor cut him off with a sharp glance. Her mind was set, she didn't want to hear any more of his protests. It was the surest way to prevent Mona from getting hurt. Even if something went horribly wrong in the attack, she would be protected, taken on board the merchant ship and delivered safely to wherever the ship was going once relieved of its load. She had made her decision, the decision the old Elinor would have made, and she needed to stand by it to show them all she was still the same ruthless, cunning captain they had elected.

"Walk with me," she ordered, handing him the map and striding out the cabin door.

The hot Caribbean sun beat down on the deck as the distant atoll they spotted came into closer view. White sand sparkled like miniscule gems against the gentle waves that frothed on the shore, and a small copse of palm trees offered the first glimpse of greenery she had seen in months. Elinor sighed, content with the relief of coming home. Though she was Welsh by birth, the tropical islands had welcomed her in a way her own land never had.

Her men were smiling, too, greeting her and Tristan with more enthusiasm than she had seen from them in weeks. She hoped to keep them smiling. The bitter resentment borne of the long journey would fade and their morale would lift after a few days in their familiar hunting grounds. Her leadership would no longer be in question once they were let loose to do what they did best: pirate.

"Go to the navigator," she said, nudging Tristan. "I need to speak with Mona."

She hadn't intended to until she saw the woman diligently cleaning the base of a cannon and was flooded with a sense of guilt. It wouldn't be right to use her as bait unless she understood what was going to happen, and agreed to it. Elinor watched Mona work for a few moments, admiring the newly formed muscles that rippled across tanned forearms. The delicate woman had hardened, but it suited her. She was more formidable than Elinor had given her credit for, and Elinor knew she would be eager to play a role in her plan for attack. She cleared her throat.

"A word, Mona?" Elinor asked.

Mona nodded and tossed her scrub brush into the bucket beside her. "Did I do something wrong?"

"Not that I've heard," Elinor said. "Have you?"

"Look if it's about last night, Tristan said I could stay on deck as long as he did. I assumed you allowed it."

"I did," Elinor assured her. "It's not that. Come with me," she said. She didn't want Mona to feel any pressure to agree to the plan in front of the crew, and she didn't want the crew to offer any unsolicited opinions until the plan was set.

Mona followed her across the deck, dabbing sweat from her brow. "It's quite warm here, isn't it?"

"You'll get used to it," Elinor replied, invoking the words from Mona's first day on the ship when she was bent over with seasickness. "And when you get to Boston, you'll long for it, or so I'm told."

She lifted a door set in the boards of the deck and descended a ladder into the first level of the belly of the ship. She placed a hand on Mona's back to steady her as she climbed down, feeling a small jolt of exhilaration to be touching her again and then Mona's booted feet landed softly on the timbers and the moment was over. Light streamed through the hole of the door in a square that illuminated Mona perfectly, her slender nose wrinkled in disgust.

Elinor chuckled. The lower deck did smell terrible, but that was to be expected. It had been weeks since her crew had last bathed, and their sleeping quarters reeked of sweat mingling with other bodily fluids.

"Glad to have your own cabin now, are you?" Elinor teased.

"Extremely," Mona agreed as they made their way between the rows of hammocks to another door. "Where are we going?"

"I need to assess the rations," Elinor said. "We're to feast tonight, providing there's enough to spare for it."

She pulled up the second trapdoor and made her way down the rickety ladder, Mona close behind. The ceiling was low enough that the taller woman had to stoop as they took in the storeroom, filled with empty barrels and crates. Elinor squeezed through the space between two of the casks, winding her way to the very back of the room. The belly of the ship was quiet, far removed from the hubbub of the upper decks, with only the faint lapping of water against the ship's planks and Mona's soft breathing behind her.

Tristan was right, the rations were scant and there was little to be considered feast worthy, but Elinor eventually found an unopened sack of sea biscuits that was mostly untouched by mice. Stashed behind another crate, she found the treasure she had been seeking– a sack of forty or more potatoes. She handed one to Mona.

"Do you know how to cook these?"

"Not really," Mona said. "I've only eaten them a few times as a child, when there was no grain to be had from rain or droughts. I know you can put them in a *cawl*."

"Good, do that. What else will you need?"

"Am I to cook then? I'm afraid I'm not very good at it," Mona protested.

"I suppose a lady of your status wouldn't be. No matter, just do your best." Elinor smiled, then, struck by impulse, offered assistance. "I'll help you."

"You? Really?" Mona was incredulous.

"Why not? It's good for the crew to see me contributing just like anyone else. And they deserve a big meal and an evening of cheer." *Anything to win back their favor*, Elinor added silently.

"But I presume you didn't bring me down here to plan a menu?" Mona asked, lowering her voice as she leaned in towards Elinor.

It would be so easy to reach out and pull her in, tangle her fingers in the mess of red hair, taste her lips again. No one would see, no one would know. Elinor crossed her arms to stop them from caressing Mona's cheek and turned away. They were so close to Nassau, so close to Mona not being Elinor's problem, or temptation, any longer. She had to be the captain, the crew was counting on her.

"No," Elinor said. "An opportunity has presented itself, but the *Revenge* may require your assistance in the matter."

"Anything," Mona said.

"You don't even know what I'm asking yet," Elinor chided. Hadn't she warned Mona not to agree to things without knowing the terms? She was far too trusting, a trait that would get her in trouble some day if she didn't change.

"It doesn't matter," Mona insisted. "I love the *Revenge* as much as I've loved any home. If she requires me now, I will do anything I can."

"Mona." Elinor sighed. "Do you understand what it is we do aboard this ship?"

"Of course I do," Mona replied, though she sounded uncertain.

"We steal to survive. We prey on ships passing through these waters on their trade routes and take whatever can be traded for coin in the ports. We kill, if necessary, and sometimes our own are killed. We are pirates."

"I understand," Mona whispered.

Elinor didn't think she did, but no one could until they had lived it. She had never thought herself capable of taking a life, until it was hers that would have ended had she not pulled the trigger first. No one had warned her how much it would change her. She was foolish to have considered the plan in the first place. Even a few moments spent with sweet, naive Mona was enough to make her regret ever considering putting the woman in harm's way. The thought of seeing her wounded, or worse, tortured like Abi, was too painful to imagine. They would sail for Nassau first, even if it displeased the crew, even if it cost her her ship.

"Captain?" Mona asked when Elinor had been lost in thought for too long. "I want to help. Really."

"No, forget I mentioned anything. It's too dangerous." Elinor spun on her heel. "I need to go tell Tristan the plan has changed."

"Wait," Mona called.

Elinor paused, certain Mona could hear her heart racing from across the room.

"I need the coin, too. Let me help, just this once, so I have enough for my passage onward from the Bahamas," Mona pleaded.

"I'll pay your way from my own pocket. I'm a woman of my word."

115

"I don't want charity from you. Let me earn it, like any of the other men on the ship. At least tell me what the opportunity is, so I can decide for myself."

Though Elinor bristled at the defiance, something in the plea gave her pause. Even if Mona was young and foolish, at least she had a spine. Out of sight and earshot of the rest of the crew, Elinor allowed the insubordination to go unchecked.

"Why should I give you a chance? You're not ready."

"What's the worst that could happen?" Mona asked.

"The ship could go down," Elinor replied curtly.

"That could happen whether I'm there or not. Me helping won't sink the ship."

"You could die."

"A better fate than the one that was decided for me in Ogmore."

Elinor cursed Mona's stubbornness, but turned back towards her. "You don't know that."

"No, Captain, you don't know. All you've known is freedom, you've always had a choice. You don't know how it is to live without that, to have the story of your entire life written by someone else without regard to your own desires." Mona's voice rose as she spoke, and Elinor heard the determination in her words. "If I died tomorrow, at least I would die knowing that I lived in pursuit of my own happiness."

Elinor could feel her resolve thawing. Mona was right, she didn't know what it was like to be forced to a life she didn't want. If she had ever disagreed with Greybrow, if he had ever asked her to do something against her will, she would have left the ship, same as any of her crew would do to her. She supposed that was what Mona had done by fleeing Ogmore, stepped off the ship captained by her father's lust for money and into the unknown of her choosing. Elinor's respect for the other woman grew as she considered what she might have done in that situation. It had taken a lot of bravery to leave a life of outward comfort and security for the unknown.

"I'm glad you left the village, then. But I still don't want to put you in danger if I can help it," she said.

"Let me decide," Mona implored, and Elinor caved. It would make everyone happy, except for her, and it was time she put others first. For the good of the ship.

"Fine. But you don't have to do this." Elinor explained the plan she had devised with Tristan. "We're near a place where Spanish merchants pass often. We would feign distress, using you to lure them in."

"What would I have to do?" Mona's eyes widened a little, from fear or excitement Elinor couldn't tell.

"Not much. Put your old dress on, stand on the deck looking distressed to bring them in close enough for us to fire on them."

"That sounds easy enough. I'll do it."

"Not so fast, Mona. The tides of battle can turn in an instant, and you'd be right in harm's way if it did."

"I'll do it," Mona repeated. "As long as I get a share, like a real crew member."

"Just this once," Elinor finally agreed.

Chapter 13

MONA PASSED THE SACK of sea biscuits up through the door to the captain, then climbed up behind her. The potatoes were too heavy for them to hoist up the steep ladders by themselves, so the captain said she would send some of the crew down to retrieve them. They passed back through the stench of the men's sleeping quarters, and blinking, emerged onto the main deck.

Mona couldn't keep the grin from her face, overwhelmed by the sweet victory she had won. Finally she had gotten through to the captain, one step closer to become a real member of the crew. She wondered when the ambush would take place, though she supposed they had no sure way of knowing when a passing ship would fall into their trap. Nevertheless, her heart fluttered with anticipation. If she performed well, she might even persuade the captain to reconsider letting Mona stay with the ship.

She saw Tristan meet the captain's eyes, noticed the almost imperceptible nod from the captain, and felt the stab of jealousy baring its fangs again. She longed for that sort of easy communication, for someone to understand her without the need for words. When the captain had called her below decks she had dared to hope the spark they had shared in the cabin those weeks earlier would be reignited and fanned into flame. Of course that spark of hope had been dashed, but Mona almost didn't care, she was so elated to be included in the captain's plan.

"Attention!" Elinor's voice halted the work on the deck as the crew noticed their return. "As I'm sure you've all noticed by now, we're home." She gestured to the island rising from the water.

The crew cheered, and Mona joined them. The sight of land earlier had brought tears of joy to her eyes, even if its sand was bright and unfamiliar, the trees unlike any she had seen before.

"So what do you say we feast tonight to celebrate our safe crossing, and then we set a trap and fill our pockets before we sail for Nassau?"

The men cheered again, and Mona wondered if maybe calling it a feast was a bit of an exaggeration. Everyone seemed in need of something to celebrate, and land was as good a reason as any. More than the meal, she was looking forward to spending time alone with the captain in the galley preparing it. She opened the door to the tiny kitchen to allow the captain to enter first, then followed her into the cramped space. The heat and humidity on the deck were nothing compared to the kitchen, only intensified by their proximity to each other. Mona swallowed hard, banishing the lump of desire that rose in her throat. They were just cooking a meal together, and it would do her no good to imagine the possibilities of anything else. She would save those thoughts for when she had returned to her cabin and stripped free of her work clothes to indulge her desires in darkness.

"Here you go, Cap." Reddy burst into the room and dumped the sack of potatoes on the tin floor of the galley. The sack split, spilling potatoes across the room. Mona scrambled to pick them up, gathering them in the hem of her loose shirt and depositing them on the galley counter.

"Thank you, Reddy," the captain said, dismissing him. She addressed Mona. "Do you think we can salvage something edible from all this?"

"Edible, certainly, but that tastes good may be impossible." Mona lifted the lid of the barrel that held salt preserved beef, filling the room with a pungent odor. Their journey was testing the limits of the preservation methods.

The captain chuckled and wrinkled her nose. "Just tell me what to do."

"We can start by boiling water and cutting the potatoes." Mona was looking around the other bags in the kitchen for something she could add to make the meal more palatable. She found a sack with a few handfuls of dried beans in it and placed it on the counter. She longed for the fresh leeks and cabbages from the manor's garden back in Wales, but the men had promised her there were fruit and vegetables aplenty in Nassau.

Mona began chopping the potatoes into cubes, cutting around the green eyes that had formed on the root vegetables during the long journey across the ocean. The captain slid behind Mona, so close that Mona could feel the heat radiating from her body. Her hand grazed Mona's hip as she slipped past, the feeling of her touch lingering long after the hand was withdrawn. Mona flushed anew, wondering if the captain knew what she was doing to her. She had to know, had to feel it, too.

Mona's eyes met the captain's. Mona thought she recognized the same yearning she felt in the intense gaze, and she quickly busied herself with dumping the chopped potatoes into water that was just coming to a boil. When she turned around the captain was right behind her, breasts brushing against hers as they spun around each other in a sort of dance made all the more intimate by the narrow space they were working in. Mona's nipples hardened into stiff peaks and she had to bite back a groan as the rough fabric of her shirt brushed against them.

"I need air," she panted as she pushed out of the room.

Mona rested her forearms on the rail of the deck as she gasped at the breeze blowing off the water. She couldn't remember a time she had ever felt so aroused just by being in the same room with someone, and she found it disconcerting. Another deep breath helped steady her nerves, though it did nothing to soothe the ache deep within her. She needed to get back to the kitchen, help finish the stew, and then maybe she could sneak away to her cabin for a few minutes to attend to herself so she could maintain some semblance of composure at the feast.

"I need you." Elinor was beside her.

Mona's breath caught in her throat. *I need you, too.*

"Do I add the beans now or wait?"

Oh. She was talking about the meal. "We'll add them now, the longer they cook the better. I think." Mona sighed and turned to go back to the hot kitchen.

Chapter 14

"ANCHOR'S DOWN!"

Elinor's order echoed down the deck of *Nimue's Revenge.* Kind winds had filled her sails, and they had reached the bay she'd identified on the map in just over a day's time. The crew on the ship were jubilant, back to cracking their normal bawdy jokes and singing shanties as they worked. Their moods had been lifted by the return to the sun and the isles, and she knew they were all looking forward to stepping off the boat.

There was a splash as the anchors were dropped, mooring the ship behind a rocky spit of land that extended into the channel between the two islands. They were hidden from view to any ships exiting the chain of isles for the open ocean. She would send a sentry to row to it and keep watch. If any ships approached, the watchman would light a torch as a signal to prepare the attack. But first, a crew needed to go ashore to scout the land for threats that might emerge from it and replenish the *Revenge's* dwindling and murky supply of water.

The men fell easily into the routine they had performed dozens of times before. Empty water barrels were loaded into a long pirogue, a narrow dugout boat made from a thick log, which was hoisted over the rail and into the water below. Tristan darted among them, barking instructions and delegating who would be among the lucky few to walk on land. He stopped when he reached her.

"Going ashore, Cap?" He asked.

"Not this time," she replied. "I can wait another week for Nassau."

"I think you should. I can keep things in order here while you're gone for a few hours." There was a sly twinkle in his eyes.

"What are you up to, Tristan?"

"Nothing, nothing at all." He flashed a mischievous grin. "I'm sending Mona though."

"Have you gone mad?" Elinor was shocked. "You can't send her out there with them. She'll get lost, and you know I don't trust them with her out of our eyesight."

"Too late," he shrugged. "She begged me and I already said she could go. It would be a shame to disappoint her now, her helping us with this ambush as it is."

"Going soft, Buell?"

"Maybe a little. She's hard to say no to when she turns on the charm. You should go ashore with her to make sure she doesn't find herself in any trouble."

"You truly are the devil himself," she said, rolling her eyes as she gave in. Spending more time with Mona couldn't hurt, especially since they were so close to their journey's end. "Make sure the cannons are well prepared, bring up extra powder from below. The trap should be set and ready to spring by the time we return."

"Aye, Captain," he said cheekily. "Try to have fun."

Once the barrels were loaded, four of the crewmen climbed aboard. Mona was last to join them, stepping gracefully into the boat as one of the crew placed a steadying hand at the small of her back. The gesture disgusted Elinor, even his hands left Mona the moment she was situated in the boat. She marched over to the pirogue and climbed in, refusing the same helping hand as it was offered to her. The pirogue jolted as the men still on deck released the ropes and began lowering them to the water.

The sandy beach beckoned from across the bay, and each of the six took up an oar to propel them towards it. Mona's clattered into Elinor's as she struggled to find the rhythm set by the stronger rowers in the agile watercraft. Elinor heard her grunting with exertion, but soon all six oars were dipping into the water in unison and the pirogue skimmed across the water. Elinor smiled to herself. The woman continued to impress her, and never gave up. It was a shame she had to leave the *Revenge*, she was the embodiment of everything Elinor wanted in the crew on her boat. Determined, hard-working, tenacious... It was exactly why she had to leave, Elinor reminded herself. No attachments.

The bottom of the pirogue scraped against reef as they rowed into shallower waters. Elinor glanced over the side of the boat and gazed into clear waters, where schools of multi-colored fish darted between great masses of bright coral, scattered from their schools by the oars plunging into the water around them. When they butted up against sand, two of the crewmen jumped out and dragged the boat to shore. Elinor scrambled on to land and turned around just in time to catch Mona as she leapt into the sand then stumbled.

"Slow down," she laughed. "Give it a moment to get your land legs back."

Mona swayed slightly, anticipating a rocking that never came. She knelt and scooped up a handful of sand, letting it stream through her fingers to become one with the beach again. Her eyes sparkled with the midday light reflecting off the ocean and the joy of having finally made it to land. Elinor pulled off her boots, feeling the warm grains between her toes. It felt like she had arrived in heaven, the dank mustiness of the ship forgotten on the shores of paradise.

"This island must be the most beautiful thing I've ever seen," Mona said, awed as she looked from the dense tropical forest to the beach and water and back again.

"It is," agreed Elinor, though Mona's unbridled joy at being there was a close second. "And they're all like this. Now you see why I hate to leave."

A gull screamed overhead, perturbed by the intruders in his home. Within moments, a flock of the birds descended on the boat, squawking their displeasure when they found no food to be scavenged.

"Water!" Griff yelled from further down the beach. "We found a river."

"Come on," said Elinor, pulling Mona to her feet. "Fresh water."

They ran barefoot across the sand as it crested, then dipped down to form the unmistakable mouth of a river that flowed down the mountain and into the ocean. Griff and the rest of the men were already hacking at the undergrowth, clearing a path wide enough to roll the barrels up.

"Brackish here, but I'm sure it's clean if we walk inland a bit," Griff explained.

"Stay alert," Elinor warned. "Just because we haven't seen signs of other people doesn't mean they aren't here."

She didn't heed her own advice, preferring to watch Mona as they walked through the lush forest that sloped gently up a mountainside. Her joy was unabated and she was practically skipping with the excitement of discovering a new place for the first time. It had been the same for Elinor the first time Greybrow had taken her ashore after she left Wales and crossed the Atlantic in search of something better.

The stream narrowed the further they moved inland, and the water deepened. After just a few minutes of walking, Griff dropped to his knees and sniffed the water. Finding it satisfactory, he cupped his hands and raised them to his lips, sipping slowly. He swallowed, then grinned.

"Clean," he said, and the six members of the party breathed a collective sigh of relief.

"Good. Fill the barrels," Elinor instructed. "Mona and I are going to explore further inland. We'll be back in an hour, maybe two."

"Aye, Captain," the crewmen agreed.

Elinor continued walking up the stream, Mona right behind her.

"Won't they be angry we're leaving them to do all the work?" Mona asked as soon as they were out of earshot.

"No," Elinor chuckled. "They wanted us to leave them alone, I'm sure of it. Probably already stripped naked and splashing in the stream. We've all been too long without a proper washing."

"Is that what we're going to do, bathe?" Mona asked excitedly.

"If we can find a good spot."

The further they got from the beach, the denser the jungle became. When their path was blocked by undergrowth, Elinor withdrew her cutlass and cut through the brush, hacking a trail through the greenery until they emerged next to a pool of water abutting a steep cliff face. Water streamed over the edge of the rock, tumbling to the earth into the pool before flowing across smooth rocks into the stream that would carry it to the sea. The forest around them was alive with insects buzzing and birds cawing through the treetops, overwhelming after weeks with only the sound of waves splashing upon the *Revenge.*

"Here," Elinor said, triumphant as she pulled back leaves for Mona to take in the scene.

"It's stunning," Mona said, and it was.

"Your bath is drawn, my lady," Elinor said, mimicking the curtsy that Mona was in the habit of performing whenever she was flustered.

Mona blushed, or maybe her cheeks were just flushed from the exertion of walking after months of relative confinement on the ship.

"I've never bathed in the wild," she said. "There's nothing in there, right? That could bite me?"

"Probably not," Elinor said. Taking the lead, she set her boots on a rock in the sun and waded into the water. "Come on, it's not even cold."

Mona pulled off her boots and followed her into the pool, gasping as the water hit her skin. "It's a little cold!"

"You'll get used to it," Elinor replied with a wink that surprised her in its playfulness. It was relieving to be away from the ship and the weight of the responsibilities she bore as captain, a freedom she hadn't realized she'd missed.

Elinor swam out until the water was chest deep, then began stripping the clothes from her body. She rinsed them until the water drained clear, then wrung them out.

"Leave your clothes here if you want," she called back to Mona as she laid her wet clothes on the rock by her boots. "They'll dry while we swim."

It took all of her willpower to turn away while Mona undressed, so she swam back to the middle of the pool, delighting as the waterfall rained water down on her head and rinsed the sweat and grime from her hair. She heard splashing behind her and saw that Mona had rejoined her in the pool.

"I've never felt so alive," Mona said, the grin she had worn since stepping onto the beach still plastered on her face. "Thank you for bringing me here."

"Thank Tristan," Elinor corrected. "It was his idea to send you ashore."

"I'll make sure to do that." Mona swam closer to Elinor. "But I wanted to thank you, as well. You didn't have to let me stay on your ship, but I'm grateful you did. I don't regret any of it."

"You've mentioned that. It's what anyone would have done, throwing you overboard was never really an option," Elinor murmured. She was entranced by the way droplets of water trickled down from Mona's hair, following the curve of her neck to slide between her collarbones and into the valley of her breasts. Her breathing quickened as she forced herself to look up again only to see Mona staring at her with the same intensity.

Elinor didn't know who reached to close the space between them, or which woman planted her lips on the other's first. For a moment, she didn't know anything except Mona's mouth against hers, teasing and tasting and then hungrily exploring beneath the cascade of water from above.

"We can't," Elinor protested weakly when they pulled apart to gasp for air. "The code."

"We're not on the ship right now. No one will ever know," Mona whispered, trailing her fingers down Elinor's spine.

Elinor shivered as Mona's touch ignited the flame deep within her. Each beat of her heart was echoed below, making her throb with agonizing need. The risks didn't matter anymore, Elinor had to have her. If she let this moment pass her by, she knew she would regret it for the rest of her life. They embraced again, laughing and kissing until time stopped mattering, the *Revenge* stopped mattering, and the world closed in until they were the only ones left in it.

"Come here," Elinor said, taking charge and leading Mona to a large rock worn smooth by the river and warmed by the sun. Not the softest bed, but it would more than suffice. "Lie down."

"Aye, Captain." Mona did as she was instructed, looking up at Elinor with lusty desire.

The words that Elinor was accustomed to hearing over and over again on the ship became an aphrodisiac when spoken through Mona's swollen lips. Elinor felt another shiver pass through her body as she let her eyes feast on Mona, taking in the rise of her chest and the soft curve of her waist before straying further down. She would take her time, taste every inch of her. If it was to be the only time they might truly enjoy each others' company, Elinor wanted to make sure to experience it fully with no regrets. The only question was where to start.

Already erect from the cool water, Mona's nipples were begging to be teased and tasted. Elinor cupped one full breast in her palm, running a thumb over the peak. Mona gasped at the sensation, rewarding Elinor with soft whimpers for more. Elinor moved her hand away, causing Mona to cry out in protest, replaced with a satisfied sigh as Elinor's mouth took its place. Mona gripped Elinor's hair to pull her closer as Elinor pushed her towards the edge of madness, tongue flicking across the nipple, circling and sucking as Mona's back arched in pleasure.

Elinor gave the nipple one last last gentle nip before moving lower, kissing her way across Mona's smooth stomach to linger at her jutting hip bone. Mona's pelvis thrust up, reaching for Elinor's touch. Elinor ran her fingers up the length of one smooth thigh before pulling away completely.

"Patience," she chuckled when Mona groaned in disappointment. "We'll get to that."

Elinor moved to Mona's other nipple and repeated the same process, teasing the tender bud until Mona cried out in desperation, begging for more. Her legs spread wide, inviting Elinor between them as she writhed with the torment of desire. Elinor kissed the soft skin of her inner thighs, then parted Mona with two fingers and plunged her tongue into the depths, tasting Mona's wetness as she lapped. Her tongue flicked up to lick Mona's most sensitive spot, grinning as Mona bucked beneath her. She increased the pressure of her tongue, circling around and around. Mona's whimpers turned into one long moan as she gave in to the pleasure, thighs quivering as she pushed Elinor's head away from her overwhelming fount of ecstasy.

Elinor returned to Mona's lips for another kiss, losing herself in the passion of the moment. When Mona's hands went to her breasts she whined at the exquisite ache that filled her. Palms roughened by hours of hard labor groped at her, squeezing until Elinor gasped, then releasing to make their way down to the wetness that slicked her thighs. One finger slipped in between her folds, stroking upwards to brush against Elinor's clit and then back down to thrust deep inside her.

A second finger joined the first. Elinor's moan was stifled by the lips still covering hers, rising in pitch as Mona's fingers worked rhythmically below. Elinor clenched around her, legs beginning to shake as the pressure built inside her. When Mona's thumb brushed over her clit again, she exploded, convulsing around Mona's hand as the wave of pleasure washed over her, releasing a warm surge of wetness that flooded the rock beneath her.

Elinor lay panting as she waited for the world to stop spinning. Aftershocks rippled through her, each spasm making her sensitive clit throb again. Being with Mona was better than she had ever imagined, and she had imagined it a dozen times or more since the ship departed Ogmore.

She reached for Mona, needing closeness in the afterglow of the orgasm. Mona stroked her hair, murmuring softly to her. Elinor couldn't make out distinct words from the lilting cadence until she realized Mona was speaking Welsh. The language flowed like the sweetest honey from Mona's tongue, an embrace in its own and a balm Elinor hadn't realized she'd needed.

"*Gallwn i aros yma am byth,*" Mona sighed. I could stay here forever.

"If only," Elinor replied. Forever didn't seem like it would be long enough to know Mona, to explore her body and make her shake with pleasure or to lie in her arms in the aftermath.

"I didn't know you spoke Welsh," Mona said, blushing.

"Of course I do." Elinor stretched, then sighed. "I was born there, was I not?"

"I've never heard you speak it."

"I haven't in a very long time. But I like it when you do," Elinor reached for Mona's hand, stroking her thumb over the callused palm.

"Then I'll continue doing it," Mona said, switching back to her mother tongue. "Why did you stop?"

"Greybrow decided it shouldn't be spoken on the *Revenge.* Too many of the crew couldn't understand it. Speaking of, they'll be waiting for us. We should be getting back soon." Elinor sighed. The ship was the last place she wanted to be.

"Surely they can wait a little longer," Mona pouted, pulling Elinor close again and running her fingers down her back.

"They'll have to," Elinor gave in easily, as unwilling as Mona to let the opportunity to be alone a little longer slip them by.

Chapter 15

Mona didn't know how she was even supposed to stand, let alone walk back to the pirogue on the beach for the long row back to the ship. All the energy she had had been drained from her— twice— by the captain. She still could hardly believe it was real. The island felt like a fever dream, intensely hot and too perfect to be anything more than a figment of her imagination. She licked her lips and tasted the captain on them. That part was real.

The captain was beside her, dozing on the warm rock in the sun with one arm around Mona's waist. Mona knew she should wake her up, but she wanted to stay in the little oasis that was all theirs for just a little longer. She wondered how many hours would have to pass before the men came looking for them, or how closely they were keeping track of the time. Sighing, she shook the captain awake.

They rinsed off again in the calm pool beneath the waterfall, then dressed in their sun-dried clothes and set off to rejoin the other crewmen who had come ashore. None of the men acted like anything was amiss as they rolled the full barrels of fresh water back across the beach, though Mona was sure the spring in her step, the peaceful glow radiating from her, and the smile she just couldn't bite back gave her away.

The captain was as calm and in control as ever. Mona wished she'd had a few more moments to talk to her, but she had transformed back into her aloof self and was silent on the walk back down the stream. Mona wondered if she was supposed to pretend nothing had happened, but how could she? Everything had changed. She'd caught a glimpse beneath the facade, felt her desire reciprocated with no uncertainty, and she didn't understand how she was supposed to ever go back. She could figure it out later though, she wouldn't allow doubt and confusion to override her bliss.

When all the barrels were loaded, Mona climbed back into the little wooden pirogue and took up an oar. She laughed a little to herself, imagining the apoplectic fit her father would have if he could see her there in men's garb rowing alongside them. He probably wouldn't even recognize her anymore, so changed from the prim and proper lady she had been. The men sang to keep the rhythm as they rowed, and she joined them in the jaunty tune about the wine and women that awaited them when their sailing was done, wondering again what awaited her there. Surely, the waterfall had changed things between her and the captain. Surely, she was reconsidering allowing Mona to stay.

Crewmen hoisted them back onto the ship just as the sun began to sink behind the island, painting the sky in streaks of orange and pink. Mona took the bowl of cold beans flavored with salt pork that was pressed into her hands. She was ravenous after expending so much energy, and the meal was as welcome as the bottle of rum that soon followed it. By the time she looked around the deck, the captain had already returned to her chambers.

Mona yawned, exhaustion overtaking the exhilaration of the day. She slipped into her own cabin and barred the door, shedding her clothes and ruing herself for not taking her nightshift to wash in the clean water as well. It was too late for regrets though, and she pulled it over her head, the fabric brushing over her skin a reminder of the way the captain had so thoroughly explored her Earlier. She shuddered at the delicious memory, letting a hand go to her still sensitive clit, another reminder of how very real it had all been. Mona slept deeply, the next morning coming too soon as she was awoken by Tristan knocking at her door.

"Captain wants to see you," he said with a smirk, and Mona knew he knew, or at least heavily suspected, what had happened between them on the island.

Her heart skipped a beat, then settled again as she remembered the plan the captain had for the *Revenge*. She probably just wanted to talk about that, make sure Mona hadn't forgotten any of the details. Yet as much as Mona tried to talk sense into herself, she couldn't help but hope that the captain was summoning her for more personal reasons.

"Is she... in a good mood today?" Mona asked hesitantly.

"Better than most," Tristan smiled. "She's about to do what she does best."

Mona had no idea what he was referring to, she could think of a thousand things the captain did best. Especially that thing with her tongue. Mona blushed as her core awoke from the memory. She paused by the rail to quiet the stirring and compose herself before facing the captain. The men were bustling about the deck as the pirogue was lowered again, this time bearing only a sole occupant. The man rowed towards the rocky outcropping that jutted into the channel beyond the bay. Wind gusted from the ocean to form choppy, whitecapped waves much stronger than the ones she had rowed through a day before. Mona peered worriedly after her crewmate as the boat was tossed to the side and water sloshed into the craft, but it righted itself and he continued rowing.

Tristan cleared his throat. "Better not to keep the captain waiting, unless you're wanting her good mood to sour."

Mona quickened her step, following him into the cabin. The room felt smaller, more intimate than it had before. She inhaled sharply as she laid eyes on the captain, unable to fully contain her desire. The captain looked away quickly to stare down at her maps.

Tristan pulled out a chair at the table and gestured for Mona to sit. He joined the captain over by the window, where they whispered for a few moments. Mona strained to hear what they were saying, but the shouts from the crew on the deck and the waves lapping at the ship covered any trace of the words the captain and quartermaster shared. Tristan nodded his agreement to something, then left the room without another word to Mona.

"Is something wrong?" Mona asked, noticing the captain's clenched jaw.

"Not yet," the captain said. "Waiting is the hardest part, now that the trap is set. We could be here hours or days until a ship appears, there's no way to tell until it happens."

"I can think of a dozen ways to pass the time," Mona said, surprised at her own boldness.

The captain gave her a sharp look. "Not on the ship. You know the rules. You'd do better to forget yesterday ever happened. I already have."

Mona felt tears well in her eyes at the captain's coldness. She hadn't been expecting any grand declarations of love, but she thought their intimacy would have meant something to the captain.

"Oh, for God's sake, don't cry," the captain admonished, but her tone was gentler. "We can't think about that now, that's all I meant. We have a battle to prepare for."

It was all Mona could think about, but she realized the captain was right. She needed to set her feelings and her lust aside to focus on the matter at hand. It was hard, though, with the captain close enough to reach out and touch, and they were all alone, and... Mona forced herself to focus.

"So what did you wish to speak to me about then?" She asked softly.

"Are you ready to play your role when the signal is given?" The captain asked.

"I am," Mona said, running through the plan again in her head.

"When the torch is lit, you don your dress and get to the prow of the ship."

"I know." Had the captain really summoned her like a child to rehash the details of a plan Mona knew by heart?

"Scream and wave but keep an eye on the masts. When the black flag is raised, get as far below deck as you can and hide. Remember where the rations are kept? Go there."

"I will."

"Good. See Tristan for your weapon when you leave, and keep it nearby at all times. Be ready to use it at a moment's notice. And Mona?" The captain stared deep into her eyes, as though she was reading Mona's very soul. "Stay safe."

The captain could pretend she had forgotten all about the tryst under the waterfall, but with those two words, Mona saw the cracks in her hardened exterior. She had felt something, too; Mona was sure of it.

"You stay safe, too," Mona whispered in Welsh, and saw the facade crumble into a flash of fear, plain as day on the captain's face. She wondered how much else the captain was holding back in order to maintain her image of control in front of her crew.

"You can go now," the captain said, turning away. "Just be ready when the signal comes."

Leaving the cabin, Mona wandered the deck aimlessly, unsure of what she was supposed to do with herself until the signal came. The men all seemed to have settled into a new routine, driven by instinct or discipline or some combination of the two. Some leaned over the railings, casting lines into the bay and shouting jubilantly as they pulled up colorful fish the likes of which Mona had never seen pulled from the seas near Ogmore. Her stomach grumbled in anticipation of the fresh meat. On the voyage across the Atlantic, fishing was too time consuming to bother with. The ship demanded full devotion from everyone.

Griff and Reddy were with two other men, sitting around a makeshift table playing cards. Mona walked over to join the other crew standing around watching the game in progress. Every so often, one of the men would glance over to the rocks, but that was the only sign they gave that they were waiting for the battle signal. Mona walked away, annoyed that no one else seemed to share her jittery anticipation.

By the second day, her nerves had calmed from anxious pacing to the occasional flutter in the pit of her stomach, and by the third the pistol no longer felt heavy at her hip, having become a strange metal extension of her body. Mona's dress had been pulled from its crate, the wrinkles smoothed as best as she could manage on the humid ship, and hung near the door to her cabin. The fourth day, just after dawn, the torch was lit.

The deck exploded into a flurry of activity around Mona as she stared at the flicker of light from shore. It was time, and all the preparedness she had felt the day before washed away as the powder boys scrambled to the storerooms and the men crouched besides their cannons. Mona couldn't see the other ship yet, but she could almost feel its presence, looming from the channel on the other side of the rocks. Fear made her blood run cold. She'd thought she was excited for the battle, but the moment had arrived and she realized with new clarity that all of their lives were at stake. Especially if she failed.

Her wits flooded back over her, and she bolted to her cabin. Ignoring the stays that would take too long to lace and were nEarly impossible to fasten alone, she pulled the dress over her head. The tight garment felt strange after becoming accustomed to the loose fitting shirt and breeches that allowed her to move so easily. The dress, with its layers of skirts, was heavy and got in her way as she tried to cross the deck quickly. The captain had been right about its impracticality. It was another aspect of her old life she wasn't keen to return to once the *Revenge* reached Nassau. But that was a problem she should worry about then. She rushed back out, belting the pistol around her waist as she went and tucking it under the gown that draped over her skirts.

Mona reached the bow of the ship and glanced up at the flag pole. Two flags flapped there, a white one signaling their distress at the top, with the Spanish merchant's flag fluttering just below. The masts of the opposing ship appeared first, gliding from behind the rocks and bearing the same white saltire on a blue background that marked them as Spanish. She couldn't see any movement on the deck of the distant ship, and didn't know if they could see her either, but she began waving her handkerchief above her head as she walked back and forth across the bow. The other ship seemed to take no notice of them as it crept on towards the horizon.

"Raise the anchors!" The captain called out behind her, the heavy chains already clanking as the weights were dragged up from the sea floor. "We're going to chase."

Mona cursed herself. They had all been relying on her to lure the other ship in, and she had failed them. She gave one last half-hearted wave of the handkerchief, frustrated at her inability to prove she could contribute to the prosperity of the *Revenge*, then blinked as the merchant vessel appeared to slow. She blinked, wondering if her mind was playing tricks on her and showing her what she so desperately wanted to see, but no, the ship really was slowing in the distance. Everyone on deck froze, as though they were all holding the same breath as they waited to see what happened. The ship began to turn.

"Hold," yelled the captain.

Mona's heart felt like it would pound through her chest as the ship crested waves and grew larger as it approached. She waved again, keeping one eye on the flagpole as she did. The two flags of distress still waved above. Time was suspended as the other ship crept closer, her handkerchief damp in her sweaty palms.

"Now!" The captain ordered as voices yelling in Spanish from the other deck came into earshot.

The pulleys creaked as the rope fed through them, lowering the white and blue flags and raising a black one in its place. Wood clattered as the hatches were opened to reveal the cannons to the duped merchants. The crew's yelling was drowned out by a boom that sent Mona stumbling backwards. Tristan caught her before she fell, and dragged her across the deck before she could properly regain her footing.

"Hide," he hissed, shoving her towards the hatch that led below deck. "It should all be over soon. We have them right where we want them."

Another boom ripped through the air and Tristan went running to rejoin the men brandishing their weapons at the side of the ship. Ignoring the orders she was given to retreat below deck, Mona crouched behind a barrel of gunpowder to watch. She unholstered the pistol at her hip and prepared a shot, bracing herself for the fight she was sure was going to break out at any second. Though the *Revenge's* cannons had fired twice, she couldn't see any damage on the opposing ship. It was close enough that she could see movement on their deck. A white flag was being raised, fluttering in the breeze as it was hoisted up the mast.

"They're surrendering," yelled the captain. "Hold your fire."

The palpable tension faded from the deck as the men relaxed. Surrender was what they hoped for, and the safest way for both crews to ensure they remained whole. Their easy smiles were back as they readied the pirogue for the crew that would board the other ship to claim their spoils. Mona wiped her hands on her skirt, then determining the risk of harm had passed, straightened and stretched. The other ship was preparing to drop their own small skiff in the water, bearing a stout, bearded man in an ornate coat that Mona presumed to be captain of the merchant vessel. Two of his sailors joined him in the skiff, and they rowed towards the *Revenge.*

The captain straightened the tricorne hat perched atop her blonde braid and stepped into the pirogue, flanked by Tristan and Griff. Dwarfed by the two men behind her, Mona thought she looked the most fearsome of all. Mona slipped from behind the powder keg to join the other men at the railing of the *Revenge* watching how the negotiations would unfold.

Chapter 16

ELINOR SCOWLED TO MASK the relief she felt at how quickly the Spaniards had surrendered, but the scowl turned real when she noticed Mona on the deck among her crew. She'd told her to get below decks once the pirate's flag was raised, and clearly her orders had gone unheeded. The fight wasn't over until the prize was secured on the *Revenge,* and there was still the chance of shots being fired if negotiations with the other captain turned sour. Elinor tore her eyes from Mona. She knew the woman would become a distraction, and she had. Tristan nudged her with an elbow, the gesture subtly reminding her to regain focus as one pirogue bobbed towards the other.

"Why is Mona on deck?" She whispered to Tristan.

"I told her to get below," he replied. "She must have snuck back up when I was distracted."

"She's not safe there."

"You can't think about that now. We've a job to finish, I'll deal with her later."

The two small boats bumped against each other, bringing Elinor face to face with the Spaniards. Their captain was a short man, just taller than Elinor, with dark hair and a scowl to match hers. The two crew he brought wore flintlock pistols, though he appeared unarmed as a show of his good faith in her not to harm him. As they approached, she noticed the Spaniards expressions turn to shock when they realized her gender.

"*Señora,*" the Spanish captain bowed to her.

"Captain," she corrected. "As I presume you are?"

He nodded. "So I have had the displeasure of falling into the Golden Cormorant's trap. You'll forgive us for thinking you were a myth."

"A great displeasure it is." Elinor raised an eyebrow, neither confirming nor denying his assumption as she wondered which of her exploits he knew her by. Her hand went to the cutlass at her side.

"No need, no need, *Capitán,*" the man stammered in his thickly accented English. "We have brought you all the *reales* on the ship, to save you the trouble."

He thrust a bag towards her, and she handed it off to Tristan. Judging by its weight, there were no more than fifty of the pieces of eight inside, far fewer than a three masted merchant ship would be expected to carry and certainly not enough to keep her crew satisfied with their day's work.

"Are you quite certain this is all the coin on your ship?" She asked, sneering. "I don't think I believe you."

"All we could reasonably spare, *Capitán,*" he amended. "Our men must be paid, too."

"I don't see how that's my problem," Elinor replied coldly. "Prepare your ship to be boarded. We shall see if you are lying to me. Send all your men to the stern. If anyone dares to raise a weapon against us, we will take your ship and send you all to Davy Jones' Locker."

The Spanish captain bowed slightly to her, frowning at the threat. She knew her crew and guns outnumbered his, with his ship designed to carry a maximum of goods at the expense of manpower and heavy cannons. He had lost the battle the moment his ship entered her firing range, and he knew it. As long as no one resisted, she would spare them their lives so they could return to port to refill the vessel with coins and goods for her to steal another day.

She yelled the orders up to the men on her ship, who lowered a rope ladder and climbed down to join her in the pirogue. A second boat was lowered, and more men filled it until she had a boarding crew of fifteen. There would be more than enough men to move quickly through the merchant ship, taking whatever treasure they could easily transport back over to the *Revenge*. All in all, it was an easy day's work, and one that would surely pay off handsomely.

Elinor led the clamber up the Spanish ship's ropes, and was pleased to see the other captain had heeded her instructions. Two dozen or so men milled about the stern, watching with disgust as the pirates boarded their ship.

"Tie them up," Elinor ordered. "I don't want any interference."

"Aye, Captain," Griff replied, moving towards them.

The sound of a musket rang out and the scent of gunpowder flooded the deck as Griff staggered backwards clutching his abdomen. Blood pooled beneath him, and he groaned. Rage burned through Elinor, blackening her vision as she drew her cutlass and stepped forward. Black smoke floated across the deck, filling her nostrils with the acrid scent of gunpowder. Metal scraped across leather as her crew drew their weapons from scabbards behind her. Elinor hadn't planned to kill any of them, but they had forced her hand.

"Who fired that shot?" She snarled, swinging the cutlass in a threatening arc before her. "Who? Give him up, or you all will die by my own blade."

None of the Spaniards moved to betray their comrade, and Elinor slowly became aware of the dozen muskets trained on her as the spots of anger cleared from her vision.

"Who?" She screamed.

"*Bruja,*" one of the men muttered, crossing himself.

Elinor shrieked as she swiped again with the cutlass. If they thought her a witch, it would only play to her advantage. She could tell they were frightened of her, even if they put on a brave show. The closer she could get to them, the less effective their long barreled muskets would be. She just needed to close the distance.

Another shot came flying from the Spanish side, the ball whizzing past to strike somewhere behind her. Tristan roared, and another surge of rage flooded over Elinor. She couldn't turn to look, didn't want to know if he had been struck. No distractions. She leapt, striking the first man in reach. He dropped his pistol with a howl of pain and fell to his knees. She thrust forward, driving the cutlass through him, then whirled around to strike again. She was a tempest of death, and she required blood to rain.

"Fire!" She screamed back to her men, not caring if she was in the line of it.

Chaos took hold of both ships as her men loosed their shots. Elinor whirled to slash at another Spaniard, and cannons boomed from the *Revenge* as the rest of her crew decided to join the fray. The Spanish ship rocked as the balls tore into its hull, impossible to miss at such a short range.

Elinor fell back as her men surged forward, their faces contorted by wicked scowls as they screamed unholy curses in every language they knew. If she didn't know them, even she might have been convinced that they were demons raised from hell. Griff lay still where he had fallen, no longer crying out. Beyond the help of even the most skilled surgeon, his glassy stare fixed on the heavens above. Elinor knelt to close his eyes. They would raise a glass to him later. It was all she could do.

She scanned the deck to see who else had fallen, and felt her muscles unclench with relief when she didn't spot Tristan among them. He was deep within the fracas, wielding his own cutlass with refined grace. The tides of the battle were turning, her men were winning despite the Spanish deception. An arm wrapped around her waist, and Elinor felt herself being yanked backwards. She heard the distinctive sound of a pistol being cocked, then felt the cold steel press against her temple.

"Enough," the Spanish captain growled behind. "Command your men to lay down their arms."

"You deceived me," Elinor replied. "You will all die. I believe I made that clear."

"I deceived you?" His incredulity was clear. "You should have taken my first offer. I would have let you live. Now all the world will know me as the man who felled the *bruja del Caribe*."

Elinor spat on the ground near his feet. She didn't fear death. She had been awaiting it, always knowing that one day it would catch up with her, a certain end even she couldn't outrun. The Spaniard pushed her forward, barking orders to his men that she couldn't understand. The fighting on the deck ceased as her men realized she had been taken captive.

"Fight, you bastards," she screamed. "Kill them all!"

Her men looked from her to Tristan, who gestured for them to lower their weapons. As long as she was held captive, his command as quarter-master ruled the *Revenge* and her crew. Cutlasses clattered on the deck as her men dropped them. Elinor stared across the water to her ship, the three masts looming in full, resplendent glory as her flag waved above the deck. The sky was a perfect, cloudless blue, the island a verdant gem looming behind the vessel that had carried her through storms and across the seas. She had done the best she could to carry on Greybrow's legacy, and in her final moments, she hoped he was proud.

Elinor became vaguely aware of screams carried across the water on the wind. Everyone turned to look as Mona leaned over the railing, sobbing as she reached towards Elinor. Elinor's stomach turned with regret. It was hard to view death as a welcome embrace when Mona was right there, begging for her to be allowed to live. A shot rang out, and she closed her eyes, holding on to the last image of the ship as she waited for the pain, and then the darkness.

The Spaniard slumped behind her, falling forward and pinning her to the deck beneath him as blood seeped warm and wet from the hole where his eye used to be. Elinor looked up, and a flash of green caught her eye on the deck of the *Revenge*. Mona smiled down at her from the other ship, the flintlock pistol still smoking in her hand, face smudged with black residue from the ignited powder. Elinor twisted, wriggling out from underneath the dead man. It was impossible. No one could hit a target from that distance, especially not from the rocking deck of a ship.

"You've lost," Tristan yelled to the baffled Spaniards. "Lay down your weapons, and pray that my captain is still in a forgiving mood."

Elinor reached for the dead captain's pistol and rose to her feet. It was time to make good on her promises. She glanced back at Mona, wishing there was a way she could shield her from what she was about to witness. Mona had seen enough bloodshed, and Elinor was sure the day would haunt her dreams, just as the men she had killed haunted hers. But maybe she could lessen that anguish.

"I feel merciful today," she said, striding across the deck and pointing their captain's weapon at the Spanish sailors kneeling before her on the deck. "Tie them all, except for that one." She pointed to the smallest of the Spanish crewmen, a boy who couldn't have been any older than thirteen. "Put them into their skiff."

One by one, the men were bound hand and foot and hauled into the waiting skiff until only the boy remained. Elinor smiled, and motioned for him to stand.

"Do you understand English?" She asked.

The boy looked up and nodded, eyes wide with horror. He tried to stand proudly, but Elinor noticed the tremble in his chin, the way his eyes avoided fully meeting hers.

"What is your name?" She demanded.

"Diego." His voice quivered on the last syllable.

"Well, Diego, you're the last man standing from your crew on a ship I don't want. So I suppose that makes you Captain Diego." She paused but he didn't reply. She hadn't expected him to. "You have some decisions to make, Captain. Your crew's fate is in your hands."

"What decisions?" Diego whispered.

"You cut them loose to let God decide their fate, join my crew, and become richer than you'd ever imagined. Or, you join them and watch your ship burn as you drift out to sea."

The boy's eyes darted from her to the skiff and back. He crossed himself and muttered what sounded like a prayer, closing his eyes briefly before reopening them to stare at Elinor with new resoluteness.

"I will go with you," he said. *"Que Dios nos perdone y proteja."*

"A wise decision," Elinor said. The boy would make a fine addition to her crew. He already showed the ability to make ruthless decisions, and might indeed become the captain of his own ship one day, if he kept learning and managed to survive. She held out her cutlass. "Now cut the rope."

"Me?"

"It's your ship, and your decision. Would you prefer to join them and I'll cut it?"

Diego took the cutlass she offered and stepped up to the length of rope mooring the ship's skiff to her side, nearly as thick around as his wrist. The men in the crowded boat were pleading in Spanish, and the boy hesitated, then squeezed his eyes shut and swung the cutlass as though it was an executioner's blade. The sharp edge sliced cleanly through, and the rope fell into the water with a gentle splash.

Elinor felt no guilt. She wasn't condemning them to death, but uncertainty. Another ship could pass through the channel before the tide drew them too far out. They could find a way to work free of their bonds and paddle themselves to shore. Maybe their God would hear their prayers and intervene. Whatever the outcome, they would no longer be a risk to Elinor.

"Show me to the captain's quarters," she instructed Diego as the Spanish skiff began to drift.

He led her and Tristan to the cabin while her crew set off to explore other parts of the ship. They needed to work quickly to catch the tide out of the bay and finally set their sails towards the island of New Providence. The captain's quarters were well furnished, and she hastily gathered gold and silver candlesticks as Tristan opened the drawers of the desk, withdrawing another purse of heavy pieces of eight.

"Knew the bastard had more than he was giving us," Tristan laughed.

"Keep looking." Elinor dragged a heavy chest to the middle of the room. She rifled through the contents, discarding the captain's personal effects and replacing them with the things that could be sold at market or to smugglers.

The first pirogue they sent over carried two of her wounded men, young Diego, and six sacks of sugar and tobacco. Her men had rigged a makeshift pulley system by stringing ropes between the railings of the two decks, using them to haul rolls of fabric and animal hides across the water. The next carried the live chickens found below deck and Griff's dead body, carefully rolled into one of the ship's sails. His sacrifice would be honored later; the crew would feast in his memory.

Elinor waited to leave the ship until all her men were back across, knowing Tristan would see to the preparations for the *Revenge* to sail on. She knelt by the dead captain whose name she had never learned, and whispered a prayer of forgiveness of her own. His one remaining eye stared blankly into the distance, watching his crew float off into the distance.

"I'm sorry," she whispered, wondering whose forgiveness she was begging. She unpinned the gold brooch on his chest and slipped it into her pocket.

"Ready, Cap?" Patch-Eyed Jack called, the last of her men remaining on the doomed ship with her.

"Aye, Jack," she said. "Let's go home."

Chapter 17

"**I** TOLD YOU SHE was lucky," Reddy told one of the powder boys.

"Aye, but was it the captain's luck or Mona's? Never seen anyone shoot like that, and they're all sayin' she never even touched a pistol afore she showed up here." The boy was buzzing with the excitement of victory.

"Might be it's both of them," Reddy replied. "But I'll tell you one thing, that's not the first time the Golden Cormorant has escaped the clutches of death. When the captain promises pay, she delivers it."

Mona thought it was appalling that they could so casually discuss luck and coin with Griff's body not even cold yet, lying a few paces away in the middle of the deck. None of the crew had even seemed to notice their numbers were one less, or that they had all narrowly escaped with their own lives. Instead, they carried on as though everything was normal, stowing their plundered goods below deck as they cracked jokes and shared lighthearted conversation. She felt as though they had watched a different battle than she, one where everything had gone right and they hadn't lost a cherished crewmate. One where she hadn't come so close to losing the

Captain. She brushed the thought away. It was over, the captain safely back on board the *Revenge*. She hadn't had to watch the woman she loved be executed just out of her reach. She had figured out a way to stop it, whether by luck or divine intervention.

The captain had gone directly to her cabin while Tristan gave the orders to let out the sails. The wind filled them, propelling *Nimue's Revenge* away from the idyllic bay and the fire blazing across the deck of the Spanish ship. Mona hurried to her place on the deck, stained black with powder from the cannons that had been fired. Any spark from the nearby ship could be caught by the wind could send the *Revenge* up in flames, and she scrubbed hastily. The work made Griff's absence all the more noticeable, and Mona blinked back tears. She had grown fond of the man, but she wouldn't allow herself to cry for him. No one else was.

"Mona," Tristan said. "Walk with me."

"The deck..." she protested weakly.

"Diego will take your place," Tristan responded.

Mona handed the mop over to the young man, remembering how lost she had felt on her first day on the ship. He took it from her with a look of trepidation, and Mona realized she must look frightful with her dress stained black where she had wiped the powder residue from her hands and her hair a mess. Did he recognize her as the one who had killed his captain? He must have thought her a monster, and Mona was seized by the urge to prove to him that she was still good, and kind. She hesitated, but couldn't think of anything to say that would matter, so she turned to follow Tristan across the deck. She was surprised when he showed her to his cabin, inviting Mona into one of the last spaces on the ship she had never been before.

"The captain owes you her life," he said as he closed the door. "She'll never thank you for it so I will."

"I just did what anyone would have done," Mona replied.

"No. What you did was stupid, and disobeyed orders. None of the men would have attempted it. But you are no man, and somehow it worked."

"I couldn't bear to see her hurt," Mona admitted. "She's too important."

"She knew the risks when she boarded their ship."

"But they tricked us! It wasn't a fair fight. They faked a surrender just so they could have a better attack."

"And we tricked them first, by luring them into our trap. There's no such thing as a fair fight in piracy. You either win or you lose, but even winning comes at a cost."

"How do you live with it?"

"Recklessly, with pockets full of gold." Tristan reached into his trousers and withdrew a handful of gold and silver coins. "These are yours, with more coming when the goods are sold at port. More than enough to get you to Boston."

"There's nothing for me in Boston," Mona said. "I want to stay on the *Revenge*. I'll work, I'll do anything. Please, let me stay."

"Even after what you saw today?"

Mona nodded. Especially after what she had seen. And done. She had killed a man, and there was no returning to the person she was. What else was she supposed to do? Go to Boston and resume to role of a lady, taking up hobbies like embroidery and prayer? How could she ever clasp her hands together or thread a needle again, knowing that the same fingers had pulled a trigger and stolen a life? Besides, if the captain was going to place herself in danger, Mona would rather be at her side than half a world away, cursed to always wonder if she was even alive. Cursed to wonder what could have been.

"That's not my decision." Tristan drank from a newly opened bottle of rum, then offered it to Mona.

"She listens to you."

"Not on this," Tristan insisted. "She still hasn't told you her reasons?"

"What reasons?"

"I've sworn not to speak of it, and I'll honor my oath to her until my last day. But I'll tell you this: the captain hasn't always been this way. She's hardened her heart to protect herself, and it will take someone stronger than I to break through her defenses."

"How?"

He shrugged. "You'll have to figure out your own way, if it means so much to you. Fight for what you want."

"But I'm running out of time. We're close to Nassau, aren't we?"

"We are, but you'll have time there as well. Once we get to port, we'll stay a while. Maybe her mind will change when you're off the ship again."

Mona blushed, a hot red she was sure Tristan would notice even in the dim light of his cabin. He definitely knew what had transpired between her and the captain on the island, and it seemed like he was on her side.

"It seems like she doesn't even like me. She said it was a mistake," Mona blurted out, immediately hoping he wouldn't ask her to clarify.

"Mona," he replied seriously. "If she didn't care for you, you wouldn't be on this ship. If she badly wanted to be rid of you, she could have handed you over to the Crown's navy, or passed you off to the Spaniards without taking their ship for them to return you or ransom you or whatever they pleased."

Mona couldn't hold back her tears any longer. "I thought I was going to lose her. I thought he was going to kill her."

"So did I," Tristan said, offering her a handkerchief. "But she's survived many a near miss, and we didn't lose her."

"Why do you do it? How do you live with it?"

"The captain and I were raised on this ship. It's all we know. As foreign as this life is to you, your life is to us."

"But you could leave it and start over. I did."

"I couldn't. I swore loyalty to my captain and my ship. I'll never abandon her. This is the life I was given and I intend to live it fully."

Mona wondered if Griff had lived it fully, or if he had any regrets in his final moments. She wished she had taken more time to know him, but though they had worked side by side for months, she had never spoken to him about his dreams or desires, so caught up was she in her own.

"Did he have a family? Griff, I mean," she asked, then clarified at Tristan's look of confusion.

"He had a wife, three children in Nassau."

"What will happen to them now?"

"They'll be paid his final share of the loot, and some extra from everyone else's when we return to port. The *Revenge* takes care of her own."

"What about his body?" Mona choked on the last word of the question.

"We'll hold a funeral tonight, celebrate his memory. It'll be as proper of a burial as we can muster. And then we sail on."

"And that's it?"

"That's it." Tristan peered at her quizzically. "Are you sure you want a life on board a ship?"

"Not any ship," Mona admitted. "But I am sure I want a life with her, a life different from what I had known, a life where I can be free. Where else can I get that? The rest, I'll get used to. Everyone else has."

"You never get used to death. You only learn to ignore it so the guilt of living doesn't eat you to your bones. If we don't keep looking to the horizon, we'll become mired in the abyss of grief. So we sail on, moving ever forward so it can never catch up." Tristan sighed and Mona saw the depths of his own grief welling in his eyes. "But one day it will, unless we die first ourselves."

Chapter 18

E LINOR RINSED HER FACE again, though the last traces of the Spanish captain's blood had long since been washed into the ocean. The crew had cheered her when she reboarded the *Revenge*, happy to have won the coins they needed for their exploits in Nassau. Happy to have won at all. She didn't deserve their praise, though. Too many mistakes had been made. She ran through the battle again, looking for where she had erred. Confidence had gotten the better of her, she had let her reputation do too much of the talking for her. The Spaniard had seen her weakness and exploited it, lulling her into a false surrender, and she had paid for it with Griff's life. She couldn't show the crew how shaken she was, though she knew Tristan sensed it and was giving her space to come to terms with the blunder.

She couldn't hide forever in her cabin, though, her crew needed their captain. Words needed to be spoken, promises made good upon. The voyage wasn't over. Elinor took a deep breath and stepped onto the deck. She scanned it, looking first for Mona, as had become her habit. She was nowhere to be seen. Elinor fought back the wave of panic. Surely she had just returned to her cabin to rest, but it wasn't like Mona to eschew work on the deck. Knocking at Mona's cabin door yielded only silence in return, and the panic grew stronger. Elinor squinted at the waves trailing behind the ship, praying the woman hadn't fallen overboard, and didn't see anything.

"Where is she? Where is Mona?" Elinor demanded, marching over to where Reddy and the newcomer, Diego, were wiping the last traces of the battle from the deck.

"Went off with Tristan an hour or so ago," Reddy said with a nod and a sly grin towards the quartermaster's door. "Lucky bastard," Elinor heard him mutter under his breath as Elinor stormed towards the cabin.

She turned to go back to her cabin. She knew Tristan would never betray her like that– he took the code of the ship as seriously as any of them– but she couldn't suppress the doubt that rose with Reddy's words. Mona and Tristan had gotten close, and there were plenty of women who enjoyed the company of both men and women. Tristan was objectively handsome, and Elinor had seen the way Mona looked at him, with eyes full of gratitude and friendship. Tristan wouldn't betray her, but if he thought Elinor had rejected Mona, if Mona went to him seeking comfort... He was only a man. Would he resist her advances? The fear and jealousy grew louder than Elinor's rational thoughts. She had to know.

Elinor stormed across the deck, trying to talk herself out of it as she went. She was confused, her thoughts clouded by panic and grief and regret in the aftermath of the battle. It would be better to wait until they emerged, and ask Tristan about it discreetly. But the crew was already whispering, making their own assumptions. She had to know. The door wasn't barred, and she flung it open without knocking. Rage blinded her as she saw Tristan's arms wrapped around Mona, embracing her. Both jumped as the door slammed open, letting go of each other to face Elinor.

"What are you doing?" She whispered, feeling the blood drain from her face as the shock and betrayal set in.

"Not what you're assuming. We were just talking." Tristan stepped in front of Mona protectively, as if to shield her from Elinor's wrath. There was no need, for Elinor's wrath would be directed at him once she could find the words to express it.

"Just talking? In your cabin, with the door closed?" Elinor's mind raced to comprehend what she had walked in on. Seeing Mona in his arms hurt, but the betrayal from Tristan, her best friend, stung the most. "I trusted you."

"And I've never abused that trust. I've no interest in Mona, and she has none in me. This isn't what it seems," Tristan pleaded.

"I know what I saw," Elinor said. "And I know what the men are saying is happening in this cabin right now."

"Elinor—"

"Captain," she corrected. "I am the captain of this ship. Address me as such."

"That you may be," He said wryly, "But must I remind you of my duties as quartermaster of this ship? Oversee the crew, settle disputes, pay out the loot, and mete out punishments when they are warranted. I was simply giving Mona her share of the take, and letting her know her refusal to follow orders in battle did not go unnoticed."

"Do you pay all our crew by wrapping your arms around them?" Elinor raised an eyebrow.

"No, that was because she needed a friend." Tristan looked her directly in the eye, and she saw real hurt at her disbelief. "Nothing untoward happened here. I swear, Elinor. On Abi."

"Mona?" Elinor asked for confirmation, though she was already softening. Tristan wouldn't have invoked Abigail if what he was saying was untrue. He had more honor than that.

"Aye, Captain," she said. "It's all as Tristan says, no more."

"Perhaps I overreacted then. My apologies." She fixed a stern glare on Tristan. He was the one who should know better. "The men are already talking, and if it's perceived you're breaking the code, it's as good as true. Make sure it doesn't happen again."

He had the decency to look ashamed. "You're right, Captain. I'm sorry."

"Both of you back to your posts, then, we've a ship to see to and a funeral to prepare."

Mona rushed to obey the orders, but Tristan lingered. His brow was furrowed and he looked troubled.

"Ellie, what was that about? You know I would never."

"I panicked," Elinor admitted. "I went to look for her, to make sure she was okay, and she wasn't anywhere on the deck. Reddy said she went with you, he implied—"

"You've had quite a day. Are you okay?"

"Bit banged up from when I fell, but still in one piece."

"That's not what I meant."

"I know what you meant. But what should I say? We lost a good man today. We almost lost the battle. I almost..." Died. Elinor's throat closed around the word, trapping it and holding it there as she trailed off.

"I was worried for you," he said.

"You shouldn't have been. The *Revenge* has to come first. You countermanded my order in battle. You should have let the men keep fighting, as I commanded. He would have killed me either way."

"But he didn't. Thanks to Mona."

"From that distance, she could have killed me as easily as the Spaniard. She didn't save me, she just got lucky. I would have figured something out." Elinor dredged up the bravado she had leaned on so many times before.

"Maybe," Tristan said. "Or maybe we'd've all been hanged."

They walked side by side to the body wrapped in the enemy sail, a sobering reminder of how close they had come to losing it all. At Elinor's nod, Tristan called the crew to attention. It was time for the funeral to begin.

"Cap's going to say a few words," Tristan opened. "Then anyone who wishes to speak, may."

Elinor swallowed. No matter how many times she did it, it never got any easier. But it was important, and what Griff deserved. She looked out at her crew, one who had been with here for mere hours, others only a few months, and the waning few who had stood behind her since she took the helm from Greybrow.

"Griff was a good man," she began without really knowing what to say. She had barely known the man, only spoken to him a handful of times and never about anything beyond the needs of the ship. "A man who was willing to do anything for his family and his ship. Fierce when he had to be, but a friend to many on and off this ship. He won't be forgotten. We'll honor his name in story and song for the rest of our days." Elinor stepped back to stand beside Tristan, gesturing for anyone else who wanted to say some words for their crewmate to come forward.

Reddy stepped up, eyes red and reeking of even more rum than usual. "He was my best friend, none truer to be found. Saved my life more than once he did, and many o' yours. I was there the first time he held each of his babes. Griff loved them more than anything in the world. Before you all, I swear on this day– which is it?" He looked sheepishly to Tristan, who whispered the answer. "On this day, August 28, the seventeen hundred and seventh year of our Lord, that I'll always look after them children, and his bonny wife, too. For the rest of my days, they'll want for nothing. Half my shares will be theirs."

"Aye, Griff was a good worker, ne'er complained a whit. As steady a shot as they come," Scab chimed in.

One by one, the men who had known Griff best stepped before the crew to share memories of the man who lay before them. When no one else wanted to speak, Elinor slipped back into her cabin and rummaged through her collection of books while the men fetched their tankards for the drinking that would soon commence. She found the book she was looking for, and, returning to the deck, passed it to Tristan. The men might accept her as a captain, but acting as a priest would be a step too far. Better for Tristan to read the burial rites from the *Book of Common Prayer*. Reddy knelt at his friend's side, wielding a thick needle to sew the thick canvas shut. Three cannonballs were tucked into the cloth at Griff's feet by three more of the crew who joined him. When the work of sewing was done, they grasped the canvas and lifted the body as Tristan began to read.

"Deliver this our brother out of the miseries of this sinful world," he intoned.

Elinor noticed Mona at the back of the crowd, tears running silently down her face as Griff was carried to the rail.

"Your grace be with us all, evermore. Amen."

"Amen," the men echoed, hoisting the dead man into the sea.

"Amen," Elinor whispered. If there was a God, surely they would all be damned for their sins, too grievous even for one who was claimed to be all-merciful. But the tradition was important to her men, so she kept it.

"*Far beyond the horizon wide,*" Reddy began singing and old shanty in a rumbling tenor.

"*Drift eternal with the tide,*" the crew joined in the song.

"*Let our brother finds his rest*
On his journey ever west
Sail on! Sail on!
'Til we reach the dawn
Sail on! Sail on!
'Til we reach the dawn."

Goosebumps prickled on Elinor's arms and her hairs raised as the full of the ship began the song again, with Mona's alto distinct against the chorus of deeper voices. They sang through the verse a third time, with many of the men crossing themselves at the end. Elinor returned the Book of Common Prayer to its drawer, and brought a freshly pillaged cask of rum out to the waiting men.

They crowded around with their tankards, eager to toast to their fallen friend and drink away the hardship of another day at sea until they remembered no more and woke in the morning to begin anew. One of the men produced a fiddle and began pulling his bow across the strings, a mournful Scotch ballad lifting to the heavens on the wind.

"To Griff," Elinor said, raising her cup and drinking deeply.

As the spirits flowed, the mood lifted into one of merriment. The crew began regaling each other with tales of Griff's feats in battle, each trying to outdo the other as they embellished details, magnifying the fallen pirate's heroics with each retelling. The sun sank lower towards the sea, and all eyes on deck turned to it as one. If someone blinked they would have missed it, but for the briefest instant the sliver of sun glowed green before disappearing into the beyond. Elinor felt the guilt weighing on her heart lighten; Griff had made it into the next world. He was free.

A wail ripped across the deck as the clutches of drunkenness and grief overcame Reddy. He staggered towards the rail only to be pulled back by the men, supporting him as they led him to a crate to sit and sob into his hands. Their camaraderie amplified Elinor's loneliness. She had Tristan, of course, to catch her when she fell. She had been so foolish to have doubted him. But as dark fell, it wasn't his arms around her she longed for. He couldn't understand, couldn't be the comfort she needed when she cried alone in the stillest hours of night. None of them could, except for Mona.

She was across the deck, laughing and crying at the same time as someone cracked a joke, at ease among the crew that had all be strangers such a short time earlier. There was a time when Elinor had fit in so seamlessly among them, a time when she was younger, bolder, not in command of the ship. The distance was of her own insistence, the bonds she'd built broken by her own decrees. She ached to break through the walls she'd erected from the pieces of grief, but she'd closed herself off too well and for too long.

"You're staring," Tristan said, sidling up behind her. "Go to her."

"I don't know what to say."

"Let your heart speak for you. Tell her the truth."

"It doesn't know what to say either," she smiled wanly. "It's forgotten how to speak."

"Give it a chance to remember," he urged, leaving as quickly as he'd come when another crewman summoned him over.

Chapter 19

MONA WIPED TEARS FROM her eyes as Rigs finished telling a raucous tale about Griff, a barmaid, a miscommunication that began with black eyes and ended in tankards of ale. The men were laughing and crying in turns as they mourned their friend in their own, peculiar pirate way. She took another swig of rum, feeling distinctly like she was being watched. Glancing around the deck, she noticed the captain's intense stare, and felt a familiar tingle run down her spine. The captain beckoned her over with a slight wave of her hand. She excused herself from the conversation and stumbled across the deck, the ship lurching and her drunkenness failing to account for it.

"Yes, Captain?" She stopped an arm's length away, unable to trust herself not to reach for the captain, knowing it would be inappropriate in front of the crew.

"Elinor," the captain said softly. "You can call me Elinor, when it's just you and I."

"Elinor," Mona breathed, tasting the name as though it were the forbidden fruit, unsure if a snake would dart out to bite her for her impudence. Her heart swelled and skipped a beat. Perhaps the captain was finally realizing her feelings. Tristan had been right. All Elinor had needed was time.

"I owe you an apology," Elinor said. "What happened on the island wasn't a mistake, and I shouldn't have said it was. It was the best day I've had in a long time. And I'm also sorry for assuming you and Tristan—"

"I forgive you," Mona responded without thinking, because she already had. All the better if Elinor had been jealous. At least it meant she cared.

"Don't," Elinor said. "I don't deserve it."

"You deserve the world, and I would give it all to you if I could. *Rwy'n di garu di.*" I love you. The words slipped out, shaken loose by the rum and a newfound appreciation for the shortness of life.

"I can't love you." Elinor sighed. "I wish I could."

"Why not?" Mona felt her heart begin to shatter anew.

"The Code forbids it."

"So change it. You're the captain," Mona pleaded. Tears welled, then broke loose to stream down her cheeks. She didn't bother to wipe them away. She couldn't. She was paralyzed, gripped in a long spasm of torment as she saw the resoluteness in the captain's hardened expression. "You can change it."

"It's not that simple, Mona. It's written in our charter for a reason. I..." Elinor swallowed, and Mona could see she was considering her words carefully. "I had a wife before, and she was taken from me because of my mistakes. This life is too cruel for love, and I'm too broken for it. I have to protect myself. If the time were different, if the place were different, there's nothing I would rather be doing, no one I would rather be with than you."

"No," Mona sobbed, feeling as though a punch to her stomach had knocked all the wind from her. "No, Elinor, please. Don't push me away again."

"Don't you see I have to? My duty is to the *Revenge,* and yours is to be safe."

"I don't care about the danger, as long as you're with me."

"It isn't about you, it's about this entire ship. Griff lost his life because my focus slipped. I've been too distracted because of you and the men deserve better."

"It wasn't your fault. They tricked you."

"I should have seen it, but I was blinded by my affection for you."

"I won't be a distraction. I won't disobey you again. Next time I'll hide, like you told me to. Please, Elinor." Mona gave one last plea, though the captain's mind seemed set.

"Go live, Mona. If you love me, don't ask to stay aboard my ship again. If you love me, go live a long life, find your happiness and grow old somewhere far from here, somewhere safe."

"I understand," Mona said.

None of it made sense. It didn't matter what she did, Elinor would never accept her. The flame of hope that guided her through all the dark and lonely nights in her cabin flickered out as though it had been drenched in water, impossible to relight. Mona ran back to her cabin, wondering how there was anything left of her body to move, so hollowed out was she by the pain of rejection. She could accept if Elinor didn't love her, but she'd all but admitted she did. It hurt worse because of it.

Four days until Nassau. Mona prayed for fast winds to fill the ship's sails and push them into the port sooner. She didn't know how she could ever face the captain again, lest she die of shame on the very spot. It wasn't fair.

Just when she thought she'd found a place she truly belonged, it was ripped away from her.

Mona slept in late the next morning. She had nothing left to prove, and nothing left to give. The ship would manage without her, as it always had. How foolish she had been to think that she could be a part of it. By midmorning, Tristan was pounding at her door, but she ignored him until he left. She lay in her bed and counted the planks in her ceiling. Twelve. Maybe when she was off this wretched ship, she would write her own tale of pirates, and tell the real truth of the matter. Tristan returned again late in the afternoon, knocking with more urgency. She tried to ignore him again. Besides the captain, he was the last person Mona wanted to see.

"Mona, at least say something so I know you're not dead," he pleaded.

"I'm not dead," she called back, her voice raspy from disuse.

"Come out. You need to eat."

She went back to pretending he wasn't there. She didn't care if she missed meals, she wasn't working for them anymore. There would be food aplenty when they arrived in Nassau. Twelve. She recounted the boards of the ceiling to be sure. Yes, twelve. The next morning, it was harder to ignore Tristan's knock and demand she come out for breakfast. The raw sting of heartbreak had faded to a dull ache, but she still couldn't chance seeing Elinor on the deck. Two more days until Nassau.

And then what would she do? The ultimate question burned hotter with each passing day. Find a hot meal first, maybe one with fresh vegetables or even fruit. Mona's mouth watered at the thought. It had been so long since she had tasted the luxury of an apple, or one of the juicy plums that ripened every August in the orchard behind the manor. Oh, how she hoped Nassau had fruit.

She didn't fully know what to expect, having heard differing tales of destruction and ruin, decadence and luxurious depravity. She would have to see to finding a room, if there was any sort of inn available in the town. New clothes would be next, and when they were acquired she would burn the ones she had so as never to be reminded of their stench, or the ship, again. The only thing there was sure to be in Nassau was more pirates. *Keep looking to the horizon and sail on.* Tristan's advice rattled in her head. She could talk her way onto one of their ships somehow and sail on, away from the *Revenge* and her cold, calculating, heartless captain.

"Come out, Mona. That's an order." Tristan was back.

"Leave me alone," she mumbled.

"I'll break down this door." His tone lacked its usual charm, and Mona could tell he was deadly serious.

She unbarred the door, and opened it, squinting in the bright sunlight.

"You look terrible," Tristan said. "Drink this."

He thrust a tankard of grog into her hands. It was only then that Mona realized how parched her throat was, and once she started drinking, she didn't stop until the whole tankard was emptied. She turned to go back into the cabin, but he slid a foot in the door, preventing her from closing it.

"The captain wants to see you. She's waiting in her cabin."

Those few words were enough to make the flicker of hope burst alive once again.

"There's nothing she needs to say that hasn't already been said." Mona fought to tamp the flame. She wouldn't fall into the trap of seeing hope where there was none again.

"She's worried about you. We all are. I told the men you've fallen ill, and they're all asking after you."

"What does it matter? I'll be gone from this ship soon enough, and then you can all forget I was ever here."

Tristan looked wounded. "What do your crewmates matter to you after almost three months at their side? I thought you were stronger than this. Let them remember you that way, not hiding in your coward's den. That's not the Mona we know, fierce and brave and reckless. Pick yourself up and finish what you started here."

He was right, of course. The *Revenge* was more than her captain, and Mona had lost sight of that. She had grown to care for so many of the crew, whom she knew to be good men. When they spoke of her, she wanted it to be with the same respect and love they showed each other.

"Fine," Mona agreed. "As long as I don't have to speak to the captain."

"You're still a guest on her ship so I can't promise that, but I'll do my best to make it so," he said, looking at her with pity. "Go to the galley and find yourself something to eat, then join Reddy and Diego at your post."

Chapter 20

"SHE DOESN'T WANT TO speak with you," Tristan reported, rejoining Elinor in her cabin.

"I don't blame her," Elinor said. "I wouldn't want to speak to me either. Besides, I don't know what I would have said. I would have just made it worse. I only wanted to see that she's okay."

"She will be. Mona's tough."

"Tristan?" Elinor asked, laughing a little to hide the hitch in her voice.

"Yes?"

"Next stowaway that finds their way onto our ship is getting tossed in the ocean straight away."

He chuckled, and drew her into a hug. "You'll be okay, too. I just hope you don't come to regret this."

"It was the right thing to do," Elinor insisted, trying to convince herself as much as him.

"None of what we do anymore is the right thing to do," Tristan said. "We've drifted so far from where Greybrow started."

"The times change like the tides. We can only change with them."

"Or are we drowning ourselves in them?"

"If we have, it's too late to surface now. But, enough waxing poetic. Is the inventory complete?" Elinor changed the subject to something less philosophical. She didn't have the emotional strength to consider morality anymore, or who she had become as a person. She just wanted to get to Nassau and find some clarity and peace again.

"Mostly. The last chickens will be slaughtered for supper tonight, good riddance to them."

Elinor laughed, genuinely amused at Tristan's contempt for the birds. Since bringing them on board, he had done nothing but complain about their noise, stench, and the extra manpower he had to allot to care for them. Elinor thought they were funny little creatures, strutting around below deck as proud as any pirate and hatching all manner of escape attempts from their quickly constructed enclosure.

"I've marked half the spirits to be sold and the other half to stay with the ship, should be enough to last until we can resupply next," he continued, "And took counts of the rest. As long as we get a fair price, we'll want for nothing for as long as we care to stay in Nassau."

"Good," Elinor said, distracted by a glimpse of Mona on the deck through her window, her copper hair unmistakable even when distorted by the rippled panes of glass. Guilt bubbled up to the surface again. She'd known her words would be hard for her to accept, but she hadn't expected Mona's reaction to be so shocked, so hurt. Elinor didn't even notice the clouds gathering in the distance behind them until Tristan pointed them out.

"Looks like our voyage will end how it began, with a storm."

THE CAPTAIN'S CHOICE

Elinor looked up at the flagpole, once again flying the colors of the Crown. It whipped in the rising wind, the *Revenge* swaying in the growing swells. Nothing came easy on the sea, but she quite thought she had dealt with enough tribulation on the unforgettable journey from Wales. The storm wasn't a surprise, common as they were in the late summer in the Caribbean, but it was another obstacle, another responsibility that fell on her shoulders to navigate.

"We need to get into deeper water," she instructed. "We're too close to land, we'll be pushed into the rocks."

She squinted, assessing the black band of clouds that stretched across the horizon. There was no way to outrun the storm, but she would try to keep them near the edge, away from the worst of the winds and waves. She had a few hours at most, and then the storm would be upon them.

"Get men on the masts, furl the sails. We won't outrun it." She frowned.

"Don't worry, Cap," Tristan said, reading her expression. "The *Revenge* has been through worse, and always lives to tell the tale."

Elinor wasn't sure that the ship had been through worse in a worse position, trapped as they were between two islands with sandbars dotting the sea. The black clouds were alarming, looming closer with every passing minute as flashes of lightning danced between them. When the storm descended and the sea roiled, the dangers around them would be all but invisible amidst the lashing rain.

"We'll survive this," he insisted.

Elinor nodded, casting the doubt from her mind. She took a deep breath, straightened her spine, and raised her chin. Her crew needed their captain at her best. Tristan held the door for her, and she forced a smile before sauntering out onto the deck.

"Winds are blowin', gents," she said, keeping her tone light. "We're going to get wet."

She strode over to the navigator, who was manning the helm, passing Mona along the way. Focused on scrubbing the deck, Mona refused to meet Elinor's eyes. Elinor swallowed the urge to order her to ride out the storm in her cabin. She would have to trust Tristan to see to Mona's safety in her stead.

"Go get some rest," she dismissed the helmsman from his station. "You'll be needed in a few hours. I'll take it the ship until the storm is upon us."

"Aye, Captain." He hurried to obey.

She took the great wheel of the ship, the wood handles smooth from years of use. It took both hands to hold the course steady, but she welcomed the physical exertion as a distraction. Her men were beginning to scale the masts to tie up the sails so they wouldn't be torn to shreds by the coming winds. One sail would remain unfurled so they could still catch the wind and keep moving, the only way to survive when waves began beating at the hull of the ship.

The gusts increased steadily throughout the afternoon, and Elinor's shoulders and forearms ached from holding the ship in position. The island to their starboard side dipped back into the sea, and she seized her window for escape before it was too late. Her hands were nEarly numb and she needed all her body weight to get the helm to turn, but mercifully it did, and the *Revenge* sailed for the deeper waters beyond. It was a small relief, but Elinor's tension eased nonetheless. At least they wouldn't find their death being dashed upon the rocks, though they were far from being out of danger.

The rain began. Elinor held her breath watching the men finish securing the sails high above her, knowing their hand and footholds were getting slicker with every passing moment. Finally, they scurried back down the masts to the relative safety of the top deck and Elinor felt the grip on her chest loosen. Even without most of their sails, the ship was easily propelled forward by the wind and the waves, their course no longer in her control.

"Take this," Tristan shouted, and handed her a hot mug of grog. "Last chance to get something warm in you until we reset the fires in the galley."

"Is everything secured?" She asked as he took the helm from her. The boat swayed, sloshing hot liquid from her cup to the deck, and she drank from it quickly before any more could be spilled.

"Aye."

"Mona?" She asked, scanning the flurry of activity below her.

"Safely below deck."

"Is there anything left to do?"

"Pray," he said wryly, glancing at the dark clouds above.

"Good. I'm going to wake Jack to take the helm."

Elinor rushed across the deck, grabbing ropes to steady herself as the ship rolled and pitched with the angry sea. She threw open the hatch and scrambled down, shaking Jack's hammock to wake him.

"Get to the helm," she ordered. "Tie yourself down. We're in for a long ride."

He rubbed sleep from his eyes, then woke fully, remembering his duty in the life-threatening situation. Elinor followed him back up to the deck. The sea seemed to be boiling around them, the water whipped into a fury that buffeted the ship from side to side. The *Revenge* stayed upright, and Elinor thanked the heavens for the heavy load they had taken from the Spaniards that helped keep them from keeling over in the water. The rain fell in sheets from the sky, drenching the deck and all who were still on it.

"Batten down the hatches," she called, as the first large wave broke over the stern.

Water rushed over her feet, nearly sweeping her off them, and she hurried to tie a rope around her waist so the next one wouldn't take her overboard. Falling into the water was a certain death sentence on most days, let alone in the midst of a storm. She worked with a crew to stretch the canvas tarpaulin over the hatches, put in place to keep as much water out of the underbelly of the ship as was possible. Her heart pounded as another wave crashed over the ship, this one taking her legs from under her. She rolled across the deck, coughing on the salt water that choked her as she clawed for purchase. The rope went taught, catching her around her ribs, and then the ship tossed the other way and she was dragged back. She cursed as she bashed into the base of a cannon and buried her head in her arms, protecting it. Tristan clung to a pole, and caught her by the shirt as she slid past him again. She scrambled to her feet, any hope of reclaiming her dignity lost to the wind.

"Time for you to get inside, as well, Captain," he said, pulling her towards her cabin.

Each step forward was a battle in itself, fighting the wind that blew steadily back. Her stomach dropped with the ship as it plummeted into the trough of a wave, then slammed back as the wave broke over them. Elinor shivered. She was drenched to her core, and the wind only made it worse. The final steps felt like furlongs, and she stumbled into the cabin exhausted when Tristan finally wrenched open the door. It was a mess, but there was no point cleaning it until the storm had passed, her books and candlesticks would be tossed back to the floor as soon as she returned them to her places.

"Are you hurt?" Tristan asked, bracing himself against the wall.

"No," Elinor said, though pain shot through her ribs every time she inhaled. "Just a bit bruised from my trip around the deck. Are you?"

"No," he said, wiping the water that dripped from his hair down his face. He was laughing. "Some welcome back to the Bahamas."

"At least we shouldn't be too far off course. The wind might even push us there sooner," Elinor said, hoping the words were true. She knew the storm was pushing north, but until the seas calmed there was no way of knowing where.

"With your luck, anything is possible. Might blow us right into the harbor."

Chapter 21

MONA KNOTTED THE THIN strip of cotton around Reddy's arm, securing the splint in place. The storm was over, but the *Revenge* and her crew were battered from weathering it. Reddy tested the bandage and winced in pain.

"Don't try to move it," she said, echoing the words a doctor had told her ten years before when she'd broken her own wrist. She knew nothing of the art of medicine, but it seemed no one else on the ship did either, so she had taken it upon herself to help the men bandage their scrapes and breaks.

He nodded, his face white with pain. He'd been thrown from his hammock as the ship tossed in the tempest, one of many men with minor injuries from the battle against a foe they couldn't fight. Mona was lucky to have emerged unscathed, having spent the last few hours with her arms and legs wrapped around a pole below deck to keep from being thrown about the crowded quarters. She tore another length of cotton and wrapped it around Reddy's wrist, adding another layer of protection for the break while it healed.

Everyone had returned to the deck except for the captain. As much as Mona tried to stop herself from looking, she couldn't help but scan the crowd every few moments for a glimpse of the blonde braid or confident swagger. Tristan would have told the crew if the unthinkable had happened to her, so she was probably just sleeping after the long evening of being battered by the Caribbean. It wasn't her concern anymore, Mona reminded herself. It never was to begin with.

The ship had miraculously sustained little damage, though everyone and everything was thoroughly soaked. One of the cannons had come free from the deck, swept overboard by a wave, but the masts were intact and the rigging held as men climbed high above the deck to unfurl the sails. They shouted excitedly down to the crew below, their words lost to the breeze. Mona tried to read their lips, then turned to Reddy, who had broken into a grin.

"What did they say?" She asked.

"Land ahead," he said excitedly. "It's New Providence. Like God Himself steered us here."

Mona squinted into the distance, and the island appeared like a mirage rising from the sea. She was ready to leave the *Revenge* and all her painful memories behind, ready to start the next adventure of her life. The word spread quickly around the deck, and the exhausted crew worked with renewed vigor, an end finally within sight. Reddy's wound as bound as she could manage, she hurried to join them in the preparations for the ship's arrival at the harbor. She swabbed the deck, rejoicing in the fact that it was the last time she would do the chore aboard the ship that had given her nothing but heartbreak.

"Pack your belongings," Tristan instructed. "You're on the first boat to shore."

She went to her cabin, the reality of their arrival setting in. Packing would be a short affair, though her possessions had tripled in her time on the ship. She folded her green dress carefully, doubting if she would ever wear it again. It was stained beyond salvation, marred with the memory of Elinor. She tucked the little purse of coins Tristan had given her in the folds, so as not to lose or draw attention to it. Those pieces of eight were her last lifeline, her way to something better. Maybe it was naive, but Mona still hoped her happiness was somewhere out there, waiting for her.

If she was to row to shore with the first boat, it showed how desperate Elinor was to be rid of her. All because another woman had loved the captain first. It was silly for Mona to be jealous of a dead woman, but she couldn't stop comparing herself to the mystery wife Elinor had so fleetingly spoken of and wondering where she fell short, wondering what the wife had offered that she couldn't. Not that it mattered. The journey was over, and it was up to Mona alone to pick up the pieces of her heart and move on.

The final thing she packed was a small, carved turtle bone given to her by Reddy earlier that day. It was a trinket for good fortune, he'd said, to aid her journey with calm seas and smooth sailing. The gift had touched her in ways she couldn't express, because he had made it with his own two hands. No one had ever done that for her before, her father and Rhys preferring to buy her things from shops so as not to waste their time that was better spent on their businesses and hobbies. As glad as Mona was to be escaping the pain of the ship, she also lamented the loss of the strange little family she had found there.

She looked around the little cabin with its sparse furnishings one last time. It was as if she had never been there. She was seized by the impulse to make a mark somehow, carve her being into the frame of the room, leave a piece of herself there to be remembered by. Instead, she sighed. She was holding on to something she needed to let go. It was time to learn how to sail on. The door thudded shut behind her. Tristan met her halfway across the deck and took the small bundle from her. The captain was still absent from the deck.

"Say your goodbyes now," Tristan advised.

"But won't I see the men again in town?" She asked, confused.

"For your sake, I hope not. The establishments they frequent are not ones a lady like yourself should find herself in."

"A lady like myself? What does that mean?" Indignation crept into her voice. He had already forgotten what she was capable of.

"High born, a lady of society. Nassau is a den of criminals, best you avoid them."

"Aren't I a criminal now, too?"

"No, because you're going to deny involvement in everything that has happened on this ship. You'll never find passage north on an honest ship otherwise. Do you understand what I'm saying, Mona? You should never speak of this crossing again."

"I won't," Mona lied. He still had no idea of her intention to continue her pirating life, and if speaking about her deeds got her closer to that goal, then she would do whatever it took. She owed no loyalty to the *Revenge* after they had shown her none.

"Good. When I order the anchors down, be ready to board the pirogue."

Mona couldn't bring herself to say goodbye, not while the *Revenge* was still sailing towards the harbor, not while she still had time, so she made her way to the bow of the ship to gather her thoughts. A pod of dolphins danced in the waves before the ship, leading the way into port. It was another sign of good fortune to come, not that Mona put stock in such things. The superstitions of sailors were almost a religion unto themselves, but she was living proof that superstitions never came true. If she'd had luck on her side, things might have been different.

Smoke curled into the sky from fires burning on shore, the sight of civilization unnerving after being so contained in a world of their own on the *Revenge*. Mona realized she no longer knew how to interact with people, especially not in such a far flung land that was sure to be different from her native Wales. She didn't know any of the customs or how people would respond to her. It had been a British colony at one point, so she supposed there must be some similarities, but the crew had told her that the last governor had been abducted by the Spanish and that the settlement had largely been abandoned.

Yet, ships dotted the harbor, some dwarfing even the three-masted *Revenge*. Nassau hardly seemed abandoned, on the contrary. It seemed teeming with life, as figures walking on the beach came into view, accompanied by the sound of a fiddle floating over the water. Mona recognized the tune, one of the many shanties she had learned to help pass time whilst working on the deck with Griff and Reddy. They had taught her so much. How was she supposed to say goodbye?

She didn't have much longer to figure it out. The port grew larger and larger until it seemed if Mona stretched far enough she would be able to reach out and touch it. Tristan was sure to call for the anchors to be dropped soon, or the ship would run aground in the shallow water of the harbor. She hurried to find Reddy, tears blurring her vision.

"I'll miss you," she said, wrapping him in a hug that caused him to stammer and blush.

"Ye'll be missed by us as well, Mona," he said sheepishly. "Good worker, you are, and an even better shot. And a good friend."

"Take care of yourself," she said. "I hope one day our paths might cross again."

"I hope it, too." He gave her an extra squeeze.

"Drop the anchors!" Tristan called behind them.

Only Tristan and Mona got into the pirogue that was lowered into the harbor. Burdened by hesitation, Mona felt like she was rowing through mud, every pull of the oar a fight to make her muscled obey and push on. She stared into the hull of carved out wood as she counted her strokes, vowing not to look up at the *Revenge* until they were too far back to see the tears spilling hotly from her eyes. When she reached one hundred, she mustered the courage to behold the ship one final time. A flash of movement caught her eye, and she briefly glimpsed the captain's silhouette moving away from the large windows in her cabin.

"Why didn't anyone else come ashore? Why just us?" She asked the question that had been burning at her, even though she feared the answer. If they meant to abandon her there and sail away on the next tide, she'd rather know sooner than later.

"I have business to attend to first."

"What business?"

"Better if you don't know," he said. "Less risk for us."

The pirogue shuddered as it hit sand, and Mona realized they had run into the beach. Tristan hopped out and pulled the boat onto the shore so the soft waves couldn't tease it back out of reach. The scent of roasting meat filled Mona's nostrils as she stepped out of the boat, followed by the deep rumble of men laughing further up the beach.

"Keep your head down and try not to attract any attention," Tristan instructed, turning towards the smoke and smells of food.

She followed him across the sand, past a row of ramshackle huts cobbled together from driftwood and what seemed to be the pieces of old ships. Some had what were clearly ship's sails for roofs, while others were covered in thick layers of leaves and lashed down by long rods. Men milled about, passing around bottles of rum and tending to small fires that burned in front of the dwellings.

They emerged onto what could pass for a road, walking into a town unlike any other Mona had seen. Some of the buildings were in ruin, their charred frames a ghostly reminder of what they had once been. Efforts to rebuild were evident the further they walked into Nassau, and the sounds of sawing and hammers striking nails echoed between the blackened husks. It was a town that had seen great tragedy, but was not put down by it.

"What happened?" She asked Tristan, trotting to keep up with his longer strides. "Is this recent?"

"No worse than the last time we were here. The bloody Spanish and French burned it all four years back. Bad luck for the folk living here, but good luck for us. Nassau is more or less ours, a safe place for our ships to rest ungoverned by any crown."

Mona noticed a stand by the road, the broad table of colorful fruits shaded by a bright tapestry. She stopped to marvel at the strange shapes, and the man lounging on a crate nearby beckoned her over with a grin and a wave.

"What will it be today, Miss...?" He asked, fishing for her name.

"Mona," she finished for him. "I don't know, it all looks so exotic and tempting. What is this one?" She pointed at a stalk that bore fruits as long as her fingers but twice as big around, their skins ranging from green to yellow.

"Bananas," he replied, amused by her ignorance. "Bad luck on a ship, but good eatings on land. Try one."

"I'd love to," Mona said. Tristan's hand clamped down on her shoulder and pulled her away before she could ask why the fruits were bad luck.

"I said not to attract attention," he reprimanded.

"I wasn't! I was just looking." She hated being treated like a child.

"I was ordered to take you straight to the inn. The captain doesn't want word of your presence to spread. It's safer for you that way, and us."

Mona sighed at the grip Elinor still had over her life, especially as it concerned her safety. "I don't have to follow her orders anymore. I'm not on her ship nor part of her crew. And I would like to see Nassau."

"It's for your own good," Tristan insisted. "You may have no further obligation to her, but I do."

Mona decided it was easier to follow than argue with the man whose loyalties lay with the captain. Nassau would go nowhere in the time it would take her to get settled at the inn, and once she was there, there would be no one to stop her from leaving. She was a woman in control of her own destiny, but she would allow others to pretend they were at the helm of her life a little longer.

Chapter 22

Elinor waited for the weight to be lifted from her shoulders as Mona and Tristan rowed away, but it remained as heavy as it had ever been, crushing her from the moment Mona had stepped on her ship. Once Tristan found passage for her, then maybe the weight would dissipate and Elinor could rest. She hoped he returned with good news of smugglers in the harbor ready to take on the *Revenge's* stolen cargo to resell in more profitable ports, and better news that he had found an ally or friend to give Mona safe passage on.

The two figures in the boat walked across the beach and out of sight. Elinor closed her eyes, committing the final view of Mona to memory, wishing she'd had the opportunity to say goodbye. But it was over, by her own doing, and the ship needed her. She paused by the door to pick up a wooden tankard, the last of the mess wreaked by the storm the night before, then joined her crew. They were antsy to be on shore, and the eager anticipation hummed across the deck as the men argued over who would bed which whore first. The only person who looked as glum as Elinor felt was Reddy. Normally the center of conversations, he stood off by himself, gazing at the shore.

"Something troubling you?" She asked.

"They'll be waiting for him," he said, sadly. "They always were, right on the beach as soon as the news of the *Revenge* spread through town. I don't know how to face them."

Elinor realized he was talking about Griff's family. "There's nothing you can say that will lessen their pain. But they'll know he died with honor."

"It should have been me. No one in the world cares what happens to me, no one's waiting in the ports when the ship anchors. Why him?"

"It's not something you can change. Find something to keep your mind busy, and eventually it will fade." Elinor patted him on the back.

"Aye, Captain," he said, still squinting towards the beach.

"Good man." She left him to his thoughts.

Tristan returned to the ship a few hours later, alone. Elinor was expecting it, but the sight of the pirogue without Mona still caused another wave of sadness to break over her.

"She's safe," he assured her. "I paid for a week at the inn, which will buy us enough time to ask around for passage to the Colonies.

"Thank you, Tristan. What other news do you have of Nassau?"

"Old Henry Rowe's here, headed for Port Royal in three days' time. He's interested in taking on some of our cargo, but the price he offered is poor."

Elinor frowned. Rowe was a good sailor, but a known cheapskate. She had done business with him before, but preferred a more favorable transaction when she could come by it.

"Are there any other smugglers here? Anyone sailing north soon?" She asked.

"Not that I heard about, but that doesn't mean they aren't here. The town is busy enough."

"Start getting the men to shore. Make sure Reddy is among the first, and give him Griff's share of the coin. He'll see to it that the widow gets it. And you keep asking around, we've men to finish paying."

"And when will you come ashore?"

Elinor shrugged. "Last. I'm in no rush."

"Nearly six months at sea with almost no reprieve, and you wish to... stay at sea?" His face said he doubted her.

She couldn't admit to him that the ship was the only thing keeping her from running to Mona and begging her forgiveness, logic be damned. He would just encourage her, but she needed to rein in her emotions for the sake of the *Revenge*. If he saw the cracks in her resolve, he would chip away at them until she crumbled and gave in to the idea of happiness again.

"I trust you to handle business on shore without me," she said.

"As you wish," Tristan said, looking none too happy about it.

"Speak your mind, Tristan." Elinor sensed he had more to say.

"I know you to be many things, Elinor, but a coward was never one of them. You're hiding."

His reproach stung.

"I'm not hiding," she protested weakly. "The ship needs me."

"As you wish," he repeated as he turned away from her. "I need to see to the crew, then."

That evening, Elinor sat in solitude on the deck of her unusually quiet ship, listening to the sounds of Nassau that drifted across the water, raucous men who had had too much to drink. She caught herself examining every high-pitched woman's giggle mixed in among the men's, unable to stop herself from wondering if they came from Mona. Frustrated with herself, she clamped her hands over her ears to block out the sounds and the unbidden worries that came with them.

The thoughts still crept in anyways, each one louder than the last. *Go to her. Tell her the real truth, that you love her so much it scares you.* Elinor wanted to scream. There was no way to captain a ship and be a wife. Mona was too stubborn, she would never agree to stay behind while the *Revenge* sailed. It wouldn't be fair to ask her to do so. *So stay with her. Abandon the ship.* It was unthinkable. Yet, she couldn't shake the idea that lingered until she filled her cup of rum and drank herself to sleep.

She spent the next morning reading books and studying her maps, imagining all the wonders of the world she had yet to behold. She'd heard Madagascar was a safe place for pirates, and the growing trade operations in the Indian Ocean made it an alluring option. And it was far away from the Caribbean. Elinor was ready for a change, a new life with new fortunes to claim where she could finally leave the heartache and tragedy of the waters she loved behind. Distance would be good, and the spices of the East commanded a high price at market. Madagascar would certainly be a profitable destination, if she could convince her crew to sail for it.

Tristan rowed back that afternoon, bearing a thick slab of roasted beef as a peace offering and reminder of what Elinor was missing out on in Nassau. He had dark circles under his eyes, a sure sign he had been up late reveling in the decadence of the isle, or maybe hadn't even slept at all.

"I found another smuggler, bound for Pensacola and offering a better price than Rowe. The men are coming tomorrow with a long boat to move the cargo over to him."

"And will he give passage to Mona as well? Pensacola might be better for her than here."

"I did enquire about that," Tristan said. "And he seemed eager to take her on. Too eager, in fact, it gave me a bad feeling. I don't think he can be trusted with the task."

Elinor sighed.

"I'll secure her a ship," Tristan said. "It just may take time to find the right one."

"I know you will," Elinor said. Tristan cared as much about Mona's safety as she did, and she was relieved he was taking the responsibility seriously. She just wished it could be faster.

"You can't stay out here the whole time. I ran into Lisbet last night," he said cautiously. "She asked after you."

"I'm sure she did, I pay her well for her services." Elinor didn't want to think about Lisbet, or any woman again, and was annoyed that Tristan had mentioned the prostitute she'd spent so much time and coin on in the past. She took a deep breath. Maybe it would be good for her to visit her old acquaintance, to block out the thoughts of Mona for a little while. And once Elinor's needs were met, maybe she would finally be able to forget the stunning, stubborn stowaway who still managed to creep into every thought.

"Anything you want us to bring tomorrow?" Tristan asked.

"No need, I've changed my mind. I'm coming ashore now," Elinor said, committing aloud to the idea before she could talk herself out of it again. Nassau and Lisbet offered a bacchanal escape into her senses where she could trade emotion for carnal pleasure. "Wait for me, I'll just be a few moments."

She rushed into her cabin to make herself presentable, running a comb through her hair, then giving up and taming it into a single plait again. The tricorne hat she wore was too plain to convey her message to the denizens of Nassau: that Captain Elinor Davies was rich for a reason and not to be crossed. A black cormorant feather was just the elan it needed, a rare prize from the luckiest of sea birds. She tied a blue silk sash around her waist, then belted her weapons low around her hips. She wouldn't hide that she was a woman, and a dangerous one. The final touch was a jacket tailored perfectly for her figure, made of blue and gold brocade, as fine as any captain in Nassau owned. It had been her first purchase as captain and she'd spent nearly her entire share of gold to have it made, but it was the type of jacket that turned heads and left no doubt about her success as a privateer.

Tristan whistled appreciatively when she emerged from the cabin. "You clean up well, as always, Captain." He winked.

"Who else have you seen?" Elinor asked, heart racing with excitement and nerves. Nassau was still her favorite port in the Caribbean, and she was suddenly anxious to step foot on the island again.

"Avery, Higgs." Tristan named two other well known English privateers that Elinor knew had become as unscrupulous as she in their quests for riches. "Most of our crew is camping near Avery's."

"Any potential recruits?" Elinor asked. Even though running short-handed meant more coins per share, she knew it was draining on her crew and she needed to replace those she had lost.

"Haven't looked yet." Tristan's cheeks reddened. "I've been busy with other things, too. Personal ones."

Elinor seized on her turn to pry. "Found yourself a lady to hold your interest longer than ten minutes then?"

The tips of his ears colored to match his cheeks. "A lady yes, but nothing so serious."

"When are you going to get serious, Tristan? Don't you yearn for a wife and family of your own?"

He shrugged. "Never really did. I love the *Revenge*, the adventure of it all. Never saw the appeal of marriage, it's just someone to support when I have better things to spend my loot on. Why tie myself to one woman when I can enjoy one hundred?"

Elinor shrugged. Despite the pain she still carried from losing Abigail, the happiness she had felt for those few short months had been worth it. She couldn't truly imagine a life without ever knowing true love, or wanting to know that love.

"Ready to go ashore?" Tristan asked.

Chapter 23

MONA HAD BEEN INSTRUCTED to stay at the inn, but she wasn't bound by Tristan or Elinor's orders any longer. There was no one to stop her from leaving her room there, the very last one at the end of the long single story building. There was no one to stop her from doing anything at all, not her father or his help, the crew of the *Revenge* or its leaders. She grinned to herself, relishing the feeling of true freedom. With so many options before her, Mona found it hard to decide what to do next. She yearned for a true bath with hot water to wash the salt of the sea from her skin, but she was equally pulled back to the little fruit stand she and Tristan had passed along their ways with its tantalizing bananas.

In the end, she opted for neither. The soft bed was too tempting, and, even though the hour was early, Mona suddenly wanted nothing more to collapse into it. She settled for a sponge bath, wiping away most of the grime and feeling as though she was washing herself of the journey and the mistakes she had made. Nassau, and all its seductions, would be there in the morning. She crawled under the sheets, wondering if she had ever felt something so soft in her life. It wasn't difficult to fall asleep, even without the ship's rocking to lull her into slumber.

Once in her dreams, Mona couldn't escape the images of Elinor any longer. Each scene was more sensual than the last, culminating in one where the captain burst through her cabin door, driven mad by lust, and pinned Mona to the bed, devouring her body and teasing the orgasms from her one by one. Mona woke in a daze and reached for the captain, only to remember she was in bed alone. Her breasts ached with a need to be touched, and she fondled them desperately in search of relief.

Little jolts of desire traveled from her nipples through her core, only heightening Mona's arousal. She bit back a frustrated moan, worried the walls were thin and the other patrons of the inn would hear her teasing herself to the brink of ecstasy. Closing her eyes, she imagined the hands tracing her nipples were someone else's, anyone's but her's. Oh, what she would do to have a mouth replace them, to have her nipples licked and sucked until her desire was released. One hand drifted lower, fingers skimming across her stomach. She shuddered, and pulled her hand away, back to her breasts to continue their ministrations. She had all the time in the world.

When she thought she had driven herself well and truly mad, when the only thoughts remaining in her head were those of completion, only then did she allow the hand to slide below. She couldn't restrain her gasps of pleasure any longer, but then again, she no longer cared. She was no longer Mona, no longer the prim and proper woman of Welsh society. She was a woman transformed, with a singular thought towards satiation.

She plunged two fingers into her warm depths, stretching to reach that magical spot where Elinor had focused her attention, the spot that would make Mona convulse and go weak with pleasure. It remained just out of reach, adding to her frustration. She stroked her inner walls as she dug her heels into the mattress, clenching her thighs and thrusting her hips forward to force her hand deeper. Slippery wetness coated her fingers, and she withdrew them to lavish attention on the little nub between her folds, rubbing in furious circles until she came with a satisfied sigh. The waves of pleasure convulsions passed through her, finally liberating her from the torture of longing.

Her first conscious thought as she rose like a phoenix from the depths of pleasure was that she didn't need Elinor. Mona didn't need anyone, except herself. It was liberating, and any residual doubt she had about her decisions faded. Newly invigorated, she decided to explore, pulling on her clothes in a rush and slipping out the door. The sun was just rising over the island of New Providence, and the little town of Nassau seemed still in the dawn.

The main road led back down to the beach, but Mona wasn't interested in returning to the shore where the *Revenge* was anchored in the distance to taunt her. She turned the other way on the road that headed towards the forested mountains. She passed through fields of cultivated crops, and wondered who was maintaining them as the entire village of Nassau seemed to be involved in the business piracy.

As she gained elevation over the harbor, she soon had her answer when curiosity lured her into following a narrow path into the woods, hoping it led to water. Even in the Early morning hours, the heat of the island was stifling and damp and her clothes were quickly soaked through with sweat from the exertion. She paused often to marvel over all the new, strange trees, so foreign in comparison to the birch, willow, and yew of Wales to which she was accustomed.

A little ways into the woods, she stumbled upon a collection of ram-shackle houses, too few to be called even a village. Mona had the strange sense she was intruding on something she wasn't meant to see, a place deliberately hidden away from the coast.

"Good morning, miss," an older woman greeted her warmly, though the corners of her mouth were pinched with suspicion. "Something I can help you with?"

"Water, if you've any to spare." Mona's throat was parched, her request raspy as she remembered her manners and dropped into a low curtsy.

"Aye, we do," the woman said, leading her to a well and pulling up a bucket. "But you didn't come a-wandering all this way just for a sip of water, now did you?" She asked as Mona drank greedily from the ladle.

"I just arrived in Nassau, I only wanted to stretch my legs on land after a long journey," Mona explained.

"So you're one of those folk overrunning our bay, are you?" The woman sneered, clearly viewing the pirates as an object of contempt. "Wouldn't expect that from someone like you."

Mona shrugged. "Well, I suppose I am. And we haven't properly met yet. I'm Mona." She paused. It wouldn't be wise to give the woman her real surname, Mona had no idea who these people were and had heard nothing about them in all the men's tales of Nassau. She offered Tristan's instead. "Mona Buell."

"Welsh then," the woman said without giving her own name in return. She gestured for Mona to return to the path by which she had come. "We don't care to involve ourselves in the business of the bay. It's unchristian, even if your devilry keeps the Spanish and French away from our little settlement."

Mona laughed, thinking of the unchristian activities she had enjoyed that very morning. The woman would probably be horrified if she knew, though Mona was certain the woman was not without sin of her own.

"Well, it was very nice to meet you, Mrs..." Mona fished for the woman's name again, and again was ignored. "Thank you for the water."

"The next time you return to this place, you won't be welcomed as kindly. We've children about, and honest people trying to make their living."

"I understand," Mona said, "And I meant no disrespect. You won't see me around here again."

She returned down the trail in the woods, reflecting on the bizarre encounter. Though the pirates claimed the island was theirs, it seemed not all of the inhabitants of New Providence felt the same way. The woman's words didn't bother her, rather the contrary. It seemed a pitiable existence, the very one Mona had fled from, bound into all the constraints of society and religion without thought to personal happiness.

The town of Nassau was finally bustling when Mona descended, as though its inhabitants had collectively decided to sleep in until the noon hour and then awaken at once into a flurry of activity. Incredible smells filled the air, and Mona decided she would walk the length of the market before picking one of the stands selling various roasted meats to quiet the growling in her stomach. She recognized some of the scents from feasts back in Ogmore, but others were completely new. She hoped she was in Nassau long enough to try them all.

The tavern offered a place for her to sit, and ale to wash her meal down, so she opted for it. It could barely be called a building, so large were the windows cut out of each wall, glassless to let the breeze flow through. A few heads turned as she entered, and one man whistled and tried to wave her over. She pretended not to hear as she slid onto a bench across the room, remembering Tristan's warning not to attract attention. She was relieved to note she wasn't the only woman in the room, though the men still far outnumbered them. One of the barmaids approached quickly when Mona flagged her down.

"What'll it be?" She asked

"A mug of ale to start," Mona said. "And what do you have to eat?"

"Just porridge or a full breakfast for now, but they're set to roast a boar for tonight. Lots more clientele will be around then." The barmaid winked, and Mona realized she thought her a prostitute, there to advertise herself to the pirates gathered there.

"I'm not..." Mona trailed off when she realized the assumption didn't bother her a bit. "Full breakfast, please."

"Right away, miss."

Mona stretched, scanning the crowd for any of the crew from the *Revenge*. She didn't recognize anyone, and wondered if the ship had already sailed away in the night. She wouldn't give into the curiosity. She didn't want to see it, didn't want to know if the ship and her captain were still in the bay. She certainly wouldn't walk down to the beach after eating, no matter how interested she was in exploring more of the pirates' expansion of the settlement.

The maid dropped off her meal, and Mona almost cried at the sight of the rasher of bacon, the two perfect eggs, a generous spoonful of beans, and a chewy heel of real bread. It seemed too luxurious to eat, but her stomach wouldn't let her stare at it any longer. She tried to force herself to eat slowly and savor each bite, but her plate was cleared in minutes, her stomach's complaints silenced. The two men at the other end of the table leered at her as she ate, but she scowled back, unintimidated. They were no different than all the men she had come to know during the voyage, and she no longer feared them.

"Leaving so soon?" One of the men growled when Mona flagged the woman down again to pay. A gold hoop gleamed from his ear, and he grinned a toothy grin that made Mona recoil.

"I have things to attend to," she replied, putting on her best haughty air as she tried to think of what Elinor would say.

"How about you attend to us, instead?" The man said, sliding a silver piece of eight across the table. "Twenty more if you come back down to the beach with me after this round."

Mona pocketed the coin and stood. "No, thanks."

The man's friend burst into laughter as the man yelled in indignation when Mona took his money and walked away, but neither of them gave effort to follow her. She meandered through the market, stopping to admire bolts of richly hued fabrics and mountains of fresh fruit. The man with the bananas was back at his table, and Mona crossed the road to him, eager to finally try the exotic produce.

A flash of gold caught her attention, followed by a bellowing laugh that couldn't belong to anyone but Tristan. Mona's heart jumped into her throat as she ducked behind one of the stalls and waited for the pair to come into sight. The captain appeared, looking resplendent in her richly colored coat. The crowd seemed to part for her as people turned to gawk at the notorious Captain Davies. Tristan was at her side, looking nearly as regal as he scanned the crowd. He bent to whisper something to the captain, then turned to walk back towards Mona. She crept back into the shadows behind the stall, heart racing as she wondered how he had known she was there. She'd been ordered to not stray from the inn, and she didn't want to see what wrath was in store for her if they caught her disobeying.

Tristan passed her and kept walking, and Mona breathed a sigh of relief. He had never noticed her in the first place. Elinor was still a few paces ahead, engaged in a lively conversation with another pirate. Mona tiptoed closer against her better judgment, desperate to hear what the captain was saying. Elinor laughed, the sound melodic to Mona's ears.

"And then the dirty Spanish bastard hoodwinked us, thought to ambush us on his own deck. My crew put him down quickly enough."

Her crew? Mona was offended. Had the shot been fired by any of the other men, his name would have been immortalized in tale or song, but the captain seemed intent on erasing her from memory.

"I'd expect no less of the *Revenge,* Captain Davies," the man chuckled. "There were rumors you'd gone down, so long it's been since you were here last."

"You know better than that, Avery. The *Revenge* never falters," Elinor responded. "I'll tell you the rest over a pint later, but for now, I've business to see to."

The man– Avery– gave a dramatic bow as Elinor continued up the road. Mona crept behind, sure the captain would turn at any moment and notice her following. They had almost reached the inn, and Mona's heart began to race. Maybe the captain was coming to see her, to tell her she'd changed her mind and wanted Mona back.

"Excuse me." A woman with flowing brown locks and a low-cut crimson dress stepped in front of Mona as she rushed down the street waving. "Elinor!"

Elinor turned, and Mona ducked behind a pile of timber boards waiting to be nailed to the unfinished wall of the building facing the inn.

"Lisbet," Mona heard Elinor say. "I was just looking for you."

"I heard the *Revenge* was back. I looked for you at the tavern last night, I was disappointed not to see you. I thought you would have missed me."

"You have no idea."

Both women fell silent, and Mona peered around the corner of the wood pile. She had to clap a hand over her mouth to contain her gasp when Elinor took the woman's face in her hands and kissed her. Tears blinded Mona as she turned to run down the street away from the moment she was never meant to see.

Chapter 24

LISBET SMELLED LIKE SHE had used perfume instead of bathwater and then doused her dress in even more of the stuff. It was a cloying scent that tickled Elinor's nose, and she pulled away to breathe pure air before the tickle turned into a sneeze.

"Mmm," Lisbet purred. "Welcome home, Captain."

Hearing a woman's voice calling her captain made Elinor think of Mona, which was the last thing she wanted. She silenced Lisbet by kissing her again, but the damage was done as the thoughts of the stowaway flooded her mind.

"Come on." Lisbet took her by the hand. "I have a house now, we'll go there. I should warn ye, I've raised my prices."

"I don't care," Elinor muttered. "I'll pay whatever your cost." Anything to help her forget.

Lisbet laughed. "Figured you would. Not that there's another girl on the island willing to offer her services to you."

Mona would, and it wouldn't cost a penny. Dammit, why couldn't she stop thinking about Mona? She'd thought seeing the whore would make it easier to forget, but everything reminded her of what she had lost.

"Nevermind," Elinor said. "I can't do this." She pulled her hand free from Lisbet's.

The prostitute pouted. "Whatever's wrong, Captain, I can fix it. I'll even give you a discount, the old rate."

"I'm not interested today, Lisbet. Go find some other sad sot to fuck." Elinor crossed her arms so Lisbet couldn't take her by the hand again.

Lisbet gave her a wounded look that Elinor was sure was feigned. She carried no illusion that the woman thought anything more of her than an easy way to make a coin. Unlike Mona, who had so willingly come to her with no incentive, whose desire was plain to see in those sparkling green eyes. Dammit, Elinor was thinking about her again. Convinced that Elinor wasn't going to change her mind, Lisbet sauntered off to approach a group of three buccaneers who had stumbled from the tavern nearby.

If Elinor was to be cursed to think of only Mona, then she would channel that into finding safe passage onward for the girl. She should have thought to ask Avery about it, but had been distracted by Lisbet. No matter, she could catch up to the other captain quickly enough; she had only been delayed a few minutes.

"Tristan!" She spied the dark head of hair weaving through the market and called out to him.

"That was quick," he said, surprised by the sight of her.

"I couldn't do it," Elinor admitted. "I'm not ready. Maybe when she's really gone."

"Doubtful," Tristan said. "I've never seen you this worked up over a woman before."

208

"Just focus. Did Avery come back by here? I wanted to ask him which direction he sails for next."

"Aye, seemed he was headed back for the beach."

"Then I'm headed that way as well," Elinor said. "Join me?"

Tristan shook his head, declining. "I need to gather our men to haul the cargo over to the smuggler. We can meet at the tavern after, I hear they're roasting a boar tonight."

Elinor could smell the evidence of the claim, the rich scent of crackling fat wafting through the air.

"Very well," she said. "Then I'll see you at the tavern later."

She walked across the soft sand, blinking as she noticed a flash of red hair in the distance. It couldn't be Mona, there were dozens of people on the island with red hair, and Mona was safely tucked away at the inn. Elinor was falling to pieces, and she didn't like it. She needed to get herself together.

Avery's camp was the furthest down the beach, past the makeshift structures and hammocks strung between trees of other privateers, some of whom she recognized and some she didn't. It seemed the population of Nassau had doubled even in the half year she'd been gone, and she was sure there were more men out on the water who considered the haven their home. The island was much like the pirates themselves, once prized by the Crown when it served their interests only to be abandoned when it didn't. Society may have given up on them, but they were proof that fortune was there for anyone willing to take it.

She finally found the rotund captain sitting with one of the youngest of his crewmen, a boy who looked no older than nine. Avery's hand guided the boy's as they traced letters in the sand with a stick.

"See, now that says Thomas," Avery explained. "Write it again, on your own this time."

Elinor smiled, the moment reminding her of how Greybrow had tutored her so many years before. She'd resented the lessons, preferring to engage in mock sword fights when the crew would deign to entertain her, but his tutelage had served her well. The boy, who Elinor presumed to be Thomas, had his face scrunched up in concentration as he gripped the stick and carefully formed the letters. She didn't want to disturb the pair, but she didn't want to feel like she was spying without their knowledge either, so she cleared her throat.

Avery looked up and nodded to acknowledge her, but waited to address her until young Thomas had completed his task. "Very good," he said, clapping the boy on the back. "You'll be moving on to a quill in no time. Run off down the beach and keep practicing while I speak to Captain Davies."

The boy complied, and Elinor squatted on the piece of driftwood he vacated. "Where'd you pick him up?" She asked.

"Off a French ship a few months back. Took him a while to come around to speaking English, and now it's time he learns to read and write it."

"You're doing a good thing for him," Elinor said, thinking of the boy Diego in her own crew. She should inquire about his literacy; it was always useful to have men who could read, write, and eventually navigate. It was another oversight among many since Mona had taken over her thoughts. "And maybe you'll find it in you to do a good thing for me, too. I need a favor."

"I probably owe one," Avery said with a wry grin that couldn't hide his apprehension. Elinor never asked favors of anyone.

"I need to find passage for a stowaway on my ship. To Carolina, or Boston. You wouldn't happen to be headed that way, would you?"

"A stowaway? I could always use good men for my crew, but I'm not running passengers. Does he work?"

"She," Elinor corrected. "She made a mistake boarding the *Revenge* and I have to get her back where she belongs."

"No. It's bad luck to take a woman on the ship. Next thing you'll tell me is she's got red hair as well."

Elinor glared at him. "You don't really believe in those old superstitions. And she does."

"Who's to say I don't?" He countered. "Never had a woman aboard, never had an issue."

"You didn't care about gender when it was a woman come to save your ass, did you?" Elinor reminded the other captain of the debt he owed her. Had she and her crew not come to his rescue, he wouldn't have a schooner to sail at all.

"Why don't you take her yourself?"

"My men preferred to come to the Caribbean. They're tired of long journeys." Elinor avoided telling the full story of the near mutiny on the crossing. "And might be it's possible someone thinks I kidnapped her, might be looking for her."

"Captain Davies, surely you didn't. Who is she?"

"I'm still not sure, but her father might be connected to some Earl who was already wanting to ask me some questions I didn't want to answer."

Avery pursed his lips and Elinor could see her old friend considering the request. Elinor hoped the lure of repaying his debt of honor was enough to take Mona on.

"I was thinking of going to the Carolina coast, that would get her back on the Crown's land at least. But I'm not sailing for a few weeks. My men need time to spend their money, to make them hungry for the next hunt."

"So you'll take her with you?"

"Five hundred pieces, plus her rations," Avery named his price.

Elinor's eyes widened and she scoffed. "Old age turning you mad, Avery? Three hundred, no more."

"Three hundred will get her to the middle of the ocean off the Florida coast," he laughed. "Can she swim? Speaks Spanish well, does she?"

"Five, then," Elinor relented. "But by God, you had better get her there safely."

Avery clasped her hand, sealing the deal. "You have my word, Captain Davies, your stowaway will be delivered to Carolina unharmed, unless God himself wills it otherwise."

"Good man, Avery. I'll deliver you the coin before you sail, we'll be here a while yet, too." Elinor wiped her hands on her breeches, washing them clean of Mona. The deal was done, and Mona was no longer to be her responsibility. The bloody weight of it was still hanging over her.

"This had better not cost me," Avery warned. "I won't forget it."

"It won't. I'll only send her with someone I trust, I wouldn't betray that." Elinor placed a hand on her heart, concealing the lie. She didn't trust Avery, knowing that as soon as their relationship was no longer advantageous he wouldn't hesitate to slit her throat. She would do the same.

"Does this stowaway have a name?"

"Mona," Elinor choked on it. "Mona Lloyd. Send word to Tristan when your ship is to depart."

"Two, three weeks, maybe," he reiterated.

Elinor stood, her most pressing business settled. "Join me for a drink at the tavern? Tristan will be along later. I'll tell you the rest of our journey."

"Another time," Avery declined. "I need to see where Thomas has gotten off to, every time he's supposed to be studying he winds up chasing crabs."

Seeing Avery's fatherly behavior made Elinor smile. It was such a contrast from his reputation as a gruff captain and fierce fighter.

"You really care for the boy," she remarked. "Why?"

"If I have any sons of my own blood, I'll never meet them. Older I get, the more I wonder who will remember me when I'm gone. And Thomas needed me. The bloody French bastards weren't treating him well at all, he was half starved when we liberated him."

"Don't you worry for his safety, raising him in this life?"

"Not if I teach him well," Avery said, glancing down the beach where the boy was playing in the waves. "All the more motivation to do so."

"I'll leave you to it, then," Elinor said, tipping her hat to the captain.

"Captain Davies." He took her hand and kissed it, winking as he spoke. "Always an experience, and sometimes a pleasure."

She walked down to the water and squinted into the distance. The men of the *Revenge* were just visible as they rowed a borrowed long boat laden with stolen goods to the smuggler's ship. Tristan would be a while yet. She could go up to the inn to check in on Mona, but she was sure the visit wouldn't be welcome. The least Elinor could do was respect her wishes. The best remaining option was to dive head first into a bottle of rum at the tavern and forget everything for a while.

Chapter 25

A s much as Mona wanted closure, she didn't want it like that. The weight of finality was crushing. Elinor had already forgotten her, already moved on. The questions raced through Mona's mind, jumping to the next before she could think one through and try to find answers. No wonder Elinor had been so desperate to get rid of Mona, she had a woman waiting for her in Nassau already. No wonder she was so eager to get to Nassau in the first place. Mona cursed her naivete. How could she have ever trusted a pirate? She should have known better.

Mona supposed it was her comeuppance. After all, she had done the same thing to Sara, her father's maid back in Ogmore-by-Sea: used her for her own, selfish pleasure without care for her feelings, and discarded her without an afterthought. Being on the receiving end of such treatment was miserable, and she wished she could have an opportunity to go back and apologize to Sara. But that, like Elinor, was a ship that had sailed on. It was what she needed to do, as well.

Mona splashed cool sea water on her face, washing away the dusty tracks of any tears she had shed for Elinor while vowing they would be the last. Leaving the island was her only option, her only way to truly be free of the captain's hold on her. And she would be damned if it was on the captain's terms when she was perfectly capable of figuring it out herself.

When she turned away from the water, she noticed an encampment of English privateers staring at her. Mustering up her most confident swagger, she approached them.

"Where is your captain?" She demanded. "I'd like to join your crew, if you've room for one more."

The men laughed.

"If it's work you're lookin' for, might be we can assist you with that. But it won't be on the *Lionsbane*," one said, leering at Mona.

She crossed her arms so he would have less to stare at. "I said, I'd like to speak to your captain."

"He's not here, but his answer won't be no different," the man said. "No ship in this harbor's going to take you on."

His crewmate nudged him. "Heard *Nimue's Revenge* is back. If anyone'll take her, its Davies."

"No." Mona's jaw clenched. "I just came off the *Revenge*. Saved the captain's life, too. I'm a good worker, know my way around a ship. Please, if your captain comes back, just tell him I was inquiring."

"Saved the Cormorant's life? Seems likely," the man laughed.

"It's true," Elinor insisted. "Ask anyone who was there."

"Might have to do that." He looked her up and down again. "If you change your mind on our other offer though, you know where to find us. Pretty thing like you could make a fortune right here in Nassau, don't know why you'd want to work on a ship."

"Nevermind," Mona said. She wouldn't let the interaction frustrate her. It was only one camp of many.

The second camp she approached responded in much the same way, but Mona refused to give up. The third camp actually produced a captain for her to speak to, even if he rejected her as soon as he saw her, laughing in her face as she plead her credentials. She was beginning to get discouraged, and as the sun got lower in the sky, the men on the beach got drunker. Their advances became more forward and the curious looks turned to outright solicitation.

"Hey, girl," a man whistled at her, his accent so thick and his words so slurred she could barely understand them.

She ignored him, deciding it was time to head back to the inn and continue her search in the morning.

"I'm talkin' to ye," he called again. "Are ye lookin' for work or not?"

"I am," she responded without turning. "But likely not the work you're offering."

"What work is it yer seeking?"

"I want to join a crew, earn my fortune." Mona raised her chin defiantly as she faced him.

"Come over here, let me look at ye properly."

Mona approached. Something in the man's stare raised the hair on the back of her neck, but he was the first on the beach who didn't dismiss her as a whore on sight. He was just drunk, she reasoned. Harmless.

"Hmm," he grumbled. "Might be able to find a use for ye. One of my men's ill and we're set to sail in two days. Do ye have your own weapons?"

"No," she admitted. "Not yet. I can before tomorrow, though." She hoped the promise was one she could keep, though she had no idea how much a pistol would cost in Nassau's black market or if the gold still tucked in the folds of her dress at the inn would be enough to pay for it.

"No need," the man said with a wave of his hand. "Plenty on board already, we'll find ye something suitable. I assume you have shot one before. What're your skills?"

"I can swab the deck cleaner than you've ever seen, and shoot a man through the eye from a hundred paces away."

The grizzled face smirked. "That so? Seems unlikely."

"It's true, ask anyone aboard *Nimue's Revenge* and they'll confirm it."

"I'm familiar with the *Revenge*," the captain said. "A formidable ship to have fought on. We'll see if your claims measure up on the water, if you're still keen to come aboard."

Mona could hardly believe her luck. She'd expected she'd have to work harder to convince a captain to take a chance on her, and it almost seemed too easy. Not only had she found a ship willing to take her on, but it was one that was leaving soon. "I'll do it," she said.

"Good. The ship's the *Bonny Lass,* and I'm her captain. Duncan Payne. We load up tomorrow night to sail for Pensacola at dawn. Don't be late, we won't wait."

"I'll be here on time," Mona promised.

"Enjoy your last night in Nassau for a while," he said, tipping his hat to her.

"I'm sure I will."

Pensacola. Mona felt the familiar shiver of excitement she'd once felt when someone said the name Nassau. Another place in another land she probably should have heard of, a place filled with unknown potential for her to grasp. She walked toward the inn, welling with pride and new-found confidence. Finally there was someone who believed in her abilities enough to give her a chance.

The scent of roasted meat and the sounds of music and laughter combined to lure her into the tavern. She was in a celebratory mood, and curious to see how Nassau came alive under the cover of darkness. The tavern was packed with pirates. Two men were standing on tables to play their fiddles, going back and forth as they bowed more and more complex tunes while the crowd cheered and bet on their favorites. She squeezed past the throng of people gathered around the fiddlers, looking for a place to sit.

A seat seemed hard to come by, each table full of pirates playing cards and cribbage, gambling away the coins they had fought so hard for. Women in various states of dress or undress, sat on men's laps, cooed in their ears, and gambled their own coin alongside them. She admired their independence and tenacity in finding their own place in the economy of the pirates, even if it was a path she wouldn't be suited for. Mona gasped when she recognized one of the women, the same woman in the red dress she had seen kissing Elinor. So it was a paid arrangement. Mona didn't know if that made it better, or worse.

A man called out her name and she turned, spying Reddy a few tables down. Two men sat with him, neither of whom Mona recognized from the *Revenge*, both occupied in a fierce arm wrestling match.

"Mona," Reddy exclaimed with genuine delight as he scooted over to make room for her on the bench. "Didn't think I was going to see you again."

She sat. "Might be the last time in a while, I'm leaving Nassau soon."

"Oh? Where to?"

"Pensacola first, then who knows? I found new decks to scrub on another ship."

Reddy looked uncomfortable. "You're joining a crew?"

"Of course, what else would I do?"

He shrugged. "Just figured a lady like yourself has better opportunities than this. Based on what you told me and Griff about your upbringing and all."

"I'm not the person I was any more, and my time at sea isn't done yet."

"Just be careful, Mona. This is a dangerous life you choose."

She sighed. She was tired of everyone telling how risky it was. Everyone except her new captain, she thought with a smile. It was a refreshing change. "I survived you lot, didn't I?"

"Aye, you did. But you won't have Captain Davies or Tristan watching over you anymore, so best you take this in case."

Mona didn't see where Reddy pulled the knife from, his movement so quick the short blade almost seemed to appear by magic on the table in front of her.

"Reddy, I can't take your knife. I can buy one tomorrow."

"Not mine, Griff's. And I think he would want you to have it. He was fond of you. We all were."

Mona closed a fist around the hilt of the knife and tested its weight while she fought back against the stab of grief in her chest. The knife fit comfortably in her hand, the blade glinting in the flickering candles around the tavern. Reddy's gesture touched her, and she looked away to blink back tears.

"Hide it well on yourself, and don't let anyone know you have it. Better to keep surprise on your side when you can."

She wrapped her arm around his shoulder in an awkward hug. "I will. Thank you, Reddy, I'll never forget this, or you."

"More ales?" The barmaid swept by, removing the empty tankards from the narrow wood table.

"And some of that roast pork you mentioned earlier," Mona said.

She'd intended to turn in early, but one ale quickly turned to four, then five, and then Mona lost count. Reddy produced a deck of dog-eared cards and taught her how to lose at piquet, the ales softening the blow of losing so much of her silver so quickly. The evening stretched on and the crowd of the tavern thinned as men made their way to more private locations with the whores they desired. Mona's pockets were considerably lighter when she finally stumbled to the door.

She woke the next morning with a pounding headache, the short walk back to the inn the night before a blur. She understood why Nassau seemed to rise later than a normal town, if every night at the tavern was like that one. The throbbing in her head got worse when she tried to sit up, but she needed to get to the market to buy things for her next adventure. If she had any money left at all. She groaned and reached for her breeches, and then patted the wadded bundle of her dress. Both clinked reassuringly. At least she hadn't wasted everything.

Nerves gnawed at her stomach, which turned unpleasantly as she tottered across the room to splash water on her face. The thought of climbing on board another ship to toss her about made her wretch, and she began to second guess the decision she had made only a day prior. Captain Payne had seemed honest enough, but what was honesty in a den of dangerous pirates? She hadn't been fully honest with him, either.

The inn offered a full breakfast, and Mona felt significantly better after eating. It didn't take her long to collect the few things she needed– a hammock, a change of clothes, a few needles and a spool of thread for mending. She traded her fine green dress for a pair of sturdy leather boots, freshly waxed to prevent the soft hide from rotting. A new belt fit snugly around her hips, holding up pants that were too large and concealing Griff's knife under a billowing shirt. She could tailor the clothes once she was aboard the *Bonny Lass*, but it would do for her most immediate needs.

A few of the *Revenge's* crewmen were loitering about town, but she ducked her head and avoided them. She arrived at the beach well before she was due, anxious not to miss the rowboat out to the ship she still wasn't fully certain she should board. Captain Payne's crew welcomed her, having been forewarned by their captain of her arrival, and one of them showed her how to wrap her belongings in the hammock, folding the canvas into a sort of satchel that was easier to manage.

"Ladies first," Payne ordered her into the little boat just as the first evening colors appeared in the sky.

Mona tried to take up an oar, but the captain batted her hands away.

"I can row," she protested.

"A fine lady like yourself? I don't think so," he said.

"What do you mean? You brought me on to work, so I'll be more than happy to share in it."

"We'll see about the tasks you're suitable for once we're on the ship," Payne said. "There will be plenty of time to work it out between here and Pensacola."

The captain remained jovial, but Mona had a creeping feeling something was amiss. She ran her fingers across Griff's knife under her shirt, a reassuring presence that reminded her she wasn't as helpless as she felt in the middle of the harbor surrounded by strangers. Whatever fate awaited her on the *Bonny Lass*, she was resolved to face it head on.

Chapter 26

"WHAT DO YOU MEAN, she wasn't there? Where could she be?" Elinor's blood ran cold and her heart dropped into her stomach as Tristan confirmed her fear.

She'd woken up late in the morning with a bad feeling that she couldn't shake as the day went on, even though nothing was wrong. Finally, she'd sent Tristan to check on Mona, just to allay the worry that had rooted itself in Elinor's mind.

"I'm sure she hasn't gone far. You know Mona's a stubborn woman, I told you keeping her at the inn wouldn't work. We'll find her." Tristan's words were meant to be reassuring, but he looked as worried as Elinor.

"What exactly did the innkeeper say?"

"Not much, unfortunately. She left yesterday morning, told them she wouldn't be needing the room anymore. They've not seen her since."

"This is my fault," Elinor said.

"There's no fault, we don't even know that anything's happened."

"I should have had her camp with the crew. We should have had a closer eye on her."

"Should have doesn't matter now, does it? Go talk to them, see if anyone has spoken to her. I'll go ask around the market. She's memorable enough, someone's sure to have seen her." Tristan said, always her voice of reason.

Elinor knew he was right, but her intuition screamed otherwise. It was too soon to panic, but she couldn't shake the feeling that Mona was truly gone, as if her very soul had become attuned to the girl's presence nearby and that connection was suddenly severed. She would go to ask the crew because there was no better option, but she already knew in her heart of hearts that Mona wouldn't be found on the island of New Providence. It was her fault, even if Tristan insisted it wasn't. She had pushed Mona away out of selfishness for her own feelings and compromised the one thing that should have mattered most: Mona's safety.

Most of her men were still lounging on their hammocks watching a pot of crabs boiling over the fire when she returned to camp. A few looked up when she walked in, but most continued dozing.

"Come to join us for breakfast, Cap?" Patch-eyed Jack asked, stirring the pot.

Elinor shook her head tersely. Normally she loved the soft crab meat that had to be delicately pulled from the shells, but that morning she had no appetite. "I need to speak with you all. Gather everyone around, this is important."

Jack gave her a wary look, but didn't argue against the order. Within a few minutes, most of her crew had gathered around her.

"Mona is missing. She didn't return to the inn yesterday," Elinor said as emotionlessly as she could manage. "Wondered if any of you had seen her around town?"

The men looked at each other, shaking their heads.

"No one?" Elinor could feel the panic rising again.

"Think Reddy might've mentioned something about her the other night, I don't rightly remember," Jack said. "Had a lot of rum that night, so things get a bit fuzzy, you know."

"Where is Reddy?"

Jack jerked his thumb over his shoulder, indicating the hammocks strung between the copse of trees behind them. "Still sleeping. Tried to wake him for you Cap, but he was proper soused last night, and that was a battle I wasn't winnin'. Can we get back to our breakfasting now? The crabs'll go tough."

Elinor nodded, dismissing the men before she stalked off through the trees. She followed Reddy's snores to the back of the camp and finally found the man asleep as Jack had said near the back of the camp.

"Reddy!" She yelled. "Get up."

He groaned and covered his ears. Out of patience, Elinor grasped the hammock and flipped it, spilling its occupant onto the sandy ground below. He stared up at her in confusion, wiping sleep from his eyes.

"Cap? What's that about?"

"Mona's gone."

Reddy scrambled to his feet. "Guess she is by now," he said, squinting to see the position of the sun through the trees. "Didn't mean to sleep this long."

"So you talked to her? You know where she is?"

"Saw her two nights back at the tavern, she said she had found employ on another ship and was leaving soon." Reddy shrugged. "Tried to tell her it was a bad idea, but she seemed set on it."

"Which ship?" Elinor asked as dread filled her.

"She didn't mention."

"And you didn't ask?"

"Didn't know I was supposed to," Reddy said. "Didn't think it mattered, seeing as how you wouldn't give her a place on the *Revenge*."

Elinor was struck with another pang of guilt. Reddy's words were carefully chosen, but it wasn't hard for her to detect the undercurrent of blame running there. She deserved it, would bear all the blame and whatever punishment came with it, just as long as Mona was safe.

"Just tell me everything you know," Elinor pleaded.

"She said she was bound for Pensacola. I did try to talk her out of it, I swear. Told her a lady like her has better options than that. But she seemed set on it. You don't think she's in trouble, do you?" Reddy was starting to sound concerned as well.

"I don't know," Elinor said.

Pensacola was where Tristan had told her the smuggler was headed, the same man he had said gave him a strange feeling when he mentioned Mona. It had to be that ship, the *Bonny Lass*, that Mona had found herself aboard. Elinor had watched it sail from the harbor on the morning tide, laden with the *Revenge's* plunder.

"We have to go after her."

"We do?" Reddy asked, and Elinor realized she had spoken the words aloud.

"I have to find Tristan," Elinor excused herself without responding to the question. It was inappropriate for her to say such things to a crew member before even consulting with her quartermaster.

She broke into a run, pushing branches out of the way as she raced towards town. Time was of the essence if they had any hope to catch the other ship on her way to the nearby Spanish colony. Tristan would know what to do, would know how to convince the men to get back on the ship they had just taken their leave from. She found him talking to one of the women selling fabric and clothing on the main street. Elinor grabbed Tristan by the arm and pulled him away mid-sentence.

"We have to go," she said, urging him to move faster.

"She was just telling me she remembered someone like Mona yesterday," Tristan complained as Elinor continued to drag him down the street.

"Doesn't matter," Elinor said. "I know where she is. Reddy saw her, she's on that smuggler's ship."

"He saw her get on the ship?"

"No, but she told him she was bound for Pensacola, and there's no other ship I know of headed that way."

"Elinor, wait," he said, pulling his arm free from her grasp. "This is what you wanted. She's on a ship away from here."

"But you said you thought something was off with the smuggler, you said you wouldn't trust Mona to him."

He shrugged. "The die have been cast this way. It seems she went of her own accord. What would you have us do now?"

"We have to go after her. I have to know she's safe," Elinor begged. "We can catch them."

"And then what? Bring her back here to start all over again? Take her onwards ourselves?"

"I don't know. I made a mistake, but I didn't see that until now. I can't let her go."

"The men have barely gotten their boots dry from that last storm and you want them to go back on the water when they still have coin to spend?" Tristan was skeptical.

Elinor knew it would be a hard sell, and having Tristan on her side was essential to getting the men to follow her. "I'll pay them from my own chest. And we'll take back our plunder and sell it to the next smuggler. Two days to double their money."

Tristan shook his head. "She made her choice, and you made yours. You have to move on now."

"I love her, Tristan. Please."

"The *Revenge* is heavy with barnacles and Payne's got a smaller boat and a long lead."

"But we're empty, we'll still be lighter. Please, Tristan. Help me convince them and I'll give you the *Revenge*." It hurt to say, but it was all Elinor had to offer. And Mona was more important. She finally understood that.

"I would never ask that of you. You don't need to bribe me with a ship, I'll always help you. As long as you're certain. I won't be party to you hurting her again."

"I'm certain," Elinor said. She knew what had to be done. "And I can't be married to a ship and a woman at the same time. So I'm choosing the latter. If she'll still have me. And giving you the *Revenge*."

Tristan's eyebrows shot up and his jaw dropped as he was stunned into silence. His eyes searched hers for the answer to his unspoken question, and she nodded. She was sure. She had never been more sure of anything in her life, and she grabbed his arm again.

"We don't have much time," she said. "We have to get to the ship."

He broke into a jog beside her as they hurried to gather the men. Her crew was waiting, their breakfast finished, scowling as the two leaders arrived.

"Reddy said you're thinking to sail?" Scab said, stepping forward with crossed arms. "We don't want to. Haven't had our fill of the island yet."

Elinor sighed, but she had known it was coming. "I know we just arrived. But this will be a short trip, if we move now we could even catch the *Bonny Lass* before nightfall. She won't be expecting us. Easy plunder."

A few of the men looked intrigued, but most stood resolute.

"Any man who joins us will receive a double share," Tristan offered. "Any man who doesn't may find himself looking for another ship."

"What's the rush? There will be plenty of other ships," Jack grumbled.

"This one carries things of personal interest to the Captain," Tristan said.

"I'll not go," Jack said. "Not had me fill o' land yet, neither."

Some men nodded their agreement, but most seemed intrigued by the idea of double pay and stayed gathered around their captain.

"We'll have to go now," Elinor said. "Pack your belongings and get to the canoes. Quickly!"

Action felt better than inaction, and seeing the men rush to gather their things made Elinor feel, for a moment, that things might be okay. Tristan squeezed her shoulder.

"We'll get her back," Elinor said, confidence returning in the wake of the morning's panic.

"I know," he said, and Elinor was surprised to notice sadness in his tone, masked by his eternal confidence in her. "But we're losing you."

The reality of her decision sunk in. If they recovered Mona from the smuggler's ship, it would be her last voyage as captain. The realization was bitter, but Elinor couldn't allow herself to think about what she would do when it was all over. She still had one last battle to fight.

Chapter 27

MONA PUSHED AGAINST THE door again. Even though it was unbarred from the inside, she still couldn't move it. She'd heard crates being dragged around after the captain had shown her to a cabin below deck, a pleasant surprise even if the room was much smaller than the one she'd occupied on the *Revenge*. The captain had told her to take her time getting settled, and that he would fetch her when she was needed on deck. The noises seemed like the normal activity of a ship about to sail and she had thought nothing of them until hours passed and the captain didn't return. She realized she had been locked in.

She pounded on the door, but the attempt was futile. If anyone was there to hear, they ignored her. Footsteps pounded above her head as the crew moved about the main deck of the ship, and she wondered if they had already forgotten about her. There was no window in the cabin, and no way for her to keep track of time. The cracks in the deck boards above let through enough slivers of sunlight for Mona to see, but she knew darkness would eventually come.

She wanted to believe it was all a misunderstanding. Perhaps no one had known she was in the room when the crates were stacked in front of the door. But the longer she was trapped, the more deliberate it seemed. She didn't know how many hours had passed when she finally heard the scrape of wood against wood again and her door swung open. Captain Duncan Payne stood in the doorway, blocking the exit with his hulking form.

"Come here," he said.

She hesitated and he lunged at her,catching her wrists in one of his massive paws and pinning her against the wall.

"Think ye can disobey orders, do ye?" He growled. "There's no place for insolence on my ship. Give ye to my men if ye disobey me again, and ye won't like that at all. I'm much kinder than them."

He was close enough to stab, if Mona could just get a hand to her waist. She struggled against his grip, but her strength was no match for his and the attempt only made him laugh.

"You tricked me," she said, filled with contempt.

"Nay," Payne said, leaning close to whisper in her ear. "You tricked yourself. You heard what you wanted to hear, not what I said. I said I could find a use for you, and I have."

Mona's skin crawled as her situation set in. Her mind raced for a way to extricate herself as the captain ran one finger down her neck.

"Such a pretty little thing." His voice turned saccharine, dripping with desire. "It's almost a shame to do this."

"Then don't," Mona whispered as the hairs on the back of her neck rose in fear.

"But then I won't have a use for ye and I'd have to toss ye off my ship. Unless that's what ye'd prefer?"

There was a way out. There had to be a way out. She just had to think of it, but he was making it hard to think clearly. She had nothing to offer the pirate to get him to let go of her, he was like a wild dog that had latched onto his prey and she wasn't strong enough to shake him off. She could only think of one thing the pirates lusted after more than women.

"My father is rich," she pleaded. "He'll pay handsomely to see me returned unharmed."

The captain paused. "How rich?"

"Very rich. And so is my fiancé, the nephew of the Earl of Caernarfon. I know he'll pay whatever you ask to have me back."

"If that's true, how'd ye end up in Nassau?"

"A mistake," Mona said bitterly. "One I'd wish greatly to reverse."

"Don't know if I believe ye," the captain muttered, but he took a step back. The greed was plain in his eyes.

"You should. It will be better for you if you did. Which would you rather be, rich or dead?"

"You're English?" Payne asked.

"Welsh."

"Same thing anymore."

"It is not," she retorted, feeling a surge of pride for her homeland. Even if the countries were united as Great Britain, she would never be English.

"Well, ye've enough sass to be titled," Payne said doubtfully, and Mona knew he was reconsidering. "But Pensacola is a Spanish fort, and they don't much like your kind around there. Mayhap could sell ye off to be ransomed though." His brow furrowed in thought.

Mona held her breath, hoping she had been convincing enough for him to take his hands off her. The captain narrowed his eyes at her and time seemed to stand still. She'd said enough, pleading more would make her look too desperate, make her look like a liar. Blood rushed back to her wrists as his grip loosened, and then he stepped away.

"We'll see if the Spanish want ye, then," he snarled.

Mona stayed silent, and finally the captain left, the slam of the door echoing behind her. She heard the crates being pushed back into place and when it fell silent again, but for the footsteps above, she breathed a shuddery sigh of relief. Why had she ever thought she could be like Elinor and work her way to acceptance on a ship? She was disappointed in her own naivete. *Don't agree with things if you don't know the terms.* Mona could almost hear Elinor speaking the words of advice from her first day on the *Revenge*. And she had failed to heed it, rushed onto the *Bonny Lass* in the fog of desperation, and had no idea what the future held for her. Little wonder Elinor didn't want her; she wasn't cut out for a pirating life at all.

Payne's duplicity was plain to see in hindsight. He'd verified she had no weapons, then guaranteed she wouldn't acquire any by promising her one after she stepped into his trap. He'd omitted any mention of paying her for the work, and had seemed all too eager to let her on board without challenging her skills at all. She should have listened to her instincts that it had been too easy.

Any longing for adventure Mona had felt was gone. The ship was no longer her ticket to freedom, it was her passage into a fate unknown. At least she seemed to have averted any immediate danger, but she had no idea how long the journey to Pensacola would be, or if the captain would eventually change his mind. She unsheathed Griff's knife from her belt and hurled it at the door, where the point jammed into the wood with a quiet thump.

She pried the knife from the door and ran her fingers over the blade. She could try to kill the captain if he returned, but what would she gain from that? His crew would likely kill her in return, or worse. Her best option was to be patient and bide her time until they arrived at the port and try to escape into the town among the confusion of unloading a ship. Imagining the Spaniards would take pity on her was wishful thinking, but she clung to the hope nonetheless. It was all she had left.

Chapter 28

NIMUE'S REVENGE FELT LIKE she was flying across the sea with wings instead of sails to catch the wind and propel them forward. Elinor stood at the helm, gripping the wheel as hard as she was clenching her jaw. No ship had appeared on the horizon yet, though they had been chasing for hours. It was beginning to feel futile, but she would sail the entire Florida coast if that's what it took to get Mona back.

"Still nothing?" She asked through gritted teeth.

"Just clouds," Tristan confirmed as he peered through the spyglass.

"Would he have sailed further west?" Maybe she had made a miscalculation.

"I don't think so. Any time gained from that route would be lost to navigating the rocks beyond the strait."

Thoughts Elinor didn't want to entertain crept into her mind, visions of the past and future that haunted her. Abi being tortured. Mona screaming in fear. Elinor unable to save either of them. She willed the *Revenge* to go faster, but the ship was already being pushed too far to keep pace.

Tristan stiffened beside her, and readjusted the spyglass. "I think–"

"Let me look," Elinor cut him off. He took the helm from her and she peered through the brass tube.

The ship was magnified through the lens, plain as the daylight fading around it, and Elinor recognized it immediately. The familiar tingle of delight that came from spotting prey spread through her.

"It's the *Bonny Lass*," Elinor said. "We found them."

"How will we approach, Captain?" He asked with a wistful smile. "I was on the *Lass*, and she's well-armed."

"In the dark of night, when his crew's drunk and unsuspecting. We need to get on board without firing any shots. Mona's on there."

"If we've spotted them, they're likely to have a spyglass trained on us as well."

"We'll turn east, so they think we're heading for land and let their guard down. Tell the men to stay to grog this evening, they can have the rum alone when we've tasted victory," Elinor ordered. She glanced through the spyglass again. The ship was slightly larger than it had been before, a good sign. If it stayed on its course, the *Revenge* would easily catch up in the cover of dark and Mona would be in her arms come dawn.

The sky darkened to a deep, clear blue, then turned black as a blanket of stars appeared overhead. Elinor's crew huddled on the deck, speaking only in hushed whispers when necessary. Their ruse of sailing east had apparently worked, because the other ship wasn't taking such precautions. The sound of men carousing on the other deck traveled across the water long before the silhouette of the smuggler's ship appeared against the sky.

She didn't need to instruct her crew; it was a maneuver they had employed with great success many times before. When she raised her arm to give the signal, they moved as one. A pulley squeaked as the three canoes were lowered down to the sea, but the noise was drowned out by the other crew. Her men followed the dugout boats, climbing down the side of the ship to take their places. Elinor joined them, taking up the first position in the first boat. They paddled swiftly to close the gap between the ships, Elinor bracing for shouts of discovery with every stroke.

By some miracle, they arrived at the smuggler's ship without being noticed. The crewmen threw hooks over the rail, long ropes trailing behind to scale the smuggler's hull. The ascent was when they would be at their most vulnerable, easiest to pick off from the deck of the ship. Elinor gripped the rough jute, realizing she hadn't yet heard Mona's voice among the chatter above.

Spurred on by worry, Elinor wrapped her leg around the rope, letting it fall across the top of her boot. Using that as a step, she was able to hoist herself up. Tristan was on the rope next to her, and she looked over at him to flash an apprehensive grin before pulling herself hand over hand until she reached the rail. She would miss the adventures with him, but she was also relieved it was her last one. The weight of responsibility would finally be off her back, and there was no one she trusted more to bear it in her stead.

"Who're you?" A man asked in surprise as Elinor hauled herself over the rail to land crouching on the deck.

"The devil herself," Elinor said, baring all her teeth to him. "Come to take my due, I have."

The man stumbled backwards, as drunk as she had expected him to be. She pulled out her cutlass and swung the blade towards him as more of her men thumped onto the deck behind her.

"Don't make a noise," she threatened the man as Tristan bound his wrists and tied him to the rail. "I don't have a reason to kill you. Yet."

Though if she found out any of them had laid a hand on Mona, she would kill them all. She glanced over her shoulder. The last two men were climbing over the rail. She beckoned them forward, and the crew fell into formation behind her, fanning out across the deck at the rear of the ship.

"Payne!" She yelled out as they marched across the deck.

Half his men were dozing, and her cry woke them from their drunken slumber. The rest were too soused to put up any sort of fight, though one gave a valiant attempt to draw and load his pistol before she slashed it from his hands. He fell to his knees, clutching his new stump of a wrist as his blood spilled across the deck.

"Payne," She yelled again, raising her voice to carry over the screams of the man she had just wounded.

Her crew circled around the group of sailors, blades and pistols aimed if anyone else dared make a move against them. Mona wasn't among them. The captain's door swung open and he staggered groggily onto the deck. His face paled slightly as he took in the commotion.

"What's all this?" He hollered.

"You have something I want, Payne." Elinor stepped closer and aimed her pistol at him.

"How could that be? You just sold me everything on your ship," the smuggler protested in confusion. He glared at Tristan, flanking Elinor. "You double-crossed me."

Tristan shrugged. "It happens."

"I'm not looking for plunder, though I'll happily relieve you of it. I know you have a woman on this ship; where is she?" Elinor was losing patience. She wanted to see Mona, whole and alive and untouched.

Payne nodded towards the hatch. "In her cabin. What do you want with her?"

"That's none of your concern. Join your men."

"Surely, that's not necessary. We can resolve this without bloodshed."

"That is yet to be determined," Elinor spat out. "On your knees, keep your hands where my men can see them."

She rushed over to the hatch, already open, and half-fell, half-climbed down the ladder, landing hard in her haste. It was dark in the belly of the ship, and she tripped over a crate as she scrambled through the cargo.

"Mona?" She called. "Are you here?"

There was no response.

"Mona?" She tried again, getting frantic.

She thought she heard a noise back near the stern, but it could have just been the men above her. She couldn't worry about them. Tristan would handle whatever happened on the deck. She just needed to see Mona.

"Elinor?"

The voice was faint, but it was Mona's and it was coming from where she heard the noise. Elinor's heart raced as she scrambled over crates and cargo. She couldn't make out a door in the darkness.

"Where are you?" Elinor called desperately.

"In here," Mona replied, the voice louder. "I think there's crates in front to lock me in."

"I'm coming." Elinor shoved crates aside, feeling the wall in front of her for a handle.

Her fist closed around wood worn smooth from years of use. Elinor pulled, and the door swung open. Mona let out a little sob, and collapsed into Elinor's arms.

"Shh, shh," Elinor consoled her, gently wiping the tears from Mona's face. "I've got you."

"How did you–?"

"Are you hurt?" Elinor cut off Mona's question with her own, more pressing one.

She felt Mona shake her head.

"Did any of them touch you?"

Mona shook her head again. "The Captain, Payne, he was going to. But I convinced him to leave me alone."

Elinor let out a shaky breath of relief. Mona was alright, she was real and there and Elinor still had her arms folded around her.

"Mona. I thought I'd lost you." Her own tears finally slipped out.

"Why are you here?" Mona sounded incredulous and guilt clenched in Elinor's stomach.

"I made a mistake and didn't realize it until you were gone. I need you, so I came to take you back."

"Need me for what?" Mona was still suspicious, and Elinor didn't blame her.

"Need you beside me for the rest of my life, if you'll have me. I love you."

"Why would I believe you? You're just a pirate like all the rest of them. A thief and a liar. How do I know you won't just use me like Payne planned to?"

"I love you," Elinor repeated, reeling backwards from Mona's anger, knowing it was deserved. "I'm giving the *Revenge* to Tristan. I'd rather have you."

"How can you say that when I saw you kissing another woman in Nassau not two days ago?"

Elinor's heart sank. She'd had no idea Mona was in the market that day. "Another mistake. It was nothing more than a kiss, and one that should have never happened. I regretted it immediately. Please, Mona, forgive me."

"You're giving your ship to Tristan?"

"As soon as we reboard her. My time as captain is done, for as long as I have you in my life." Elinor felt for Mona's hand, and took it in her's.

Mona responded by pulling Elinor forward and kissing her hard, as though she might find the answers she sought in the passion of the moment. Elinor kissed her back, feeling more whole than she had ever felt in her life.

Chapter 29

I T WAS A DREAM within another, Mona was sure of it. Her deepest desires had come to the surface in her slumber to torment and tantalize her, only to be ripped away the moment she opened her eyes. She kept them squeezed shut, desperate to hold on to the memory of kissing Elinor a little longer. Even after the explanations from Elinor, it didn't seem possible for her to really be there.

"I've been gone a long time," Elinor said, pulling away. "We should go up. The crew is waiting."

"Do we have to?" Mona asked, leaning in for another kiss. She still wasn't ready for the dream to be broken.

"Aye, unless you want them to come looking for us," Elinor giggled as she lifted her chin to meet Mona's lips again.

"I don't care if they do. I still can't believe you're here."

"I am. Let's go home, Mona." Elinor took her hand and guided Mona through the dark maze of crates, letting go only to climb up the ladder, then immediately retaking it when Mona reached the top.

"Mona," Tristan greeted her with a broad grin. "Good to see you again."

She returned the smile as it started to sink in that it all might be real. "You too, Tristan."

"I searched the cabins up here," Tristan continued, looking at Elinor. "Not a bad take of coin, plus all their guns that aren't bolted down. Shall we take the cargo too?"

"It's your call," Elinor replied. She wrapped her arm around Mona's waist and pulled her closer. "I have all I came for."

Tristan looked to the *Revenge's* crew. "What say you all?"

A few men shrugged, but none seemed eager to take on the extra labor of hauling the goods back to the ship only to have to do it all again when the goods were resold.

"I'll just take my share of the coin, if that's what you're asking," Reddy spoke, and the other men mumbled their agreement.

"So it's settled. We'll return to the *Revenge*."

"Tristan," Elinor waved him over. "Get Mona into a pirogue, I have one last thing to attend to."

"Aye, Captain," Tristan said. "Come on, Mona." He offered his arm as though Mona were still some lady of society.

"I want to stay with Elinor," Mona insisted. If she let Elinor out of her sight, Mona was afraid she would be gone.

Elinor hugged Mona close to whisper in her ear. "Go with him, I'll be right there. I just need to speak with Payne. I swear, it's the last time I will ever put my duty before you."

Mona saw nothing but truth in her eyes, shining in the moonlight, so she followed Tristan to the stern. Over her shoulder, she saw Elinor withdraw her cutlass and advance towards the captain that kneeled on the deck, surrounded by the crew of the *Revenge*. She had to finally take her eyes off

Elinor when faced with the ropes required to rappel over the side of the ship.

Walking over the side of the ship with nothing but a frayed rope to keep her out of the sea terrified Mona, but it was the only way off the *Bonny Lass*. She gripped the line until her knuckles were white, but somehow managed to inch her way down the side of the ship and into the canoe, Tristan encouraging her the whole way.

"You alright, then?" Tristan asked when they were finally settled in the canoe, and Mona knew he was asking about more than her rope-splintered hands.

"I'm alright," she answered.

The rest of the men clambered off the ship, Elinor among the last of them. She knelt behind Mona in the canoe, and Mona leaned back into her, still marveling that the captain was really hers. Elinor stroked her hair, almost lulling Mona to sleep as she lay against the captain's chest.

"What happens now?" She murmured as the men began rowing.

"Whatever we want to happen," Elinor replied. "I thought we would go back to Nassau, at first. Unless you'd rather go somewhere else?"

"Nassau suits me fi–," Mona said, cut off by another kiss to a chorus of cheers from the crew around them. She still had so much she wanted to ask, but in the moment, she would have followed Elinor anywhere.

Back on the *Revenge,* when the anchor was raised and the ship turned to sail back south to the pirate haven, Elinor called for all the men to gather on deck. Mona stood beside her as the captain clutched her hand, and Mona could tell she was apprehensive about what she had to say. Tristan stood at Elinor's right side.

"I wanted to thank you all," Elinor began. "It's a lucky captain indeed to have a crew as brave, as loyal as you. It's been an honor to sail with you all."

The men turned to each other in disbelief, looking for confirmation that their ears weren't deceiving them. Mona still could scarcely believe that Elinor would give up her beloved ship herself.

"The time has come for someone else to helm the *Revenge*. I've found the only treasure I need." She looked at Mona, who felt her cheeks redden at the open affection. "Tristan will be a fine captain for you, perhaps even better than I've been. He's got a sharp mind for battle, and you'll never want for spoils." Elinor paused, and Mona saw her swallow hard to fight back the tears that welled in her eyes. "It's been an honor to sail with you."

Mona squeezed her hand as Tristan spoke. "The honor has been ours, Captain Davies."

The men shouted their agreement, cheering for their captain who had seen the ship through nearly a decade of victories.

"Just Elinor now," she replied softly with a half smile. "The men seem happy enough with my choice of successor, no one spoke against you."

"They trust you," Tristan said.

"I suppose I should remove my belongings from your cabin, Captain?" Elinor asked.

"You'll do no such thing. You should stay there until we reach port. It's plenty big for you and Mona, and I'm in no rush to move in. A captain isn't made by his quarters."

"Thank you, Tristan," Elinor said, tightening her grip on Mona. "For everything." She had so much more to say to him, and she would in due time, but she knew he understood her meaning.

"Always," he replied, and Mona was shocked to notice he had tears in his eyes as well as he embraced them both.

Elinor led Mona to the cabin, barring the door behind them. Mona reached for her, desperate to be wrapped in her arms, to be reassured again that everything was real.

"I'm sure you still have questions for me," Elinor said, holding back.

"They can wait. I just want to be near you." Mona pulled Elinor to the bed. "Are you okay? I know how much this ship means to you."

"Not as much as you mean to me." Elinor brushed away a strand of hair that had fallen into Mona's eyes. "The *Revenge* will manage without me, but I can't live without you." The kiss lasted forever but was still over too soon, then Elinor was pushing Mona down on the bed.

"What about the code?" Mona asked.

"Not my ship, not my problem." Elinor's reply was muffled as she buried her face in Mona's neck, kissing and biting at the soft skin there until Mona's body begin to tingle. "God, I missed you."

Mona closed her eyes, lost in the sensations of pleasure that jolted from her neck to spread warmly through her body and overwhelm her with longing. She clung to Elinor's waist, sliding a hand beneath the hem of her shirt to caress the smooth skin underneath, thumb brushing across the pebbled flesh of Elinor's nipple. Elinor's chest rose as she inhaled sharply, then she pushed Mona down on the bed. Their mouths met again and this time it was Mona who gasped as Elinor's hand slid down to cup Mona through her breeches. Mona ground against the hand, desire building with the friction that teased but fell short of satisfying her. She fumbled with her belt, desperate to remove her breeches so Elinor's deft fingers could do their work, but Elinor stopped her.

"What's the rush?" She asked huskily. "We have all the time in the world."

The ship rocked as a wave hit it, and Mona whimpered with need, knowing that Elinor intended to build her up until the desire could no longer be contained within her body, the growing sensations an exquisite torture that promised the explosive relief she craved. Elinor's finger slid over the seam of her breeches again. Mona wondered if she could feel her wet readiness through the garment that posed such a frustrating barrier.

"I need you," Mona pleaded. "All of you."

"And all of me you shall have, now and forever. *Rwy'n di garu di,*" Elinor whispered. *I love you.*

Chapter 30

AUGUST, 1708

ELINOR SAT BACK IN the shade of the tarp stretched above her stall at the market, nearest to the beach. Nassau was quiet in the mornings, but she didn't mind the slowness that allowed her to put her feet up and listen to the sound of waves splashing gently against the sand just a few dozen paces away. Sails were folded and rolled around her, and coils of ropes dotted the yard she had claimed for herself and Mona.

None of it had been easy. They'd spent months contending jealousy and resentment, building trust and defining their dreams. It had taken Elinor a long time to warm up to being vulnerable, but once she allowed herself that freedom her capacity to love had grown into something incomprehensible. She didn't fear it anymore. Mona had given her time, and been willing to work through all the complex emotions together.

As if she'd been summoned, Mona appeared just up the road, basket laden with fresh fruits and smoked fish.

"I was just thinking about you," Elinor said, greeting her with a peck on the cheek.

"Thinking what?" Mona asked.

"Just how lucky I am. I never really believed I was until I met you, but now I know I'm the luckiest woman alive."

Mona smiled. "I could say the same thing. Back in Wales, I never would have imagined a life like this."

"No regrets, I hope?"

"Of course not. Do you want a banana before I put these inside?"

"No, I already ate. I'll take a kiss though," Elinor said, rising to claim one.

Mona giggled and blushed as she always did when their lips met. "Close the stand for a little while," she urged. "Come inside with me."

"Later," Elinor said, though the temptation to drop everything and take her to their bed was strong. "A ship just came in, I need to stay here."

"We can make it quick," Mona said.

"No we can't," Elinor laughed. "We never do."

"I know," Mona said, laughing as she kissed Elinor again before she walked inside the shack they had built together.

It was a temporary home with a driftwood frame and thick canvas sails for walls, but it was theirs until they could build a larger house on the land. She glanced down to the harbor, dotted with ships. Nassau continued to grow, each month seeming to bring more privateers turned pirate than the last, and there would be a place for her and Mona to make their fortune without sailing as it did. After the house was built, she could expand her shop to be the first and only place the pirates visited when their sails needed mending or their rigging replaced. Yes, she was truly lucky. A hand at

Elinor's waist startled her. Mona had returned to her side and was staring out at the sparkling blue water beside her.

"I know you still miss it," Mona said.

"Sometimes I do, but I wouldn't trade my life with you for it." Most days the call of the sea was quiet, but it was still there, a part of her that would never truly vanish. Only Mona was worth giving it up, and Elinor never regretted that decision.

"Who knows? Maybe we'll find ourselves out there again someday, though I'll admit I'm in no rush for it."

"I hope not," Elinor said. "We have bigger dreams for now. The house, the shop, a family..."

"In due time. For now, I'm content to just be with you."

Elinor squeezed her hand.

"Look, there's Lisbet," Mona said, nodding towards the path. "I saw her at the market earlier and invited her round for tea." Against all odds, Mona and Elinor's former paid paramour had formed a fast friendship once the jealousy was out of the way, finding a shared purpose in feeding the stray cats that prowled the town.

"Guinevere had her kittens under the veranda at the inn," Lisbet announced happily as she swept into the yard. "I'm pleased to report that the mother and nine babies are doing well. Well, nine that I could count, anyway."

"Oh, I'm so glad you found her," Mona said. "We'll save some fish from the supper you can take back to her later. You are still coming tonight, right?"

"Of course I am. I got some good French wine from a customer the other day, I'll bring it by."

"Which one is Guinevere?" Elinor asked, looking at her wife in amusement.

"The calico with three legs that always comes around the tavern at noon. We've been looking for her for days." Mona's eyes sparkled with delight and Elinor couldn't help but soften at her joy, even if she did find it a bit ridiculous to make so much fuss over a cat.

"Found you a new customer, too, Elinor," Lisbet said. "Reckon he'll be coming down today after he sleeps off the night I gave him. Captain by the name of Stillwell, sailed in two days ago."

"Much obliged," Elinor thanked Lisbet. The arrangement benefited them both, since Lisbet had close access to the men that came off the ships with one priority in mind, and Elinor was happy to pay her a portion of the profit to funnel the valuable traffic her shop's way.

"Is there anything I can do to help you get ready for tonight?" Lisbet asked.

"I don't think so," Mona said. "I've got meat stewing already, and bread and fruit from the market. Won't you join me for a cup of tea inside, though, and we can leave Elinor to her work?"

The two walked off, chatting animatedly about cats again, and Elinor sat down to assess a tear in one of the sails she had recently acquired, taken off a French ship by a pirate. It would be a difficult thing to salvage– a cannonball had rent it nearly in two– but she could cut it down and sew up what she could to make a serviceable sail for a smaller vessel. The smaller scraps could be sold at the market, where other resourceful vendors might sew them into sacks or stretched around sticks for would-be painters to try their hand at the craft.

Tristan sauntered up just as she was tying off the last stitch. He walked around the sail, laid flat on the ground, and picked up the side opposite

Elinor. They folded it together, meeting in the middle to swap corners and repeat the process. When it was done, Elinor added the sail to the stack, and turned to leap into Tristan's arms.

"I didn't think you were going to make it," she said. She had invited him to the dinner party a few weeks earlier, the last time the *Revenge* had been in Nassau.

"I wouldn't have missed it." He grinned. "Are you ready?"

"I think so," Elinor replied, feeling the nerves for the first time that day.

"Having doubts?" He teased.

"Never," Elinor sighed. "But what if she is?"

"She's not. She loves you."

Elinor glanced towards the shack to make sure Mona wasn't watching before reaching into her pocket and pulling out the ring. None of the gold or jewels for sale in Nassau had been adequate for what she wanted, so she'd had the ring made especially with Mona in mind. Delicate emeralds the same color as Mona's eyes glinted from the gold band etched in Welsh. *Am byth*. Forever.

"Do you think she'll like it?" Elinor asked.

"Of course she will." He picked the ring up to examine it closer. "It's perfect for her, just like you are. And if she says no, you always have a place on the *Revenge*."

She'd been so caught up in her own life, she'd forgotten to ask for news of her old ship. She assumed they had been successful in their latest exploits since they had returned to harbor. A quick once over assured her Tristan was in one piece and no worse for the wear.

"Any great new tales of adventure?" She asked, curious about where the *Revenge* had been and who it had encountered. She was surprised to see the look of worry flash across Tristan's face.

"Aye, always. I'll tell you later, after the party."

"Tristan." She raised an eyebrow. "What are you keeping from me? Just tell me now, so I'm not worried about it all night."

"I'm sure it's nothing," he said, still stalling.

Elinor crossed her arms, not knowing why he bothered. She would win the battle of wills, she always had.

"We were boarded near Tortuga. The navy is looking for Mona, and you. I told them Captain Davies was dead, but I don't know if they believed me."

"We always knew this could happen. It was one of the reasons I had to step down from the ship."

"Just lay low for a while. They'll never find you here, even if they suspect. The port is too well defended by us now, the navy wouldn't dare approach."

"That's exactly what I plan to do. I have everything I need here, and we're safe."

"Good," Tristan said. "Now what needs to be done for tonight? Do you know what you're going to say?"

"Yes, just help me get the table ready, if you haven't got better things to do."

He helped her drag the table to the center of the yard, then pulled stumps into place around it to serve as chairs. They went inside to fetch plates and candles, and Mona shrieked in delight as she saw Tristan. Elinor used the opportunity to slip away and retrieve the new tablecloth she had purchased as another surprise for Mona, hidden under the bed for weeks until the moment was right.

"Keep her distracted," she whispered to Tristan as she brushed past. She didn't want Mona to see the table until everything was ready.

Mona was oblivious to Elinor's preparations though, filling Tristan in on everything that had happened in the port since he'd left. She didn't notice the package Elinor clutched as she slipped back outside.

Elinor's heart beat faster as she spread the rich purple tablecloth out. It was almost time. Tristan rejoined her as she laid fragrant white flowers in a trail down the center of the table, bearing the candles and plates. The sun was setting, and the guests would be arriving soon.

"The stew's rea..." Mona burst from the house, trailing off as she took in the scene set in the yard. "This is beautiful, Elinor. But what's it all for?"

"You," Elinor said, feeling like she should have done more to decorate.

"I love it." Mona kissed her lightly. "I love you."

She had planned to wait until later, to make a speech declaring her love before all their closest friends, but Elinor couldn't wait any longer. She needed to know, and the moment was right as the sun dipped towards the horizon and colored the sky with glorious, tropical clouds of orange and pink. The candles on the table flickered in the salty breeze that loosed a strand of copper hair from Mona's braid. Elinor reached up to tuck it behind her ear, then let her hand linger on Mona's cheek.

"Mona," she whispered, eyes misty as she was overwhelmed by love. "From the day you came into my life, you've taught me so much. I've become a better person because of you. I believe in happiness again because of you. And I can't imagine a future that doesn't include you. I want to wake up every morning at your side, and fall asleep each night with you in my arms. I love you, Mona Lloyd, with my whole heart. *Am byth.*" Elinor pulled the ring from her pocket. "Will you marry me?"

"Of course," Mona said as she held out her hand. "Nothing would make me happier."

Elinor slid the ring on Mona's finger as she breathed a sigh of relief, then pulled Mona close to kiss her deeply. The waves splashing in the background were silenced, the air around them still. Their tongues met and swirled, and two became one, separate from time and space, alone in the universe of their own making.

Tristan cleared his throat and Elinor jumped back. She had forgotten they weren't alone. When the haze of passion lifted, she realized Lisbet, Reddy, and more of their friends had arrived and were gawking at them from across the yard.

"Welcome," Elinor called, blushing at having been caught in such an intimate moment. "Mona and I have something to tell you all." She looked to her fiancée.

"We're getting married!" Mona squealed, a grin splitting her face as she held up her hand. The emeralds sparkled in the candlelight, but Mona's eyes sparkled brighter. "Elinor just proposed."

"Congratulations," Lisbet said. She ran over to look at the ring.

"Well done," Tristan said, clapping a hand on Elinor's shoulder.

Reddy came over to shake her hand before disappearing with Mona to help carry out the pot of stew so the feast could begin. Elinor uncorked a bottle of rum and filled the cups on the table, thinking about the toast she would make. There was so much to say to all of them, but there would never be enough words to fully convey the gratitude she felt that evening, surrounded by friends who had become family and the most beautiful woman in the world soon to be her wife. It was more than she had ever dared dream of, and she truly was the luckiest woman alive.

Author's Note

This book is a blend of history and my imagination. Where it was possible, I tried to keep dates and places historically accurate, but *Nimue's Revenge* and Mona, Elinor, Tristan, and the rest of her crew are all figments of my imagination. While we know women pirates like Anne Bonny and Mary Read were active during the Golden Age of Piracy in the Caribbean, there are otherwise very few records of women aboard these ships. It is hypothesized that many more women worked aboard these ships disguised as men, so the real number of women pirates is lost to history.

Most pirate ships did adhere to a code, designed to maintain order and camaraderie among the crew. Pirate ships were more democratic and egalitarian compared to their naval and merchant counterparts. The crew had a say in many matters, and the captain and quartermaster held nearly equal power on this ship, though their roles were different. Mutiny was a very present threat if the crew became displeased with the way the ship was being run.

The places mentioned are all real. Nassau was home to what would be known as the Pirate's Republic, a haven for some of the most famous names in history like Blackbeard, Stede Bonnet, Black Sam Bellamy, and of course, Anne and Mary. This story takes place a few years before Nassau developed fully into a pirate haven. Prior to the 1710s, the island of New Providence was colonized by the British and destroyed in multiple raids by opposing fleets. Many British privateers seized the opportunity to base their operations there, as it was an island largely ungoverned and with few inhabitants.

In *The Captain's Choice*, I tried to bring this time period back to life while imagining what it would have been like if women had played a greater and more open role on these ships and what unique challenges they might face. I hope you enjoyed my creative interpretations of life at sea and exploring the islands of the Bahamas while falling in love.

About Author

WREN TAYLOR is a sapphic romance novelist. A passion for history and stories of empowered women serve as her primary inspiration when writing. She lives in the Pacific Northwest with her two dogs. When she's not dreaming up her next book, Wren enjoys cooking, painting, gardening, and enjoying the natural beauty of the world.

The Pirate's Pursuit

Coming February 2023

The Sapphic Seas series continues in an all new adventure with characters you already love, and some you haven't met yet!

Nassau, 1710

Lisbet Clarke knows how to fend for herself in the growing pirate haven of Nassau, and is quite content doing it. When a woman from her past steps back into her life, she is forced to finally contend with old memories and betrayals. Yet, she can't help but wonder what might have been had things ended differently a decade prior.

Printed in Great Britain
by Amazon

24387423R00152